ALEXA GRACE

Deadly Relations

Alexa Grace

This ebook is a work of fiction. Names, characters, places and incidents are products of the author's imagination or are used fictitiously.

Any resemblance to actual events or locales or persons, living or dead, is entirely coincidental.

Cover design by Christy Carlyle of Gilded Heart Design

DEDICATION

For my amazing, loyal readers

CONTENTS

ACKNOWLEDGMENTS

A special thank you to Sgt. Adrian Youngblood of the Seminole County Sheriff's Office, Major Crimes Unit, who patiently answered my questions and reviewed each chapter for accuracy as I wrote this book.

I am also grateful to Lieutenant Patrick J. Flannelly of the Lafayette Police Department for answering my questions specific to Indiana.

Thank you also to the wonderful experts at Crime Scene Writers.

Any mistakes here are entirely mine.

Thank you to my editor, Vicki Braun, who painstakingly edited this book.

Much appreciation goes to the Beta Reader Team who devoted their personal time to review each page of this book: Karen Golden-Dible, Carolyn Ingham-Duncan, Gail Goodenough, Melody McAllister Novellino, Kelsey Summer, Barrie MacLauchlin, Rhonda Dennis, Kelly Struth, Nate Kitts, and Cindy Lawyer.

Thanks also to Melissa McGee, Megan Golden, Nancy Carlson and Karen Golden-Dible for their help and support.

I want to express my appreciation to my family and friends. Without their love, encouragement and support, this book would not have been possible.

1 CHAPTER ONE

He hid his car in the woods and hiked back to the house. He'd been planning what he was about to do for a long, long time. The first seed of the plan was planted when he was seven years old: Mama locked him out of the house for wetting the bed, just as the school bus arrived with his classmates hanging from the bus windows, laughing and taunting him, as he stood outside in his soiled pajamas. The plan strengthened with each beating with the long, black, leather belt Daddy left behind after the divorce. The beatings grew more frequent, and just about anything could inspire one, whether it was a stolen snack before dinner, or because she had another one of her headaches.

His was a plan that had been honed and perfected over the years. He'd put in time for practice, too, unfortunately for the five women he'd killed over the years. What surprised him was how much he enjoyed killing the women. It was anger that motivated him, but each killing gave him a sexual release like he'd never had. He'd become proficient at murder. Three of the women had not even been discovered, he'd hidden them so well. The other two would become cold cases soon. As Mama always said, practice made perfect.

He entered the old farm house and laid the jug of kerosene he'd carried from his car down on the linoleum floor.

He pulled a pair of latex gloves out of his front pocket. Then he stood back and took a good look at the woman, lying on her stomach, strapped to the kitchen table with duct tape. He'd removed her panties and flung her dress up so he could reenact a scene that was repeated throughout his childhood, up until the time he'd grown big enough to fight back. It was a scene that played in brilliant Technicolor in his nightmares every night.

"Good choice livin' in the country, Mama. A good five miles between farms makes things that much easier for me. No one's going to notice the fire until it's too late," he said, laughing as he walked into the kitchen.

"Oh, what is it you're trying to say? Hard to talk with duct tape stretched across your face, isn't it?" he asked as his mouth pulled into a sour grin.

When she noticed he had Daddy's long, black, leather belt in his hand, she started to whimper. Mama knew what was about to come. Hadn't she done it to him a million times before?

"I even remember the chant, Mama," he told her. "You repeated it with every beating, so how could I not remember it?"

He popped the belt, the crack echoing through the small house. Mama flinched as he moved closer.

"Little girls are pure and go to heaven. But little boys are dirty and go to hell." His voice grew husky, changing back from the imitated falsetto. "Isn't that what you would say, Mama?"

He pulled the belt over his shoulder, whipped it down across her buttocks, and laughed at her muffled screams. "Oh, Mama. Does that hurt?" He pummeled her with the belt until her flesh was so bloody it looked like raw hamburger. He checked her pulse. The bitch was still alive. But that would be remedied soon.

He strode into the living room to a vintage red kerosene lantern Mama owned, in case the house lost electricity during a storm. He slammed it to the floor. Rivulets of the oil ran over fragments of red shattered glass, sinking into the old carpet covering the floor.

Going into the kitchen, he pulled a hypodermic needle out of his pocket and jabbed it into his mother's neck. "This will make you too drugged to move, Mama. Got to get you off this table and into a living room chair. It'd be a little suspicious if somehow enough of you was left after the fire, and it was discovered you were duct-taped to your table."

He watched her a few minutes until she lost consciousness, and he was sure the drug had taken effect. He then carried her into the living room and deposited her in her favorite easy chair. For good measure, he found a book nearby, opened it and placed it on her lap, so that it would appear Mama was enjoying her book when the "accident" happened.

Opening the kerosene jug he'd brought, he poured it over his mother and around the living room. As he headed for the front door, he pulled a book of matches out of his jeans back pocket. He struck a match, and when it lit, tossed it near his mother. He stood back as the room exploded with flames. He dashed through the door and watched from the driveway as the inferno engulfed the small house. Aroused, his hand flew to his member and massaged it as ripples of heat became a tidal wave. He moaned aloud with the erotic pleasure he always got when he'd slain his prey.

In no particular hurry, he walked to his vehicle, turning to watch the fire occasionally as he went. When he reached the woods, he spotted his car a short distance away. It was stuffed with moving boxes. He'd accomplished the one thing he wanted to do since childhood. He'd destroyed evil.

He'd leave Ohio for his new job in Indiana. It was time for a fresh start.

2 CHAPTER TWO

A tear slid unchecked down Jennifer Brennan's cheek as she stared at the casket of her baby's father, while the minister spoke words of support. She didn't hear a word.

The end of the long Indiana summer was nowhere in sight. A September breeze rustled leaves in the tall oak trees surrounding the cemetery, cooling her skin, which was heated by the bright sunlight and rising temperature. The humidity was thick, temperature at least eighty degrees, and no shade near the gravesite. Wiping moisture from her forehead with the back of her hand, Jennifer thought about her baby.

Had he lived, her baby boy would have been five years old. Once Jennifer had learned she was carrying a boy, she'd named him after her father, Tim. She was eight months pregnant and shopping for a baby crib with her mom, Megan. Feeling bigger than a barn, she waddled instead of walked. They'd found the perfect baby bedding set called "Stars at Night," with stars and prints in shades of warm blues, yellows and browns. It matched the light yellow walls they'd painted the week before in baby Timmy's room.

They only needed a crib. They were in Foster's Furniture on Main Street when the pain started radiating from her back to her belly button. She used the breathing techniques she'd learned in childbirth class and thought she might be having false labor pains. It was too soon. She and her mom were following a saleswoman to the back of the store to see a vintage-looking oak crib when a wave of pain slammed into her like a freight train. Jennifer had moaned and leaned against a dresser for support, her legs feeling like they might give out. Her panties became wet, and she felt something trickling down her leg, into her shoes. She looked down to see blood. Jennifer remembered screaming before she lost consciousness. She'd lost her baby.

Paul Vance, Timmy's father, had been her world for two years when they both attended Indiana University in Bloomington. There was a time when she thought she loved Paul more than life itself. Christ, she used to think he was her soul mate. All that evaporated the night she told him she was pregnant with his child.

Jennifer grieved for what could have been if things had been different between Paul and her. It was the unanswered questions and doubts that made it hard. Could things have been different if Paul's reaction to her pregnancy had been joy instead of anger and fear? Was she wrong to have expected delight when they were both juniors in college, with Paul on a football scholarship, a professional football contract hanging like a bright star in his future? Was she wrong to refuse his marriage proposal?

Right or wrong, she'd associated Paul Vance with the living nightmare that ensued after that night. Had it not been for Paul's abandonment when she'd needed him the most, she would never have had thought about giving her baby away, nor would she have gotten involved with an illegal adoption agency that resulted in her abduction — and probable murder, had she not escaped.

It wasn't just that she couldn't forgive Paul. She couldn't trust that in the future, when things went wrong, he would stand by her — and do the right thing. In the two years immediately following their son's death, they'd tried to recapture the love they once had. She blamed herself for each failed attempt to get back together. He'd destroyed her trust and she couldn't get past it — no matter how many times Paul begged her.

Jennifer remembered the last time she'd seen Paul. He'd arrived for a visit as handsome as ever, and happier than she had seen him for a while — since before the Indianapolis Colts had benched him for a knee injury. He'd been picked up by the Tampa Bay Buccaneers and was ecstatic. He was in such a good mood; he took her to Deer Run State Park, where they hiked and had a picnic. They'd spent hours together hiking and swimming.

When they returned, Paul showed no signs of leaving until the society page fell out of the Sunday newspaper they were reading. Paul was on the front page, photographed with his model girlfriend of the moment. Paul made a beeline for the door and the visit ended. Jennifer knew their relationship was over, and probably had been for some time. Neither of them wanted to admit it, but it was time for both of them to move on.

The next day, the first of September, the small private plane he was taking to Tampa had engine trouble. The plane went down thirty minutes after takeoff, thus ending Paul's young life.

She felt her father's arm around her shoulders as the minister handed her a long-stemmed red rose. Shakily, she moved to the casket and placed it on top. "Good-bye, Paul."

Jennifer followed her father as he led her mother and her to the awaiting black limousine. Her cousin, Frankie Hansen — who was more like a sister than a cousin — followed them, along with her husband. Lane Hansen carried their three-year-old daughter, Ashley.

Jennifer had already heard from Paul's attorney, who

announced that Paul had left a great deal of money for her in a trust. That's what men like Paul did, Jennifer thought, they spent money and set up trusts to relieve their guilt. Did that mean Paul had finally felt responsibility for abandoning her when she needed him most? It didn't matter anymore. She didn't want his money.

From the car, she glanced back at the crowd of people leaving the gravesite. County prosecutor Michael Brandt and his wife, Anne, each held the hand of one of their five-year-old twins, Melissa and Michael, Jr., and headed toward their car.

The entire county sheriff's department attended the ceremony in force and stood near a line of trees nearby. Each of the deputies was wearing his or her dress uniform out of respect for Jennifer Brennan, who was now a detective on their team, and for their sheriff, Tim Brennan. A black band stretched across their badges. Like most law enforcement agencies, they were a family who supported their own.

Blake Stone stood in the distance and gazed at Jennifer as she lingered near the casket. Watching Jennifer was not a new thing for Blake, he'd been watching her from a distance since the first moment he saw her five years before. Jennifer had been missing. Her father, his sheriff, beside himself with worry and fear, had summoned Blake and his scuba-diving team to search Monroe Lake near Bloomington. Monroe Lake was the cell tower area where Jennifer's cell phone had pinged for the last time. They'd hoped to find evidence of what had happened to her in the lake.

Blake remembered gazing at Jennifer's photo and praying they would not find the beautiful young woman at the bottom of the lake. His prayers were answered. Her car was discovered, but there were no signs of Jennifer. He was telling a teammate how glad he was she was not in the lake when he heard a woman's voice behind him. He'd turned to find himself face-to-face with one of the most beautiful women he'd ever seen. A blast of desire had hit him so strong it nearly knocked him off his feet. Jennifer Brennan stood before him, in the flesh, very pregnant and very much alive. Though he'd never acted on it, he'd fallen hard for Jennifer that day.

He watched as Jennifer, her hand shaking, slowly laid a rose on the casket. Even from a distance, Blake could see the tears that stained her pale face. It was all he could do to just stand there and not run to her. He wanted to enclose her in his arms and kiss her until she forgot any pain Paul Vance had ever caused her.

But that was the last thing he could do. Jennifer was a detective on the sheriff's investigations team, as was he. He couldn't have a relationship with a peer, especially if the peer was his sheriff's daughter.

He clenched his jaw as he thought about Paul Vance. If there were ever a man who did not appreciate what he had, it was Paul Fucking Vance. How in the hell could the bastard have allowed Jennifer to go through her pregnancy alone? The prick was nowhere to be found when they'd buried Timmy. Big football star, Paul Vance, had plenty of time for the many women it was rumored he was involved with, but he was too busy to attend the burial of his baby? Though he'd never met the man, Blake hated Paul Vance.

Seven Months Later

Sweat beaded on Jennifer's forehead as she tossed and turned. The nightmare had returned. She was locked in a small room, walls lined with royal-blue foam soundproofing. She jumped to reach the window, but it was too high. Trying the door again, Jennifer discovered it was locked. Icy fear twisted around her heart as she began to shake. The walls were moving in closer; the room shrinking so small it was suffocating her. There wasn't enough air and her lungs squeezed with pain.

Suddenly there was the sound of a key turning in the lock of the door. The doctor monster was coming to take her baby. She couldn't let that happen. He entered the room with a scalpel in his hand. It was her own scream that jolted her from sleep.

Jennifer awoke, panting in terror with the sheets bunched in her hands. It had happened again. The damn nightmare was back. Turning on the lamp on her bedside table, she looked around the room. No blue foam covered the walls. She wasn't abducted. Jennifer was in her own bedroom that she'd decorated in pale yellow and white. Everything was okay. At least that's what Jennifer told her family. Her kidnapping had happened a long time ago, so why did the nightmares continue? Why couldn't she let it go? She got out of bed and opened a window. A surge of freezing March air filled the room and she slammed the window down.

Jennifer looked at her alarm clock. It was almost four in the morning. She didn't have to be at work at the sheriff's office for hours, but she got out of bed and headed for the shower. She didn't want to risk having another nightmare.

Because she didn't feel like making breakfast, Jennifer grabbed her coat to ward off the chill of the March morning and headed for the Sugar Creek Cafe. The place was a favorite for the police and firefighter crowd, and was so packed, she was lucky to find a table. After a few minutes, she noticed her favorite waitress, Catherine Thomas, bearing down on her with a full pot of hot coffee.

"Catherine, you're a lifesaver. I need my caffeine fix."

"I hear ya," the waitress said as she filled Jennifer's cup to the brim. "Are you eating alone this morning?"

"Yes, and I'm starved. I'll have your "Country Special" with the eggs scrambled, along with a glass of orange juice. And keep the coffee coming."

Catherine nodded and took off for the kitchen, as Jennifer unfolded her newspaper. She'd barely finished the front page when Blake Stone plopped down in the chair across from her, making himself at home at her table.

"Good morning, Jennifer," he said as he grinned mischievously. "Thanks for saving me a place at your table." He removed his black leather jacket and placed it on the chair next to him.

Blake shot her one of his devastating smiles and she didn't blink, but her stupid heart skipped a beat. He needed to focus his gorgeous self on someone who had more appreciation of his ripped body and natural good looks. It wasn't that she hadn't noticed him. How could she *not* notice the hottest detective on her team? It was just that he was forbidden fruit. It was career suicide for a female cop to date at work, not that she dated at all these days.

Besides, her dad was the county sheriff, and he definitely wouldn't approve of her dating a man on her team. Hell, her dad didn't approve of her being a detective. He'd made it very clear that police work was the last thing he wanted for his only daughter. But Jennifer's abduction had changed her. She wanted to make sure that what happened to her didn't happen to others. Jennifer completed the police academy training after her college graduation, then joined the sheriff's department, first as a deputy, and after a promotion, a detective.

"Oh, but that's the curious thing. I didn't." She aimed a glare at Blake that he ignored as he studied the menu.

"I'm starving. Where's our waitress?" asked Blake.

Magically, Catherine appeared and chastised, "Jennifer, you told me you were eating alone. I didn't know you were expecting Mr. Hotness, here."

Jennifer rolled her eyes as Catherine poured Blake's coffee and took his order. She glanced at Blake. He was wearing his detective "uniform" of a starched white shirt, tie and dark pants. The shirt stretched across his chest and arms, revealing the hard muscles beneath. To most people, he was damned intimidating, but she'd never felt that way about him. She still remembered the day she saw him at the lake where his scuba team was searching for her car. Her first thought was that he was the most gorgeous man she'd ever seen with his hard-muscled body, dark hair and eyes the color of espresso. But it was his smile that impressed her the most; it was brilliant and filled with warmth. Jennifer was sure he melted a lot of hearts with that smile. But she'd pledged hers wouldn't be one of them.

"Catherine, when do you start classes at the Police Academy?" Blake asked, and then sipped his coffee.

"January 10! Eleven more months and I can't wait." The young woman glowed with excitement.

Before Blake could respond, his cell phone vibrated on the table. He picked it up, looked at the display and said, "Excuse me, ladies, I need to take this." Grabbing his jacket, he maneuvered through the breakfast crowd, so he could go outside to take the call.

"I don't blame you for being excited about going to the academy. I loved it," said Jennifer. "How's your boyfriend going to feel about you being away all that time?"

"Nicholas is just going to have to get used to it." Catherine paused for a moment then continued. "If I thought for a second that I had a chance with the hot Italian hunk you're having breakfast with, Nicholas would be history. Are you dating him, Jennifer?"

"No. Of course not." As soon as the words left her lips, she realized she had said them too loud and too empathically. A couple of deputies nearby turned to look at her. Damn it. The last thing she wanted to do was to add to the rumor mill.

Jennifer studied the young woman and wondered if Catherine and her boyfriend were getting along. She'd seen them together and they seemed so much in love. Of course, if anyone knows that looks are deceiving, it's a detective. Jennifer knew from experience that things aren't always what they seem.

"Just wondering," Catherine said. "I've seen the way he looks at you when you're not watching. I think he has a thing for you."

"Nope. There's no 'thing,' Catherine. Just co-workers. That's all."

Jennifer felt her face heat as Catherine headed back toward the kitchen. The waitress returned a short time later with a huge tray balanced on her shoulder with both breakfast orders. Blake followed her toward the table.

Starving, the two detectives dug into their food. Blake was shoveling it in like it was the first meal he'd had in days.

"Hungry?" she asked.

"Worked out this morning and ran three miles, then lifted weights," Blake said as he stole a biscuit from her plate, even though there was a basket of them on the table.

"Hey!" She said, smacking his hand.

He grinned mischievously as he split the biscuit in two and put a dollop of apple butter on each slice. There was something intimate about the way he slid one half onto her plate and he took a bite out the other. "I heard you took down the kid who was robbing all the 7-Elevens."

"He's not a kid. You make it sound like he was an elementary school student. He's a twenty-two-year-old brute."

"I heard you flipped him on his stomach and had the cuffs on him before your partner could get out of the car."

"So what? Dick was calling for backup." Jennifer's partner was an older man, in his late fifties, and she got defensive when anyone questioned Dick's abilities. He was a damn good cop and she was lucky to have him as her partner.

"What's up with Dick lately anyway? He seems distracted, like he's got something on his mind."

"He's private. I guess if he wants me or anyone else to know what's going on with him, he'll tell us."

He'd noticed her a week ago and had learned her name was Catherine Thomas. He'd visited the cafe every day since, purposely sitting at a table in her section. He watched her as she talked with another waitress at the coffee stand. She swiped a section of sun-lightened brown hair out of her eyes with the back of her hand and tightened her ponytail tie. She was young, in her twenties, and full of self-confidence, as was evident by the way she blatantly flirted with him and deliberately brushed against his body as she poured his coffee. His mama would have said the girl was a whore just asking for it.

Catherine Thomas was young, but not too young to be considered prey. Not too young for what he had in mind for her. He clenched his jaw at the thought. He was an idiot to think the urges would magically disappear just because he'd moved to a new town, new state. The impulses had returned so strong last week, when he noticed this girl, it nearly rocked him out of his chair. Shit! He could never resist the urges. Never.

Catherine headed toward him toting a full pot of hot coffee, her hips swaying seductively as she walked. His chest tightened as his blood pressure rose and a roiling heat filled his belly. Quickly wiped the sheen of sweat from his brow, he clenched his jaw as he fought for control. He moved his chair closer to the table in an effort to hide his burgeoning erection.

"Hi, handsome. Coffee?" asked Catherine.

When he nodded, she reached across him for his cup and brushed her breast against his arm, sending a fresh shot of lust shooting through his body like a bullet.

"Are you new to the area? You must be. With a face like yours, I'd have remembered you." Catherine shot a wide grin at him.

He ignored her question, focused on the menu and said, "I'll take the omelet with cheese, mushrooms and steak with an order of hash browns." He closed the plastic menu and handed it to her as he reached for his coffee. As she moved back toward the kitchen, he noted her athletic build and firm ass. He became aroused anew as he thought of what he'd be doing to her soon — very soon.

Jennifer grabbed a pillow to put over her head. Damn it. It was Saturday, her day off, the only chance to sleep in. Who in the hell was hammering? The pounding stopped for a moment, then started back up again. Shit! She threw her pillow across the room, giving up on sleeping in, but determined to find out who was being so loud, so early. Slipping on her white terrycloth bathrobe, she opened her bedroom door. It was then she realized, it wasn't hammering she had heard. Someone was pounding frantically on her front door. Jennifer ran down the stairs and whipped open the door.

Julie and Fred Thomas, who lived about four blocks from her, stood on her front porch, both looking as though they hadn't slept all night.

"Where's your dad?" Fred demanded, looking past her into the house.

"Why are you looking for my dad?"

"He's the fucking sheriff, isn't he?" Fred was wide-eyed and his face red with fear or anger or a mixture of the two. "He's not answering his door."

Jennifer knew her parents had gone away for a fishing trip, but said nothing. It was none of Fred Thomas's business. Besides, she was a freaking detective. Why had it not occurred to Fred that she might be able help him?

"Fred, stop it. Calm down," Julie pleaded. She gently pulled on her husband's arm.

"What's going on? Why are you two so upset?" Jennifer had known the couple for years and they were two of the happiest people she knew. Whatever had them this upset had to be serious. "Come in." She showed them to the living room where they sat on her sofa. Jennifer sat on an easy chair close by.

Fred scrubbed his hands over his face. "It's Catherine. She didn't come home last night."

"Well, maybe she had a good reason. Maybe..." Jennifer began. She almost suggested that Catherine had probably stayed the night with Nicholas. They'd been seeing each other for at least a year. She stopped herself. Fred and Julie Thomas were pillars in the Methodist Church. Catherine may have hidden their relationship from them.

"No, it's not like that. She calls. She *always* calls. That damn cell phone is plastered to her like super glue."

"Could she be with Nicholas?"

"Jennifer, we know when she stays the night with Nicholas. She calls so we don't worry. Something is wrong, I tell you. I can feel it. A mother knows." Julie sank further into the sofa, giving up on composure, and sobbed into her hands. Fred slipped his arms around her shoulders.

"Okay, let's stay calm and talk about when you last saw

Catherine."

"I saw her early last evening. She was going for a run." Fred began. "I remember seeing her standing by the small table we have near the front door. She was putting her keys and cell phone into her pocket. She turned and smiled at me, and then she left. I should have stopped her."

"Honey, how could you have known to do that? Stop beating yourself up." Julie scooted closer to Fred and held his hand. They both looked small and frightened. "We're both thinking worst case scenario and we need to stop."

"We want to report Catherine missing," stated Fred. "What do we need to do?"

Jennifer grabbed her coat and keys. "You need to complete an official missing person document at the sheriff's office. Come with me."

Later, at the sheriff's office, Jennifer peered through the one-way glass as Blake Stone talked with Fred and Julie Thomas in the interview room. Blake was lead detective on call, so if this turned into a missing person case, it was his.

"When was the last time you saw Catherine?" Blake looked directly at Fred when he asked the question. Fred seemed angry and hostile as he sat in the chair across the table from him.

"Damn it all, I just gave Jennifer Brennan that information. We're wasting valuable time!" Fred shouted, pounding his fist on the table.

"Fred, I need for you to answer the question so that we can file an official missing person report so we can find your daughter." Blake's voice was low in an effort to calm Fred.

Julie put her hand over Fred's and squeezed. "Honey, answer Detective Stone's questions."

Tiredly, Fred sighed and said, "I saw Catherine around dinner time last night, so it must have been around five o'clock. That's the time my wife always has dinner ready. I was coming down the stairs when I saw Catherine standing near a small table we have near the front door. We have a bowl on the table where we put our keys when we come in the house. Anyway, I noticed Catherine, dressed in running clothes, so I surmised she was going for a run. She ran whenever she could to stay in shape."

Blake held up his index finger to interrupt and asked, "What did the clothes look like?"

"I'm sure she was wearing a red zipped hoodie, white sweatpants and her white Nikes."

"Okay, now continue. Tell me what you saw Catherine doing."

"She already had her cell phone in her hand when she pulled her keys out of the basket and put them both in her pocket. She noticed me and smiled, and then she left out the front door. That's the last time I saw her."

"You mentioned a cell phone and keys. What about her purse? Did she carry a purse? If so, where is it?"

"No, she didn't have her purse. I found it in her bedroom this morning."

"Mr. Thomas, we're going to need Catherine's purse for any bank or credit cards. We can use those to determine if there's been any activity since she was last seen."

"Oh, sure. You can have the purse. No problem."

Blake looked toward Jennifer on the other side of the one-way glass as if he could see her and nodded. That was his way of assigning her the task of getting the purse, then running any credit or bank accounts to see if either had been used recently.

"Thanks. After we finish talking, detective Brennan will drive you and your wife back home. We appreciate you giving the purse to the detective, so she can start tracking any transactions that may have occurred."

"If it will help you find Catherine, you can have anything in the house."

"Would you mind if Detective Brennan does a walk-through of Catherine's room?" asked Blake.

"No, of course not."

"Where does Catherine usually go when she runs?"

Fred thought for a second, then said, "I think she usually runs at the high school track. Though sometimes she does run in the neighborhood."

"Has Catherine ever run away or disappeared before? Even for just a day or so?" Blake doubted that Catherine had run away, but it was a question he had to ask so he could rule it out.

"No. Absolutely not. Catherine is a good kid. She calls us if she is running late or going somewhere. Always. Without fail." Julie responded emphatically.

"Does Catherine have a drug problem?"

Fred exploded. "You can't be serious! Hasn't Catherine been waiting on your table at the cafe for a couple of years? Does she look like a druggie to you?!"

"Okay, Mr. Thomas. Calm down. I have to ask the question."

Blake directed his next question to Julie, who was infinitely calmer than her husband.

"How has Catherine seemed emotionally lately? Upset about anything? Any problems with her friends?"

"No, not really. Most of her college friends are away for the summer, so the only one she really hangs out with is Nicholas Connor. I think the two are getting along.

Catherine hasn't said anything about being upset with anyone." Julie replied.

"So Nicolas Connor is Catherine's boyfriend?"

"Yes, they've been going together since they met in college. Fred and I think they'll eventually marry. He's a nice young man."

"Who else might have seen her yesterday?"

"Well, she worked her shift at the Sugar Creek Cafe, so her co-workers and anyone eating there would have seen her. I think she worked until three o'clock. She didn't come home until around five o'clock."

"What about Nicholas? Have you talked to him about Catherine's whereabouts?"

"I called him this morning, as soon as Fred told me that Catherine's bed hadn't been slept in. Nicholas said he talked to her at the cafe, after he got out of school around four o'clock. He's a kindergarten teacher at the elementary school. He said that was the last time he saw Catherine."

"Okay. We'll talk to Nicholas. I need you to fill out some paperwork that will ask you for very specific information that will help us find Catherine. We need her cell phone company and number; and the make, model, color and year of her car. I also need for you two to think carefully and list anyone that may know where Catherine is, because we need to talk to those people." Blake paused and looked toward Jennifer through the one-way glass again. "Jennifer Brennan will take you home as soon as you complete the paperwork."

"Please find her. Catherine is our only child. She's all we have." Julie begged, tears dripping down her cheeks.

"I assure you both we'll do our best to find her."

Jennifer emptied Catherine's purse on her desk, neatly organizing and inventorying each item. There was a J.C. Penney credit card, VISA card, and a bank debit card. Armed with each account number, Jennifer's fingers flew over her computer keyboard. She didn't notice Blake standing in her cubicle until he cleared his throat. He startled her, and she jumped in her seat.

"Damn it, Blake. Can't you make a little more noise?"

He just shrugged and stared at her computer screen. "So you're running Catherine's cards?"

"Yes, I ran the J.C. Penney account first. No changes since last December 23rd when Catherine was probably shopping for Christmas presents. The VISA card was used last month at a Starbucks store in the mall. The bank debit card was used to fill her car with gas yesterday at 3:10 p.m. at a Shell Gas Station on Third Street. That was the last time it was used."

"I got the cell phone history," said Blake. "Her last call was at five thirty from Nicholas Connor and lasted less than one minute. The last ping from her phone to a cell tower was near Deer Run State Park one minute later. Nothing since then. It looks like she may have turned her cell off after the call from Nicholas," said Blake.

"Are you thinking what I'm thinking?" Jennifer asked.

"Let's go have a talk with Nicholas."

In the parking lot, Blake opened the passenger door of their unmarked car for Jennifer. "Let's head over to the high school track first. Her dad said she was going running."

Blake drove and Jennifer scouted the area on the way to the high school. It was Saturday and the March weather was warmer than usual, so there were a lot of young people about. When they reached the track, there were a number people running, but mostly jocks. No sign of Catherine.

Though they'd work together for a couple of years, it was the first time Jennifer had been alone in a car with Blake. She usually rode with her partner, Dick Mason, who was on vacation. Jennifer didn't know if it was the subtle scent of musk and man, or the way he kept glancing at her that made her senses alert and her heart beat against her ribs. When she didn't think he was looking, she checked Blake out. His massive shoulders filled the jacket he wore, his thigh muscles strained against his khakis.

Blake had a ruggedly handsome face and dark features that spoke volumes about his Italian heritage. The man was hot. She'd give him that. Actually, she'd give him more than that. He was the first man in five years that she was remotely attracted to. Not that she was going to do anything about it. He was a member of the same investigative team she was. No relationships allowed. Period. It was career suicide for a female in law enforcement, and there was no other job she'd rather do.

"How do I rate?" Blake said, breaking the silence.

"What?" She said, startled by his abrupt question.

"You've been staring at me since we left the high school. So how do I rate?"

At first she froze, speechless. After a long moment, she said what usually worked in situations like this, "I don't know what you're talking about." She focused on looking out the window so he wouldn't see how red her face was.

They next stopped at the Sugar Creek Cafe to see if Catherine had reported for work, but no one there had seen her. The waitresses who had worked Catherine's shift the day before were off. Jennifer and Blake would have to return the next day to interview them.

Jennifer scanned the restaurant and noticed Nicholas Connor, Catherine's boyfriend, sitting alone in a booth. She and Blake joined him.

"Hi, Nicholas. Good to see you," said Blake as he waited for Jennifer to slide in the booth seat. He took off his jacket and tossed it across the back of his seat. "You're just the guy we're looking for."

"Nicholas, we're looking for Catherine. Do you know where she is?" Jennifer studied his face. Nicholas looked surprised to see them. But why wouldn't he be? It wasn't like they lunched with him on a regular basis.

"No, I haven't seen her since Thursday afternoon. Why are you looking for Catherine?" His eyebrows rose inquiringly.

"Her parents said she didn't come home last night. I thought she might have been with you."

Nicholas looked annoyed. "Catherine's mom already called me this morning. I'll tell you what I told her. No, we didn't see each other last night."

Jennifer noticed that there was no eye contact when Nicholas responded, which made her wonder if he was telling the truth. Something was off with him, but she couldn't pinpoint what — yet. "What about yesterday afternoon?"

"Yeah, I saw her at my house after her shift."

"Why didn't you mention that before?" asked Blake as

he shot Nicholas a don't-yank-me-around glare. A couple of diners at the next table stared at them, and Jennifer poked him in the ribs.

"You asked me if she spent the night."

Blake leaned across the table. "Listen, asshole, if you're going to play games with us, we can move this little talk to the sheriff's office."

"No, that won't be necessary."

Jennifer dove in with a question, "So, what did you do last night, Nicholas?"

"I stayed home alone, ordered a pizza and watched TV until late."

"Anything good on TV? What did you watch?" Maybe Nicholas was telling the truth, maybe not. Jennifer was placing her bets on not.

"Watched the Pacers vs. Miami Heat on ESPN."

"Cool, was it a good game?" One look at the Pacers ESPN schedule on her laptop would make or break his story. In addition, there was only one pizza place in town that delivered, so a quick call to them was in order, too.

The next day, Jennifer attended a staff briefing at the station, led by Sgt. Lane Hansen, her boss. With the exception of her partner, Dick Mason, who officially was on vacation, the entire department was in attendance to discuss the girl they would search for.

"Our missing person, Catherine Thomas, is five feet and six inches tall and weighs 115 pounds with an athletic build. She is Caucasian with light brown hair and blue eyes. She was last seen on Thursday by her parents in their home prior to leaving for a run. She drives a white 2010 Honda Civic. The license number is in your report." He nodded at Jennifer as a signal to give the information she'd collected to the group.

"I ran Catherine's credit card and bank records," Jennifer reported. "No recent activity on her credit cards. The bank debit card was used to fill her car with gas yesterday at 3:10 p.m. at a Shell Gas Station on Third Street. That was the last time it was used."

Blake Stone spoke next. "I did Catherine's cell phone history as well as the cell tower report. The last ping from her phone to a cell tower was near Deer Run State Park at 5:31 p.m. No activity since then. It looks like she may have turned her cell off after a call from her boyfriend, Nicholas Connor."

"Half of you will search the park today covering every trail. Call in if you find anything relevant," Hansen ordered. "The other half will perform their regular duties."

An officer in the back row raised his hand to speak.

"Sir, what about the park's security cameras? Shouldn't we get their videos?"

"There are no security cameras at the park," Stone said. "They didn't make the budget cut last year. There are lights in the parking area, but no cameras or lights anywhere else in the park."

Catherine Thomas awoke from a drugged sleep with every bone in her body aflame. Breathing in and out triggered a torturous throbbing in her head.

She wanted her mom. Though in her early twenties, Catherine had always needed her mother most when she felt ill. Though she rarely got sick, she knew something was very wrong.

She shivered as the cold seeped into her consciousness. Why was she freezing? Where were her blankets? Catherine tried to move her legs but they seemed frozen in place. She attempted to stretch her arms, but couldn't. Her eyelids felt heavy and swollen and she feared the pain that would accompany opening her eyes to the light. But she had to find her mom. Catherine slowly opened her eyes to inky blackness. Was it night time? Her facial muscles flexed involuntarily and she realized something was tied around her eyes. It was then she remembered.

She and Nicholas had had another fight. This one was

a doozy, and she'd slapped him, leaving an ugly red mark across his jaw. Though he hadn't admitted it, she *knew* he was seeing someone else. He'd been distant and his usual insatiable desire for sex had diminished so much it was practically nonexistent. There was someone else, and he didn't have the balls to tell her.

Consumed with anger, Catherine had rushed out of his house and drove home to change clothes to go for a run. Running had become her salvation. She ran when she needed to think or to drive away her demons.

She'd changed into her running clothes and was pocketing her keys and cell phone when her dad appeared in the hallway. Catherine remembered smiling at him. For a second, she'd been tempted to throw herself into his arms for one of his special bear hugs. But, instead she'd hurried to her car so she could make the most of the remaining light of day.

Catherine's original plan was to run at the high school track like she usually did, but once she got there and saw the number of people running, she'd changed her mind. She'd needed some alone time, so she'd backed her Honda Civic out of the lot and headed toward Deer Run State Park ten miles away. If she hurried, she could get her exercise done before the park closed at nightfall. She'd feel better about her fight with Nicholas. Running made her feel better about everything.

Once inside the park, Catherine had studied a sign that listed each trail and the degree of ruggedness. She'd chosen trail number ten, which was advertised as moderately rugged and would give her a good workout. Maneuvering between several groups of people leaving the park, she'd reached her trail and started out in a jog on the narrow, dirt path. Catherine noticed few people on the trail, and that was fine with her. She valued her alone time and concentrated on the exercise.

Catherine hadn't gone far when she reached a wooden platform built over a deep ravine. Peering over the railing, she saw the river surging below and a deer drinking on its bank. She continued down the trail, alternating between jogging and walking, depending on the terrain. It was unseasonably warm for March, and the scent of the tall pine trees and ferns filled her senses. Catherine was calming. With or without Nicholas, she was going to be okay. She was stronger than she gave herself credit for. Who needed Nicholas? She'd go to the Police Academy in eleven months and start the career of which she'd always dreamed.

Catherine slipped as she made the descent to what the park labeled as the "Ice Cave." She slid a few feet on her bottom, but was able to stop herself by grabbing a sapling. Pulling herself up, she assessed her injuries to be just some scratches and scrapes on the back of her legs.

Her senses went on alert. Catherine felt as if someone

35

were watching her, but when her eyes scanned the wooded area, she saw nothing. She continued on the path down the hill.

Once she'd reached the sandy bottom, she stood before the Ice Cave. A twig snapped. Spinning around, trying to spot any danger, she heard the crackling of dry undergrowth with each step as someone approached nearby. Was someone following her? Catherine launched herself into the next section of the trail, cursing herself for being so angry with Nicholas that she lost all thoughts of personal safety. When she hiked, she always had her small stun gun and a pocket knife with her. Sticking her hands in the pockets of her sweatpants, she felt only her cell phone and keys. She turned her cell phone on only to find there was no signal. Damn. She turned if off again and shoved it back in her pocket.

Catherine pushed on as the path wound around a steep hill. On one side of her was a thick forest of trees and vegetation, on the other was a slope that led to the rushing creek below. She stopped frequently to look back, but saw nothing. Figuring she was at the half-way point of the trail, she pushed forward and prayed she'd make good time getting to the end.

The sun was waning in the horizon in hues of orange, pink and red. Daylight was running out, and she quickened her pace as she brushed a spider's web from her face. The crunch of brittle leaves and twigs behind her continued, but each time she searched the thicket of woods, she saw dark shadows sheathing the trees as the light diminished — but no humans in sight.

Turning a bend, Catherine lost her footing again and tumbled down the descent of the dirt path. She crashed face-down to the bottom of the slope, knocking the wind out of her. She lay on her stomach for a short while as she sucked in air to fill her lungs.

Catherine *felt* him nearby, rather than saw him. She rolled over and looked up at him. She recognized him. Thank God. She'd seen him at the cafe. Catherine smiled at him as he offered his hand to help her up. Grasping his hand, she pulled herself up and was about to thank him for his help when he swung her around, slamming her body against his, gripping her in place with his left arm locked around her neck. Catherine's eyes widened in terror as she noticed the hypodermic needle in his right hand. An explosion of pain rocked throughout her body. Her world went to black as he plunged it in her neck.

Her heart slammed against her ribs with the memory. Where was she? She tried to move her arms and legs again, but it was impossible. The effort to move caused the structure she was lying on to creak and rock. Catherine moved her fingers to scratch at the surface and realized she was secured on a long, wooden table. He had her strapped to a wooden table, with a dark blindfold stretched across her eyes! She couldn't move. She couldn't see. What was he going to do to her? A primal scream started in the depths of her chest and rushed through her throat until she discovered her mouth had been sealed shut with tape, muffling the scream into a moan.

3 CHAPTER THREE

Jennifer left the Sugar Creek Cafe, where she'd filled her thermos with hot coffee. She walked down Main Street toward the county sheriff's building, where Catherine Thomas's latest search efforts were being organized. March had been fickle thus far, alternating between unseasonably warm or frigid weather. Today, it was chilly, so she tightened the belt on her coat and lifted her collar as she walked against the wind that whipped her hair about, stinging her face and eyes. Though she'd never admit it, she was exhausted and had averaged around four hours of sleep per night since Catherine went missing. When she wasn't in her car searching for Catherine, she was sitting in front of her computer using the methods Frankie had taught her to look for a missing person. Her cousin, Frankie, was a private investigator with an expertise in technology, and Jennifer had worked for Frankie prior to going to the Police Academy. But Frankie's sure-fire methods hadn't worked to find Catherine.

One look at the gray clouds overhead confirmed what the TV weather guy had said. There was a chance of rain today. At least, she hoped it was just rain. If the temperature dipped below thirty-two degrees, there was a good chance they'd get freezing rain, or what people called "black ice." That made the roads treacherous to drive, let alone search for a missing person.

The majority of the businesses in the historic downtown area were located on Main Street for six blocks or more. Most of the buildings had been built a hundred or so years before. They'd been preserved by massive renovations and modernization as time went on.

The wind was playing havoc with Catherine Thomas's missing posters, which peppered the trees and light posts. Lining the inside of nearly every shop or restaurant window was the poster for the world to see, with the silent prayer that someone would find her. Fred and Julie Thomas worked tirelessly to get the word out about Catherine's disappearance.

Jennifer gritted her teeth as she thought about Catherine. She'd been abducted. Though there was no evidence, she was sure of it. Catherine had been taken against her will, just as Jennifer had been taken years before. The girl was looking forward to going to the police academy.

She was not a runaway. There was no way Jennifer would believe Catherine left on her own volition. She had an ominous feeling that time had run out, and their chances of finding Catherine alive were nil. Catherine's parents hadn't lost hope of finding her alive, but Jennifer had. She knew the more time that elapsed, the less likely they would find Catherine alive. Like most detectives, Jennifer knew that time and again when they didn't find the missing person within forty-eight hours, it was likely the person was dead.

It was Thursday and Catherine had been missing for five days — a time period painfully realized by every member of the county sheriff department. The staff took it personally. The sheriff, each of his officers, and all the admins wore a yellow arm band that matched the yellow ribbon tied around a huge oak tree in the Thomas's front yard. People don't go missing on their turf, on their watch.

So much time had elapsed that most of the sheriff's team had lost hope that Catherine was alive, just as Jennifer had. The sense of loss made them more determined to find her body so they could focus on what happened to her. While there was a lot of information they'd gain by finding a dead body in terms of prosecuting a killer, there was a lot more satisfaction in finding the missing alive.

Fear ran rampant, as was evident by increased calls to the station. Paranoid citizens were reporting suspicious strangers, or strange noises outside their homes. High school girls, much to their distress, found themselves with early curfews and increased parental surveillance. Local restaurants were filled with anxious chatter about Catherine, and gossip ran rampant. People were angry, too, firing blame at the county sheriff's office for not finding Catherine.

For the first time since Jennifer could remember, people were locking their doors at nights and leaving on their outside lights. The quiet street she lived on was usually dim at nightfall, with only a few street lamps to light the way. Since Catherine went missing, the street was flooded bright by house, porch, and garage lights.

As Jennifer approached the sheriff's building, Jeeps, trucks and ATVs filled the empty parking lot nearby. More than one hundred people, some with hunting dogs, gathered to search for Catherine Thomas the third time since she went missing. The Ladies' Aid group from the Methodist church had set up a tent and was handing out bottles of water, donuts and sandwiches to volunteers who shuffled by.

Jennifer watched as Blake Stone divided up the search area and assigned teams to each one. Her father, Frankie, and Lane Hansen stood nearby, waiting to join the search teams. Frankie had brought her Giant Schnauzer, Hunter, which had been trained in search and rescue. The dog had found and rescued several people over the years, including an Alzheimer patient who'd wandered from a nursing home. Hunter found the elderly man lying near a creek, nearly dead from hypothermia. The dog covered the man's body with his own to provide warmth until help arrived. If anyone could find Catherine, it was Frankie and Hunter.

Blake divided the group in half. Searchers were assigned in teams of twos and threes to a deputy who would lead their efforts.

Fifty were assigned to search the Northwest corner of the county, which was mainly farmland and wooded areas. The other fifty searchers would comb Deer Run State Park, where Catherine's cell phone pinged for the last time. They'd searched the park two times before, but found nothing. Today, the searchers would focus on areas only lightly covered by the last searchers.

She and Blake were assigned to stay at the command post, and the searchers would communicate their findings to them with cell phones and two-way radios.

Jennifer knew the moment Blake noticed her approaching the group because a wide smile spread across his face as he nodded at her. It was the same irresistible smile he wore every time he saw her. Electricity passed between them for a moment, before he turned to talk to Fred Thomas. As much as she tried to fight it, there was something going on between them. She just wasn't certain what it was.

A reporter from the local paper shot a photo with his camera, while a deputy handed her dad a microphone so he could instruct the group.

"Most of you know who I am. For those of you who don't, I'm Sheriff Tim Brennan. I'm joining you to search for Catherine Thomas today. Before we leave to search, there are a couple of things I want to communicate to you.

"You've all been given a photograph and information about Catherine Thomas. Your assigned deputy will be handing out a topographical map of the particular area your team will be searching today. Each team will be equipped with cell phones, two-way radios and a GPS unit to report any find that may be significant to locating Catherine.

"If you should find anything out of the ordinary, like pieces of clothing or an object that is out of place, call the item to the attention of your deputy, who will determine its significance, flag it, and call it in.

"I want to thank each of you for volunteering your time to find this young lady."

Jennifer watched as the last of the vehicles left, carrying searchers to their respective areas. She tiredly sat down on a folding chair and poured a cup of coffee from her thermos. Before long, Blake sat down beside her. He wrapped a small plaid blanket he'd retrieved from his car around her shoulders.

Surprised, she glanced at him, but he was already focusing on the topographical maps he was taping to the table. Each map was marked with that search team's focus.

"Blake, do you think they'll find her today?"

He stopped what he was doing to look at her. He waited a moment before he responded. "If they do, I doubt if they'll find her alive. I think she's been abducted and the one who did it has either already killed her, or soon will, because of the posters and media attention."

"Why haven't we found her body?"

"We have too much ground to cover. She could be in a shallow grave somewhere that could take years to discover."

"I didn't see Nicholas Connor among the searchers. Is he here?" asked Jennifer.

Blake opened his laptop and pulled up the searcher roster and searched for Nicholas's name. "His name's not here. So why wouldn't a missing girl's boyfriend join a search to find her?"

"Good question. Remember when he told us he was home alone that night watching a Pacer and Miami Heat game on ESPN?"

"Yeah, he said he ordered delivery pizza and watched the game."

"Well, I found the ESPN Pacer schedule on the Internet, and there was no Pacer game on ESPN that night. In addition, I talked to the kid who delivered the pizza and he said that Nicholas was not alone that night. The kid saw a woman with short, light hair and too much makeup sitting on his sofa."

"Sounds like we need to bring Nicholas in for a little visit."

He leaned against the window frame of his cabin, peering up at the sky. Where was the fucking rain? He'd had Catherine Thomas in his cabin for five days too long. Clouds in drifting shades of gray stretched across the sky, giving him hope it would rain soon. God bless the rain, his mama always said, for it washed the earth. Rain would also wash a crime scene of trace evidence, and he was all for that.

A grin creased his face. He was damn good at what he did. Sure, he prided himself on the way he hunted and secured the bitches, the prey, but the kill itself and aftermath was apparently pure genius. In all his years of killing, not once had he even had a sniff from law enforcement. No visits, no questions, nada. That was how proficient he'd become after he'd gotten caught the first time.

He was twelve and kicking the shit out of the family dog in the backyard when the five-year-old neighbor brat, Sally Billings, wandered into his yard. She became hysterical, screaming, sobbing for him to stop kicking the dog. He had to stop her from screaming; he had no choice. So he'd thrown her over his shoulder, kicking and shrieking, and locked her in the tool shed so he could run to the house and get his father's belt. He returned to the shed, pulled her panties down, and beat her with the belt as his mother had beaten him. He'd counted ten lashes until she promised not to tell anyone what he'd done to the dog. Hysterically, she'd begged him to let her go, so he did, confident that the fear of another beating would keep her quiet.

It wasn't even three hours later that the little bitch ratted on him to her parents, and he was charged with battery, convicted and slammed in the secured juvenile detention facility for six months. But that punishment was nothing to what Mama delivered after he'd served his time. He'd learned his lesson. From that point on, once he'd secured his prey, no one got out alive.

As for the killing aftermath, it was his own sheer genius that inspired him to wait for rain until he dumped the bodies. He'd seen on some forensics TV show how rain could wash away key trace evidence. So he'd put a damper on his impatience and wait for rain before saying good-bye to his latest prey.

He threw another log in the fireplace and headed toward the kitchen. As soon as he entered the room, the Catherine bitch started whimpering. He walked around the wooden table where he had her face-down, naked and strapped to the table with duct tape. He'd fed her cereal a couple of hours before and cleaned up the table where she'd defecated after her last beating with good old Dad's belt. The rain was coming and it wouldn't be long until she'd breathe her last breath.

It was nightfall, and finally the rain started coming down in sheets, drenching anything and anyone in its path. The searchers had gone home for the night, finishing another disappointing search for Catherine Thomas. They found nothing, leaving most to wonder how the girl could have vanished without a trace.

The next day, Dick Mason returned to work. He and Jennifer had just had an unpleasant run-in with an intoxicated husband who chose to beat his wife so badly she'd had to be hospitalized. The poor woman had the misfortune of asking her husband where he had been for the past twelve hours. Jennifer and Dick had gladly handed the husband to a deputy, who whisked the man off for an up-close and personal visit in the county jail.

They were waiting in line for coffee at a Starbucks drive-thru when Jennifer's cell phone buzzed.

"Jennifer, this is Blake. A deputy just found Catherine's car. He's securing the scene and is waiting for the crime analysis techs."

"Where's the car?"

"Deer Run State Park."

"What? How could her car be at Deer Run State Park? We've combed that park three freaking times!" She was incredulous. How in the hell could anyone miss seeing Catherine's car in the parking lot?

"That was my first thought," Blake responded.

"Where are you, Blake?"

"I'm heading there now."

"So are we."

Jennifer shoved a wad of bills to the Starbucks barista at the window, took the two coffees and gunned the car in the direction of Deer Run State Park.

Once they reached the park and entered the parking lot, even in the driving rain, they couldn't miss the 2010 white Honda Civic. It was sitting under a street lamp that bathed the entire parking lot with bright light. The crime scene investigation van was there, as was Blake's black SUV.

Jennifer and Dick grabbed their yellow rain slickers from the back seat and jumped out of the car to race toward Blake, who was now waving at them.

"Have they found anything?" Jennifer wanted to know. The crime techs hadn't been on the scene for long, but there was always a chance they'd found something important early on.

"Not yet," said Blake. "But Karen Katz thinks the car has been wiped down. She can't find any fingerprints, including Catherine's."

"You're kidding," said Jennifer as she peered inside the car.

"Wish I were. She said the car is fucking spotless, including the trunk."

"There is no way a busy young woman like Catherine Thomas would have a spotless car." Dick added.

"Oh, hell no," exclaimed Jennifer. "Mine hasn't been spotless since I drove it off the lot."

A silver minivan raced into the parking lot, nearly ramming the deputy's car at the entrance, its brakes screeching as it came to a stop near them. Fred and Julie Thomas jumped out of the car and rushed toward them, sliding on the rain-slickened pavement. Julie lost her footing and slammed to the ground on her hip. Fred continued running, not even stopping to help his wife.

"Where is she? That's her car! Where's Catherine?!" Fred was in hysterics.

Dick ran to help Julie, who still lay on the ground

where she fell, sobbing as the rain pelted her body. Dick checked to see if she had any injuries, then persuaded her to wait in the minivan.

Blake pulled Fred away from Catherine's vehicle. "Fred, you can't be here. This is a crime scene. Drive Julie home, and wait to hear from me."

"My baby. My baby's gone." Fred melted his knees in hysterics, crying so hard his entire body shook. Suddenly, he started gasping for air and held his left arm as he screamed in agony.

"Jennifer, call dispatch and get an ambulance out here, stat."

As she called, Dick used his umbrella to shield Fred from the driving rain. Blake leaned over Fred and tried to talk him down. Julie, now on her knees next to Fred, sobbed hysterically. Helplessly, Jennifer watched Fred writhe in pain as they waited for the ambulance to arrive.

Fred Thomas had gone to that dark place parents go when they lose a child. Jennifer had visited that place the day the doctor told her that her baby was stillborn. The dark swallowed her whole for months as she grieved her loss, blaming herself for her baby's death, certain that she was being punished for her initial decision to give him away to strangers. God was punishing her for not wanting her baby more, for not fighting harder to keep him until her abduction knocked some sense into her. She understood Fred Thomas's pain, more than she wanted.

The next morning, the rain continued to pelt the windows of Jennifer's kitchen, as she poured cream into a steaming cup of coffee. A loud hammering on the front door startled her, and the cup flew from her hand and shattered into a million pieces on the floor.

She ran to her living room and jerked open the front door. Dick Mason stood on her front porch.

"A group of Cub Scouts just found a body in Deer Run State Park."

"I'll get my rain slicker."

Dick raced the ten miles to the park in the driving rain and nearly lost control when the car hydroplaned near the park entrance. There were no police cars or emergency vehicles in the parking lot and they realized they were the first responders.

"Come this way," said Dick, as he raced toward the park suspension bridge. "Dispatch said a conservation officer called it in. He's on trail number ten near the Ice Cave."

Jennifer looked down at her flat-heeled leather shoes
and wished she'd thought to bring her hiking boots.
Freaking great. She'd hiked the trails of Deer Run State Park
many times with her dad, and sometimes by herself. She
knew trail number ten was one of the more rugged trails
with steep hills, deep canyons, and sandstone cliffs. She and
her dad had taken this trail to see the erratics, which were
pieces of bedrock from Canada that had been moved there
by glaciers. The downpour of rain guaranteed the trail
would be difficult, even treacherous, with the wrong type of
shoes.

They raced across the park's suspension bridge, then
entered the muddy trail at a fast walk. The area was quiet,
with only the sound of rain drops hitting the leaves of the
tall trees and pelting the hoods of their yellow, sheriff-issued
rain slickers. Dick's feet skidded as they hit a curve in the
path too fast, but he regained his balance and moved
forward. They'd reached the steep hill that led to the Ice
Cave, when Jennifer slid in the mud, lost her balance, and
fell face-first down the hill. She struggled to fasten onto
something to break her fall. She latched onto a sapling for a
second, lost her grip and slid the rest of the way on her
stomach until she landed at the bottom. Dick rushed down
the hill as quickly as he could in the slippery mud to pull
Jennifer to her feet.

She was covered with muck that clung to her face and

hands, and soaked her pants and shoes. Trying to clean herself off, Jennifer wiped her muddy hands on a scarf she'd pulled out of her pocket. She turned away from Dick, not wanting him to see she was hurting from the fall, as well as the scratches and cuts that covered her face and hands. Dick turned her around and wiped at the mud on her face.

"I'm fine, Dick. Stop hovering. We're close to the cave, let's keep going."

They'd gone only ten feet or so, when Jennifer saw five Cub Scouts huddled like frightened baby ducks around their wide-eyed troop leader. Several feet from them was the conservation officer she assumed called in the body. Then she saw her, a young woman lying on her back with her arms folded across her breasts, her hands pressed together as though she were praying. The rain ran rivulets down her naked body; her eyes were open, cloudy and opaque, blankly staring into space. Her face was swollen and her body had a purplish cast, but it was Catherine Thomas.

Bile rushed to Jennifer's throat and she swallowed hard. She tried to blink away the quick tears forming in her eyes, reminding herself that she was a professional. This was not the time to get emotional. She could do that later, when she was alone. She had to stay in control so she could secure the scene. Jennifer knew that trace evidence was critically important as it could definitively link an individual or object to the crime or accident scene. Since the body was uncovered, the rain was washing critical trace evidence away.

Suddenly Jennifer became so enraged she shook with anger as she screamed at the conservation officer, "Where the hell were you when they did the training on crime scene preservation? You couldn't fucking cover the body?! Gee, do you think the rain might be washing away valuable trace evidence?! And why the hell haven't you moved the Cub Scouts and leader away from the scene!"

The conservation officer just looked at her with a blank expression, which had the effect of pouring gasoline on her anger. She jerked off her rain slicker and carefully laid it across the top of Catherine's body. Dick Mason removed his, and she placed it over the bottom half. The conservation officer, hands in his pockets, watched them closely, but didn't move or say anything.

Jennifer yanked her cell phone out of her pocket and called Lane Hansen. "I need back up at Deer Run State Park. We have a body here."

"Shit, is it Catherine Thomas?"

"Yes, Lane. I think it is."

"I'm on my way. What do you need?"

"Dick and I are the first responders. We need the coroner and crime scene techs. It's vital that we get a deputy ASAP at the Ice Cave on trail number ten to secure the scene. The crime scene has already been compromised by the rain, Cub Scouts and who knows what else. We need to make sure it's secured before anything else happens. We also need a deputy at the park entrance to prevent anyone from entering. This deputy needs to get ID, addresses, and phone numbers from anyone leaving the park. Our killer may still be here."

"I'll give Blake Stone a heads up. He should be there any minute."

Blake Stone appeared and quickly assessed the situation. He turned to the two deputies following him, "Take the Cub Scouts and leader away from the scene, back to the parking lot. Get the leader's statement, then find out why the hell she had these kids out here in this rain. Then get the Cub Scouts' names and phone numbers, and find their parents to pick them up. We can call them in later to make a statement with their parents present. Make a call to Pat Brown, our victim's advocate counselor. Those kids are going to need to talk to someone."

Dick pulled the conservation officer aside. They walked several feet away. Jennifer couldn't hear what they were saying, but the ranger waved his hands as he talked as if he were angry. Dick was trying to calm him down, but soon the ranger pushed at Dick and stomped up the trail. "I'll get his statement," Dick called to Jennifer as he ran after the ranger.

Blake touched Jennifer's arm, "Is it Catherine?"

When she nodded, Blake pulled back the rain slicker covering Catherine's face. A drop of rain hit Catherine's eye and as if it were a tear streaming down her cheek. That's when Jennifer lost it. She rushed into the woods, bent down and heaved until she lost the contents of her stomach. Catherine was dead. She'd never see the bright, young woman wait on her table again, or hear the excitement in her voice as she talked about going to the police academy.

Jennifer turned to see Blake at her side. He gently touched her back and she gravitated toward him. His strong arms encircled her like a warm blanket. She pulled him closer, melting against the warmth of his hard body. Nothing had felt that good for Jennifer in a long, long time. Something heated inside her as she breathed in his warm, male scent. They stood like that for a long moment, until Jennifer noticed the arrival of two crime scene technicians and a deputy who was putting up yellow crime scene tape. She gently pushed Blake away.

He brushed her hair out of her face to examine the cuts and scratches on her cheeks.

"Jennifer, are you okay?"

"Yes, I am so sorry about that. I'm a professional. That shouldn't have happened."

"You're a professional, but you're human first." He walked her back to the crime scene.

Bob Goldberg pulled out his camera and walked the perimeter, taking photographs of various aspects of the crime scene. There was no such thing as taking too many photos, as they'd learned the hard way during a past case. He approached Catherine's body and took photos of various angles as he got closer and closer to her.

Karen Katz, with her hands in her pockets, also walked the perimeter looking for anything, no matter how small, that might be connected to the crime. She walked past Jennifer and Blake and said, "This is the secondary crime scene. She was killed somewhere else and dumped here." She walked back to the body, lowering herself to her knees as she looked at Catherine's face and neck.

"So how'd she die, Karen?" Jennifer asked as she wiped a wet strand of hair from her eyes.

"Did you see her neck?" She motioned for them to come closer. "See the deep grooves and bruising around her neck? I'd bet my next paycheck she was strangled with some kind of ligature. Doc Meade may even be able to tell you what type he used."

"What about time of death?" asked Blake.

"This is only a guesstimate. The doc has the final word on that. But judging by the stiffness or rigor mortis of the body, I'd say eight to twelve hours ago." She paused and looked at her watch. "It's 9:00 a.m., so that puts it between 9:00 p.m. last night and 1:00 a.m. this morning. Keep in mind, the rain and cold weather slows down the process. It's forty damn degrees today so my estimate could be off a bit. But, like I said, Doc Meade has the final say on time of death."

"I heard my name." Doc Meade appeared with two of his assistants. Jennifer had known Doc Meade through her dad since she was a child. The good old country boy demeanor hid a brilliant coroner who had helped solve too many cases to count. "Jesus Christ, that's Catherine Thomas. Isn't it?"

Jennifer nodded and shuddered as a chill ran up her spine. She crossed her arms to warm herself. She was freezing. The dampness of her clothes felt like it was seeping into her very soul.

"I was still hoping we'd find her alive," Doc Meade said. "Damn it. I watched that girl grow up. She and her parents never missed a Sunday at church. Once she was old enough, Catherine sang in the choir. And that girl could sing."

He left them to do a precursory exam of Catherine's body, asking his two assistants to carefully move her body onto the body bag, so the two crime scene techs could examine the ground underneath.

"Wait a minute! Turn her over," shouted Doc Meade. It was obvious that the coroner had noticed something. They gently turned the body over. There were severe bruises, abrasions and lacerations on Catherine's buttocks, back and thighs. "The sick bastard beat her with something. Christ, he tortured her. This poor girl suffered before she died."

Jennifer watched as the two assistants moved Catherine into a body bag. They placed the body on the stretcher they'd carry to the parking lot, where the coroner van was parked.

Following them, Doc Meade looked back and asked, "Are both of you going to attend the autopsy? I'll start at ten o'clock tomorrow morning."

Blake looked at Jennifer and said, "It took a lot of rage to beat a woman like that."

"Which makes me wonder if this was personal? Did the killer know Catherine?" Jennifer asked.

"Another angle is that he has hostility toward all women, and took that out on her."

"He posed the body, Blake," Jennifer said. "He made her look as if she were praying. Are we dealing with a religious fanatic? Or is the killer trying to communicate something to us?"

"Maybe he's telling us that at the end she prayed for her death?"

Jennifer shrugged her shoulders. "Why pose her naked body out in the open?"

"Because he knew she'd be found. The bastard thinks he's smarter than we are, and he's pretty sure he's not going to be caught. I think he wanted us to find her."

"Do you think he's done this before?"

"I don't know, but I can promise you that we're going to find out." Blake paused, knelt down and sniffed where the body had laid. "Now I know what that smell is."

"What?"

"Bleach. I think he bleached down her body. That tells us the sick freak know something about trace evidence."

"You think he's in law enforcement?"

"Maybe. Or it could be he's a big fan of forensic TV shows."

"Do you think Karen was right when she said

Catherine was killed somewhere else?"

"The damn rain makes it difficult to say. But my guess is that Karen's right and she was killed somewhere else and dumped here."

"Thanks to the dumbass in the conservation officer suit, the scene's been compromised."

"Yeah, but I still say she was dumped. No sign of a struggle. The rain wouldn't have washed away everything."

Jennifer stared at Blake. What kind of monster were they up against?

There was no let up with the drenching rain as they hiked trail number ten back to the entrance and then the parking lot.

When they reached Blake's SUV, he looked down at Jennifer, and rubbed his thumb across a streak of mud on her cheekbone. "How about if I take you home so you can wash up and change clothes?"

Jennifer didn't answer right away. She was thinking about how good it felt to be in his arms. She wondered how it would feel if he kissed her. Was she insane? The last thing she needed right now was to get involved with another investigator. This might be the biggest case of her career.

Did she want to jeopardize it by getting emotionally tangled with Blake?

"I see my partner waiting for me." She walked away, heading toward the vehicle where Dick sat inside.

At first Blake thought he imagined it, but no, it was fear that crossed Jennifer's face when he'd asked to take her home. What the hell? He'd worked with her every day since she'd joined the department. Then it hit him. She had feelings for him and it scared the crap out of her. Feelings that made things a lot more complicated — for both of them.

Jennifer got into the passenger side of vehicle, and Dick handed her a towel. She wiped at her face and hair as he drove through the parking lot and onto Route 40 toward town.

What was wrong with her? Why didn't she let Blake take her home? Stupid question. The man radiated testosterone and she'd been going through some serious withdrawal. Try five years of withdrawal. A man hadn't affected her like this since she'd first fallen for Paul. Every time Blake came near her, her senses went on alert and her body reacted — whether she wanted it to or not. Besides jeopardizing the case, she reminded herself she was the sheriff's daughter and Blake was on her team. Several good reasons she should distance herself from the sexy detective.

Something was wrong with Dick. The two of them had driven ten minutes without Dick saying a word. In other cases they'd worked, he couldn't wait to compare notes with Jennifer and debate theories about the crime. His jaw clenched, he stiffly sat behind the steering wheel.

"Did you know that jerk conservation officer? Is he new? I've never seen him before." Jennifer asked.

"He's my son." Dick said the words so quietly, they were barely audible.

"What did you say?" Jennifer was incredulous.

"The conservation officer. He's my son."

"Son? You've been my partner for how many years, and you're just now mentioning you have a son?!"

"It's not something I'm proud of," Dick began. "His name is Damon. He's twenty-seven-years old. I hadn't seen him since the day I left him and his mother, over twenty years ago. Then last week, he shows up out of nowhere and sits down at my table at the Sugar Creek Cafe."

"What did he say?"

"He just said he wanted me to know who he was and that he'd moved here from Ohio. He has a lot of anger toward me, and I don't blame him. I was a terrible excuse for a father."

"I'm sorry, Dick."

"I wish I could turn back the clock and do things differently. I was so young. Back then, all I knew was I couldn't get away from his mother fast enough."

"Where is your ex-wife now?"

"Damon said she still lives in Ohio in the same house. He says I should go visit her." Dick paused for a second. "That will never happen. The woman is toxic. I was a bastard for leaving my kid to fend for himself."

"What did he say about the crime scene?"

"Damon said the Scout leader called the ranger station with her cell phone right after they found the body. He was the conservation officer on duty so he took the call. Damon said he was so shocked to find the body the way it was, that he wasn't thinking. He knew better than to leave the body uncovered like that in the rain, but he just wasn't thinking."

Jennifer frowned but said nothing. She didn't believe Damon's story and was surprised that Dick did. She knew for a fact that all area conservation officers got training on how to preserve a crime scene during their first week on the job. Jennifer knew because Karen Katz taught the class.

He sat in his Jeep and watched as the bitch detective with the big mouth and her sorry excuse for a partner drove out of the parking lot.

Detective Jennifer Brennan had a lot to say about the way he didn't secure the crime scene. Her anger reminded him of his mama and the way she'd screamed at him when she thought he'd done something wrong. Of course, with Mama, everything he did was wrong.

That bitch detective had better hope she was never in the wrong place at the wrong time, because he'd snatch her up in a second. She'd find out how stupid he was at the receiving end of his belt.

Jennifer Brennan thought she was so fucking smart. Little did she know she was no match for him. She didn't have a chance in hell of ever catching him. He wished he could see her face when she discovered he'd left no evidence she could use to track him.

What was amusing was dear old Dick's lecture to him about preserving a crime scene. Neither he nor his bitch partner had an inkling of how brilliant he was to wait for the rain before he killed Catherine and dumped her body. Bye, bye trace evidence.

4 CHAPTER FOUR

On Monday morning, Jennifer raced to Michael Brandt's prosecutor office near the courthouse for a meeting he called to discuss Doc Meade's autopsy findings. Even though she and Blake had attended the autopsy, Michael wanted them to attend the briefing to provide insights, and to answer questions about the case. Jennifer knew her dad would be attending, along with Lane Hansen.

She flew up the marble stairs to the second floor. Jennifer was one of those people who was always early, no matter what the occasion, but she'd stopped by her office, lost track of time, and was now running late.

Michael, Lane, Blake, Doc Meade and her dad were already seated around the table when she reached the conference room, so she slipped in and took a seat next to Blake as quietly as she could. Her dad glanced at her with a concerned expression. Her parents worried too much, and she felt guilty about it. The last thing she wanted was to cause her parents concern. Ever since her abduction five years before, they'd taken overprotectiveness to an all new level. But since Catherine's abduction, she had more of an understanding of a parent's fear of something bad happening to his or her child.

As if sensing how much she needed it, Blake picked up the pot near him and poured hot coffee into Jennifer's mug and handed it to her. She whispered her thanks and took her first sip. He must have showered just before the meeting because his hair was still damp. She breathed in his masculine scent of fresh soap and the outdoors. A sudden visual of the two of them bathing each other in her shower shot to the forefront of her brain, and she felt her face heat, along with other parts of her body. Of all the inappropriate times for an erotic vision of Blake, this topped the list — especially since among those seated at the conference table was her dad. She shook her head as if to remove the image.

Jennifer looked around the long, cherry wood conference table and wondered why her partner Dick hadn't arrived. She'd never known him to miss a meeting. Jennifer had tried to call him earlier, but he hadn't answered, so she left a message on his voice mail.

Michael cleared his throat and aimed his first question

at the coroner. "Doc, what were your findings with Catherine Thomas's autopsy?"

Doc Meade drained his cup of any remaining coffee and began. "The cause of death was strangulation with a ligature, breaking the hyoid bone. Judging from the inch-and-a-half width of the groove in the victim's neck, I think the ligature was a belt. In fact, there is bruising that suggests the shape of a metal belt buckle on the back of her neck, as you can see." He pulled a photo out of a thick file folder and passed it around the room.

"If you'll bear with me, I'd like to do a demonstration. Lane, your belt looks to be the right width. May I borrow it?"

Lane unbuckled and pulled off his belt and handed it to him.

"Jennifer, since our victim was female, would you please volunteer to help me." After she nodded, he directed her to lie face down on the conference table as the rest of the group stood around the table. He placed Lane's belt around Jennifer's neck and pulled it through the buckle until it was snug.

"Judging from the buckle marks on back of the victim's neck, I believe she was lying face-down either on the floor or on top of a table or bed. The killer approached her from behind to strangle her with the belt. You'll notice that as I stand next to her, the belt is pulled at an angle, which would have caused a different marking on the victim's neck." Doc Meade climbed on the table. "That is why I believe he straddled her, like this, from behind as he pulled the belt tighter and tighter until the victim died.

He helped Jennifer get off the table, handed the belt back to Lane, then continued. "Thankfully, death would have come quickly after the onset of unconsciousness which is only ten to fifteen seconds."

Blake leaned forward and asked, "What about the injuries to her buttocks, thighs and back?"

"It's likely the killer used the same belt he used to kill the victim to cause the severe bruising, abrasions and lacerations to her buttocks, back and thighs." He passed around another photo. "See the linear marks connected with a curved end? These are indicative of the belt being folded in half, with the looped end being used to strike the victim. Since the wounds are in varying stages of healing, she suffered many beatings."

"Oh, my God," exclaimed Jennifer as she shuddered. "I don't even want to imagine the pain she endured during those beatings."

"The pain of the beatings with the belt was significant enough to cause the victim to bite her lip so deeply, it was practically severed."

Tim shook his head angrily. "I've been in law enforcement for thirty years and I've never seen such brutality. We need to find this sick bastard and lock him up where he belongs."

Lane nodded his head in agreement then asked the doc, "Did you find anything that suggests Catherine was tied down?"

"Yes. There is bruising on her wrists and ankles from being restrained. In addition, we found residue from tape on her wrists and ankles. I sent a sample of the residue to the lab. My guess is that the tape used was duct tape — and he used it to restrain her for the seven days she was missing."

He got up to fill his cup with more coffee then returned to the table. "I'm convinced she was also restrained during her murder because there are no fingernail marks on her neck to suggest she struggled to remove the ligature or belt."

"Was she raped?" asked Michael.

"Yes, there was vaginal tearing that suggests the victim was raped. There was no biological evidence; therefore, it is likely the killer wore a condom." The coroner tiredly rubbed his hands over his face. "There's a good possibility that the killer was raping her at the same moment he was strangling her with the belt."

"So this killing could be sexually motivated?" asked

Jennifer.

"That is your job to discover."

Lane squirmed in his chair, agitation evident on his face. "Tell me you found some trace evidence or something that will help us find this freak."

"The body was found nude and had been washed with what looked like regular bath soap. There was residue in her hair. We're sending a sample to the lab. The body was also washed down with bleach. Each of her nails were cut and scrubbed with bleach. I'm sorry, there's not much to go on."

"Time of death?" asked Michael.

"Anytime between 9:00 p.m. last night and 1:00 a.m. this morning."

Blake's face reddened with anger. "Whoever did this was playing with us when he left Catherine's car in the Deer Run State Park parking lot. That's why it wasn't seen before. It wasn't there. We searched that park three fucking times. Someone would have seen it."

"I agree," said Jennifer. "He left her car there after he completely wiped it down. There were no fingerprints, not even Catherine's. Which makes me wonder if he might be in law enforcement? Look at how hard he worked to eliminate the trace evidence."

"Maybe, Jennifer," said Tim. "But keep in mind, since TV programs like CSI have gained popularity, there are a lot of amateur forensics experts out there. Criminals are using these programs and the Internet to learn how to hide their crimes."

"I agree," said Lane. "Remember how Charles Beatty, the serial killer who tried to kill Anne, washed down every victim with bleach. He was a computer technician. We can't rule out the killer might be a cop, but I don't think it's wise to turn our entire focus in that direction."

"Any suspects?" asked Michael.

"We're looking at Catherine's boyfriend, Nicholas Connor. He has no alibi for the day she went missing. He also hasn't participated in any of the searches for her. We're talking with Catherine's friends today to find out more about their relationship," Blake offered.

In the parking lot outside Michael's office building, Blake stopped Jennifer. "So where's Dick? Wasn't he supposed to be at the autopsy and this meeting?"

"Yes. I tried calling him, but got no answer. I left a voicemail."

"Well, since you're without a partner today, how about helping me interview some of Catherine's friends?"

"Sure."

"Hungry? I thought we'd have lunch at the Sugar Creek Cafe and talk to the owner and some of the waitresses Catherine worked with."

Jennifer grabbed her laptop out of her car and joined Blake in his SUV. "I was thinking. We've done a criminal background on Nicholas but didn't find anything. He's been teaching at the elementary for about a year. Wonder why he left his last school? Most teachers stay for years at the same school to get tenure. Let's find out what his fellow teachers have to say about him."

"Good idea. The more information on him, the better."

At the cafe, Jennifer ordered a breaded tenderloin sandwich with fries and a sweet tea. She studied the young waitress who took Blake's order. With brown hair tied in a perky ponytail, she looked like she was the same age as Catherine, and just as friendly with a contagious smile. She introduced herself as Brianna Hayden, and promised to take a break and talk to them, as soon as she put their order in.

Jennifer noticed several people staring at the large flat-screen television on the far wall. They were watching her dad's press conference to announce Catherine's murder. A couple of waitresses tearfully hugged each other after hearing the news. The cafe owner, John Isaac, shook his head as if in disbelief.

Brianna returned a short time later with their drinks. Jennifer motioned for her to sit on the chair next to her. Visibly shaken, Brianna sank into her chair.

"I can't believe she's dead," Brianna said, as tears slowly found their way down her cheeks.

Jennifer lightly touched the waitress's hand to comfort her. "Brianna, we need to ask you some questions about Catherine. Were you two friends?"

"Yes, we became friends about a year ago when she started working here. We hung out after work sometimes."

"What was your impression of Catherine's relationship with Nicholas Connor?"

"I'm not the best person to ask about Nicholas. I don't like him very much." Brianna frowned as she nervously folded and unfolded a napkin.

"Why not?" asked Blake.

"I didn't think he was good for Catherine. She was so sweet and naive, and he is so *not*. Sometimes I think he purposely picked fights with her. I never witnessed them fighting, but the way Catherine talked, it sounded like he got a kick out of upsetting her."

Jennifer's eyebrow rose as she glanced at Blake, and then asked, "Were they arguing a lot?"

"Yes, especially after Catherine overheard some of the

other waitresses talking about how Nicholas was frequenting the area bars at night without her. I heard he was spending most of his time at the Hoosier Sports Bar."

Jennifer noticed John Isaac tapping his watch as he glared at Brianna. "Oh, it looks like my break is over. I'll see if your food is ready."

John moved to their table, sitting in the chair where Brianna sat. "Terrible news about Catherine. Hated to hear it. She was a good kid. Is that why you're here, to ask questions?"

"Yes," answered Blake. "How well did you know Catherine?"

"Pretty well."

"What did you think of her relationship with Nicholas Connor?"

"I told her to break up with the pompous asshole, and you can tell him I said that. Catherine told me she was in love with him. But Nicholas was cheating on her every chance he got. He's supposed to be this upright citizen, elementary teacher. If you ask me, he's a prick."

"It doesn't sound like you like him very much," noted Jennifer.

"I don't."

"Do you think he had anything to do with Catherine's

death?"

"I wouldn't rule him out. That's for sure."

John left abruptly to help a customer at the register. Blake looked at Jennifer. "What do you think?"

"The cheating bothers me. Maybe a fight they had about it turned violent."

"I wonder if she caught him in the act. Remember the pizza delivery kid said a woman was with Nicholas when he delivered the food the night Catherine disappeared?"

Thirty minutes later, Blake and Jennifer were headed down Route 40 toward the elementary school where Nicholas Connor taught. With Blake focusing on the road, Jennifer gazed at him. He was wearing a gray T-shirt and jeans with a black leather blazer. The man was buff, his hard chest straining against the fabric of his shirt. She remembered how good he felt when he hugged her at the crime scene, his warm body pressed against hers. He definitely worked out, but she wondered why she'd never seen him at the Sheriff's Gym.

"See something you like, Jennifer?"

"Not sure what you're talking about," she said, looking away. Damn it. She couldn't believe he caught her staring at him again. Jennifer turned to look out her window so he wouldn't notice how hot her cheeks had become. She was acting like a school girl, or one of the female deputies who ogled him. What must he think of her?

He stopped for a traffic light. After a long moment, Blake said, "Jennifer, I like the color of your hair, it's the same color of the wheat in the farmer's field I pass on my way to work. Your eyes, the color of whiskey, are expressive and intelligent. I can always tell when you have an idea or question." He paused for a second. "Naw, I don't check you out either." He grinned mischievously and focused his attention on the green light and getting through the intersection.

His words came out of nowhere and sent her heart pounding an erratic rhythm. She shouldn't be so pleased.

By the time they reached the elementary, school was out and there were few cars in the parking lot. They entered and made a beeline for the principal's office. Sarah Hill, vice principal, was pulling a file out of a huge green filing cabinet when they entered. Once they introduced themselves, she motioned for them to sit in her office across the hall.

"We'd like to ask you some questions about one of your teachers." Blake began.

"I imagine the teacher you want to discuss is Nicholas Connor." Sarah sighed and took off her reading glasses.

"I've heard that Catherine Thomas was found murdered. I know they dated. So what do you want to know?"

"Tell us what you know about Nicholas." Jennifer urged.

"I know I wished I'd never hired him three years ago." Sarah said as she circled her desk to close the door for privacy.

"Why do you say that?" asked Jennifer as she glanced at Blake, whose eyebrows raised inquiringly.

"It wasn't long after he started teaching here that I got a visit from some parents who had some interesting information about Nicholas." She began. "They were friends with a family whose kids attended the high school in the corporation where Nicholas last taught in Salem, Indiana. There were rumors that he'd had a sexual relationship with a sixteen-year-old student."

"Were the rumors substantiated?"

"Not by me, and I tried," said Sarah, her voice laced with frustration.

"The sixteen-year-old's parents found a dresser drawer filled with suggestive love letters from Nicholas, along with a collection of romance books, each with the theme of a young girl who runs away with an older man. Nicholas and the girl had been meeting after school at his apartment. Her parents called the school, then the police. He was held overnight, but was never charged."

"Why wasn't he charged?" Jennifer asked, her lips pressed together in anger.

"The parents dropped the charges. They didn't want their daughter's reputation smeared. They moved out of town."

"What did the school corporation do?"

"I imagine they didn't have enough ammunition to fire him, so they probably made it clear he should find another place to teach," said Sarah.

Incredulous, Jennifer asked, "But when you called them for a reference, didn't they tell you about this?"

"That's the thing. They gave him a good reference." Sarah said with a smirk. "I guess if they hadn't, they might never be rid of him. So now I'm stuck with him and I'm watching his every move."

"Has anything happened here?" asked Blake.

"No relationships with high school girls that I know of. He's dated a couple of female teachers who work here. Neither one went out with him for very long because they found out about his long-term relationship with Catherine."

"Do you think Catherine knew Nicholas was dating these teachers?" Blake wondered.

"Who do you think told the teachers about their

relationship?"

Walking out to the car, Jennifer seethed with anger. "The bastard is a pedophile. They should have nailed him in Salem. There's no way he should be teaching school."

"It pisses me off, too. But there's not much they could do if the parents dropped the charges."

"It makes me that much more eager to interview him again — this time for Catherine's murder."

"That's a stretch, Jennifer, between preying on high school girls for sex, compared to torture and murder. We need more information. Brianna said Nicholas was spending a lot of time at the Hoosier Sports Bar. Let's find out who he was spending it with."

There were so many cars parked outside the Hoosier Sports Bar that Blake had difficulty finding a space to park. Inside the bar was the after-work crowd. Jennifer checked out the dining area, looking for Nicholas Connor, then scanned the bar, but she didn't see him.

"If there's anyone who can tell us what Nicholas was doing at this place, it's the bartender." Blake said and he led Jennifer to two empty bar stools.

Blake got the bartender's attention and she moved to

them. "What will you have?"

"Two sweet teas."

"Seriously? How about a couple of Long Island Teas?"

Blake took out his badge and laid it on the bar. "We're from the sheriff's office. Just the sweet teas and some information when you get back."

Jennifer noticed the bartender's mouth slip into a sour grin when she eyed the badge. The woman quickly turned her back to them as she prepared the iced teas. The bartender looked to be in her twenties with short, spiked platinum-blonde hair and heavy makeup. When she returned, she delivered the teas then turned to leave, but Jennifer glanced at her name tag, then caught her hand. "Patti, we need some information. It will only take a few minutes of your time."

"Listen, the bar is really busy tonight. I really don't have..."

Jennifer cut her off. "We can talk here or down at the station. Your choice."

She glared at Jennifer then asked a male bartender at the other side of the bar to watch her area while she took a break. "What do you want to know?"

Taking out her small writing pad, Jennifer asked, "What's your last name, Patti?"

"Simpson. Patti Simpson."

"Any relation to Butch Simpson?" asked Jennifer.

Patti blinked and swallowed uncomfortably. "Yeah, he's my husband."

Jennifer knew Butch Simpson. He was considered the town bully and never had a conflict he didn't resolve with his fists. Butch had been in and out of jail since he hit puberty. Most people feared his vicious temper and steered clear of him. She didn't want to imagine what it would be like to be married to the guy.

"Do you know Nicholas Connor?"

Patti nervously rubbed at a spot on the bar with a wash cloth. "Yeah, I know him." She said softly.

"We hear that Nicholas hangs out here a lot. We're wondering who he's hanging out with."

Patti's looked down as her eyes darted to the right, and Jennifer knew the next words out of her mouth would be a lie. "To tell the truth, I never noticed who Nicholas was hanging out with. It's a big place and on the weekends, it's packed, so your guess is good as mine."

She was definitely lying, and Jennifer resolved to find out why.

Blake moved in with a question. "Patti, have you seen Nicholas come in here with Catherine Thomas?"

She licked her lips, looking down again. "I suppose I might have seen them once or twice. Lots of people come here."

Three men arrived and sat at the bar. Patti's counterpart was at the far end of the bar mixing drinks. "Listen, I have a job to do. Are you finished with your questions?"

"For now."

Patti rushed off. Jennifer was far from being finished with questioning Patti Simpson. She was lying and Jennifer wanted to know why. She looked at Blake for his perspective, "What do you think?"

"She's lying through her teeth. Grab your glass. We're moving to the other end of the bar. Maybe her bartending partner will be more forthcoming."

Harry Brooks, the male bartender, eyed them curiously before asking them if they'd like another drink.

"Just information," responded Blake as he showed Harry his badge. "Nicholas Connor? Do you know him?"

"Of course, I know him. He comes in here a lot — usually later in the evening. What do you want to know?"

"We just want to get a sense of who he hangs out with," said Blake.

"He used to bring his girlfriend, Catherine, in here a lot.

But that changed after the fight."

"What fight?" asked Jennifer. They'd already learned that the two had argued a lot, but no one mentioned they did it in public.

"About a month and a half ago, Nicholas and Catherine were sitting in that booth over there." Harry pointed out a booth not far from the bar. "I heard a commotion and looked over in time to see Catherine throw her drink in Nicholas's face. They screamed at each other until I walked over and asked them to quiet down or they'd have to leave. Catherine shoved her plate of food in Nicholas's lap, grabbed her purse and ran out of the bar. He cleaned himself up and ordered tequila shots until closing. That was the last night I saw him in here with Catherine."

"Have you seen him hang out with anyone other than Catherine?"

"Yeah, but I'm surprised Patti didn't tell you when you were talking to her."

"Why's that?"

"He spends most nights sitting at the bar chatting with Patti."

Nicholas Connor was finishing his fried chicken dinner at the Sugar Creek Cafe when Blake and Jennifer located him. He didn't say much on the ride to the station, but the scowl on his face spoke volumes.

When they arrived at the station, Blake asked a deputy to put Nicholas in an interview room.

"Are we leaving the bad boy to stew about his situation?" asked Jennifer.

"Yup. Let's leave him in there for thirty minutes."

Julie Thomas sat in Fred's room at Memorial Hospital. She'd been there since his heart attack in the parking lot when Catherine's car was found. He'd had to undergo heart bypass surgery. His condition was guarded, and the doctors warned that the news of Catherine's murder could kill him in his fragile state. So she'd waited, holding Fred's hand and praying he'd regain his strength. Julie was so tired and worried that she felt numb.

She closed her eyes to rest for a minute. Julie remembered how proud Fred had been when Catherine was born. He'd walked the hospital floor, carrying a box loaded with Cuban cigars that he passed out to whomever he encountered. They had been so young and happy. Fred had turned out to be a wonderful father, supporting Catherine in everything she did. Julie blinked as tears ran down her cheeks unstopped. Christ, she missed Catherine. Her little girl had grown up to be her best friend. How empty her life had become in such a short time.

Julie's cell phone tune sounded. She jerked it out of her purse and went into the hall, fearing the noise would wake Fred out of his peaceful slumber. Before answering, she glanced at the display and froze when she saw the name "Catherine Thomas" in black letters on the small screen. Icy fear twisted around her heart, her body trembled, as she lifted the phone to her ear. She struggled to say something but the words wouldn't come.

"Bet you thought this call was from Catherine, didn't you, Mama?" The male voice was deep and absolutely emotionless as he taunted her.

"Who is this? Where did you get Catherine's cell phone?"

"Where do you think? Found your number in her favorites."

"You bastard! Why did you hurt her?" She gasped, realizing a shiver of panic.

"Mama, I just wanted you to know that good girls don't always go straight to heaven. Sometimes they get to visit hell first. I made sure of that with your Catherine."

The call disconnected and Julie Thomas leaned back, screaming a piercing cry that bounced off the walls in the quiet hallway, until she lost consciousness.

Lane stood with Jennifer and Blake, watching Nicholas Connor through the one-way glass. Lane had been briefed and observed the man in the other room, who was biting his fingernail and pacing. Finally, Nicholas sat down.

"Think he's been in there long enough?" asked Jennifer.

After Lane and Blake nodded, Jennifer entered the interview room while Lane and Blake watched.

Jennifer sat in the chair directly across from Nicholas. She felt his eyes on her, but didn't look up until she retrieved a small writing pad and pen from her jacket.

"Hello, Nicholas. Sorry I kept you waiting. You wouldn't believe all the things I have to take care of with this murder case. You heard about us finding Catherine's body, right?"

His eyes wide and face flushed, Nicholas nodded.

Jennifer looked down at her pad for a second then asked, "According to my information, you were a no-show at the search organized to find Catherine last weekend? Is that right?"

He nodded again.

"Now, maybe it's just me, but I find it odd that a long-time boyfriend wasn't there to help search for his girlfriend's body. I mean if I'd been in a relationship with a guy that went missing, I'd be the first one at a search organized to find him."

"I had plans I couldn't get out of." He was starting to sweat and wiped across his forehead with the back of his hand.

"What kind of plans?"

"I'd already committed to chaperoning the high school debate team at a meet in Terre Haute."

"How many members of the high school debate team are female, Nicholas?"

"I don't know. I guess eleven or so." He replied sharply, acting as if she were asking a stupid question.

"I'm asking because I hear you have a thing for high school girls." Jennifer asked, holding her temper in check.

"I thought we were here to talk about Catherine?" Nicholas was eager to change the subject.

"Did Catherine discover that you have a thing for high school girls? Is that why you two argued?" asked Jennifer.

"Who said we argued? We got along just fine." Nicholas eyes were blinking at her, then suddenly he looked down. He was lying.

"That's not what I hear, Nicholas. I have witnesses who say you and Catherine quarreled a great deal." She chided.

He just stared at her.

"Just a second. It seems like there was another question I wanted to make sure I asked you." Jennifer flipped through her notepad until she found a page. She tapped on it with her fingernail. "So on the night Catherine disappeared, you say you were home alone watching the Pacers vs. Miami Heat game on ESPN?"

"That's right."

"Hmm, that's where I get confused, Nicholas, There was no Pacer game on ESPN that night."

Nicholas glared at her.

"Another thing, when I talked to kid who delivered your pizza, he said when he arrived you were not alone."

"He's lying." Nicholas spat.

He was getting rattled, just like she wanted.

"Is he? If he's lying, then he had a vivid imagination. He told us he saw a light-haired woman wearing a lot of makeup sitting on your sofa. "Catherine never wore a lot of makeup, did she? I wouldn't describe her hair color as light, either. "

"He's mistaken." Nicholas said the words but wouldn't meet her gaze.

"I'm thinking that you had a date that night. You ordered pizza. Maybe you found a good movie on TV and got cozy with your date on the sofa."

"No, you're wrong. I was alone."

"Yeah, I think you were getting cozy with your date and Catherine caught you. She wondered if you were cheating, and now she was sure. Once Catherine arrived, your date left. That's when you and Catherine had a fight. Maybe it was the worst fight you ever had. Things happen. The fight turns violent and before you know it, Catherine is dead. Is that how it happened, Nicholas?"

He jumped out of his chair. "No! That didn't happen!"

"Calm down and sit down," Jennifer hissed.

"Okay, I was with someone. But no one can know about it. She's married. Her husband will kill both of us. He was out-of-town and we spent the night together."

"If she's your alibi, I've got to have her name, Nicholas."

"You don't understand. If I tell anyone and he finds out, he'll kill us both."

"Okay, then," She said as she closed her notepad. "I'll get a deputy to take you to your cell."

"All right, all right. It was Patti Simpson."

A loud knock sounded on the door. With her eyes glued on Nicholas, Jennifer opened the door and stepped into the hall where Blake waited.

"Why did you stop me? It was going well."

"We have to cut him loose."

He had to be kidding. "What the hell? He's got guilt written all over his face."

"Yeah, he does. But I don't think it's about Catherine's murder."

Jennifer shook her head with confusion. "What are you talking about, Blake?"

"The killer just called Julie Thomas with Catherine's cell phone."

"What?!"

Blake pulled Jennifer out of the hallway and into the small room with the one-way glass. "We tracked the cell phone's ping at a tower near the Thomas house when he called. He's either turned off the phone or removed the battery. We've gotten nothing since."

"So you think he was at their house when he called?"

"It looks that way. He must not have known the Thomases are at Memorial Hospital."

"Why would the killer call Catherine's mother?"

Jennifer was incredulous. She'd never heard of a case where the killer phoned the victim's mother. It was the definition of cruelty.

"It sounds like the prick called to taunt her. He said something about good girls don't always go straight to heaven and that he made sure Catherine got to visit hell first."

A quick and disturbing thought flicked through her brain. "At the crime scene, remember how the killer posed Catherine's body with her hands folded together, as if she were praying?"

"Yes."

"Is he communicating that just Catherine needed to visit hell before going to heaven? Or is he saying that all women should?"

"Somehow, I don't think he's just referring to Catherine, which makes it that much more critical to catch this sick freak before he kills again."

Lane entered the room and touched Jennifer's arm. "Hey, have you heard from Dick today?"

"No, I called him earlier but got no answer. Why?"

"Dispatch just sent an ambulance out to his place."

"Oh my God. Why?" asked Jennifer, her heart racing.

Lane shrugged his shoulders. "Don't know why. His

neighbor called it in."

Jennifer nodded and raced out of the building to the parking lot; Blake was close behind. Outside, he grabbed her arm and led her to his SUV. "I'll drive."

Blake flew his SUV out of the parking lot, flicking on the lights and siren. Jennifer shivered, as a wave of apprehension swept through her.

"Was Dick out sick today?" asked Blake

"I don't know. I haven't heard from him. That's why I think something must be wrong. Dick always calls me," Jennifer began. "I should have checked on him earlier. I don't think he's missed a day of work in twenty years. My intuition told me something was wrong, but I ignored it."

"Stop blaming yourself, Jennifer. We don't even know what's wrong." He held her hand, intertwining his fingers with hers.

Blake raced through town, hitting all the green lights. He didn't slow down until he hit County Road 47, a gravel road that ran through farm fields that would soon be filled corn and bean plants. Once they passed the Maffett farm, they could see the swirling lights of emergency vehicles lining the sides of the road. Blake hadn't even brought the SUV to a stop, when Jennifer jumped out of the car. She rushed ahead, flashing her badge at a deputy who tried to stop her. She needed to find Dick. He had to be okay.

"Jennifer, stop," called Blake as he raced after her.

She ran down Dick's long driveway panting so hard she thought her lungs would burst. Jennifer had to reach Dick and see that he was okay.

She grabbed the arm of the first EMT she saw. "Dick Mason lives here. Where is he?"

The EMT only shook his head. "I'm sorry."

An older man, face crinkled from working years in the sun, stepped forward. "Are you Jennifer?"

"Yes." Jennifer was numb. Dick couldn't be dead. She wiped at the tears blinding her vision.

The man took her hand in his, and said, "I'm Carl Freeman. I own the farm up the road." He paused as a deputy ran past them. "Dick's told me all about you. Dick and me usually shared a beer in the evenin' on my porch. He'd tell me about his day, and I'd share mine. Hell, I think we've been doing that for more than ten years. Kind of our ritual. He was mighty proud of you, Jennifer. He said you were a good detective."

She bit her lip and asked, "Do you know what happened?"

"Just what I saw. Dick hadn't been over to see me in two days. This was unusual so on my way to town this morning; I stopped in to check on him. As soon as I got close enough to the house, I noticed exhaust smoke seeping out from under his garage door. I jumped out of my truck, lifted the garage door and turned off his car. Dick wasn't in the garage so I went through the open kitchen door and walked through the house calling his name. The air was so thick with exhaust I had trouble breathing so I opened up the front door and living room windows. I found Dick on his bed. He was already gone. There was a cup of coffee and a prescription bottle on his bedside table. Little pills were strewn everywhere, on his bed, on the table, on the floor. Found out from the EMT, the pills were Valium. Don't know how many Dick took."

"Are you saying Dick committed suicide? No! He wouldn't do that."

"Jennifer, I wouldn't have believed it either, but I saw it with my own eyes."

"Was there a note?" asked Jennifer.

"Yes, it was on the kitchen table. It said, 'I'm not the man people think I am.'"

Blake reached Jennifer and gathered her into his arms, holding her snugly against him. He stroked her hair and said, "Jennifer, it's going to be okay."

Sobbing, she pushed at his chest. "No, it's not going to be okay. Dick was my partner. I'm supposed to be his backup and protect him when he needs me. But I wasn't here to protect him. I sensed something was wrong and did nothing. I should have found a way to make him talk to me."

Dick Mason was to be buried in the same cemetery as her baby, Timmy, his headstone overlooking the Wabash River. It was a gray, misty morning, the weather almost as depressing as the occasion. The entire sheriff's department was in attendance in dress uniform, each wearing a black band around his or her badge to signify the loss of a fellow law enforcement officer. Standing next to Frankie and Lane, Jennifer listened as a man played "Danny Boy" on his bagpipes next to Dick's coffin, which was covered with the American flag.

Jennifer hated funerals. She'd always been a private person, and the public good-bye ceremony was too much for her emotions. It brought back memories of the day she buried her baby boy. Jennifer quickly wiped a tear away with the back of her suit sleeve and felt Blake squeeze her hand. She glanced at him and wished she were wrapped tight in his arms, pressed against the warmth of his hard body. Jennifer couldn't forget how Blake had held her at Catherine's crime scene, and how right it'd felt to be in his arms. And she'd tried.

Jennifer was going to miss Dick Mason more than anyone knew. It was Dick who'd patiently shown her the ropes when she made detective. He did it for *her*, and not to impress her dad. Dick didn't give a damn that her father was sheriff. He wanted her to succeed and had told her that many times.

Jennifer thought she'd known Dick inside and out until the day she discovered he had a son. She thought they'd shared everything about themselves. Why did he keep that a secret from her? Perhaps he was ashamed of the way he'd left his son with his ex-wife years before and never looked back.

Dick's estranged son, Damon Mason, was standing on the other side of the coffin and Jennifer couldn't stop staring at him for some kind of sign that he and his father had made amends. But he showed little emotion that revealed they had.

Damon was good-looking in a rugged kind of way, with a long, lean body like his father's that stood tall and straight. His tanned skin reflected his occupation as a conservation officer and his preference for outdoor work. His eyes were blue, but more of an ice blue, with little warmth to them. His expression during the entire funeral proceedings was as blank and unreadable as it had been the day she'd seen him at the crime scene.

Damon was her partner's only family member, but she couldn't bring herself to comfort him. There was something off about him, and she couldn't figure out what. She'd pulled his statement about why he didn't secure Catherine

Thomas's crime scene. He'd written exactly what Dick reported, that he hadn't discovered a body before and he'd become so upset he screwed up the procedures. Okay, maybe she should cut him a break for Dick's sake. But that wouldn't be soon. She was still pissed that valuable trace evidence, which might have led them to Catherine's killer, was washed away by the rain.

Sheer luck and his genius was a powerful combo. If he weren't surrounded by so many mourners, he'd bust a gut laughing his ass off.

Dear old Dad had invited him over for coffee. Said he wanted to talk, to get to know him better. That was a laugh. He sure wasn't interested in getting to know his son better twenty years ago when he abandoned him. Did the bastard really think he wouldn't pay for deserting him and leaving him with a sadistic lunatic?

The house was way the hell out in the country. He thought he'd never find it. Once he did, he found himself on a long driveway leading to an old farmhouse that had seen better days. His father was waiting for him in the front yard.

He'd excused himself to use the bathroom while his dad made coffee in the kitchen. That's where he saw the prescription bottle of Valium in the medicine cabinet and his plan was born. This day would be his father's last. He couldn't believe he'd been that fucking lucky. But luck didn't have anything to do with the genius of the plan.

He stuffed several Valium in his hand, and then went to the kitchen where his dad was pouring coffee into two mugs. He offered to carry the mugs to the living room, while his dad carried a plate of cookies. Halfway there, he told Dad he needed some milk for his coffee, turned and carried both mugs back to the kitchen. He dropped the Valium in his father's mug, and poured milk into his.

It wasn't long before dear old Dad was too drowsy to talk. And being the good son he was, he'd helped the older man to his bedroom. He then returned to the kitchen, grabbed a kitchen towel, lifted Dick's mug and placed it on his bedside table along with the bottle of Valium. Spilling the pills was a nice touch.

Grabbing some car keys he found in the kitchen, he went into the garage and started up the Crown Victoria. The car had a full tank of gas! Luck was with him again. He found a pen and paper and wrote a note he left on the kitchen table. All those years playing with a box of old letters from his father that Mama had kept paid off. He'd spent hours tracing and retracing each of the letters in the sentences that Dad wrote. He knew his father's handwriting better than his own.

He slipped out of the house through the front door, carefully wiping the knob with a kitchen towel. The rest, well, was history.

Of course, that hadn't been his original plan, which was to abduct his father, strap him to a table and give him a taste of what his mother had done to him for years, thanks to his desertion. How he would have enjoyed it.

5 CHAPTER FIVE

Exhausted, Jennifer couldn't remember a time she was more pleased to be in the comforts of her home. It had been one of the longest days and nights she'd ever lived through. She locked the front door, then took off her coat and put it in the coat closet. Glancing at her wall clock, she noticed it was already nine o'clock.

If there was one thing she detested, it was a funeral. Hell, she hated saying good-bye, period. Jennifer didn't want to think about how much she was going to miss Dick. Actually, she didn't want to think at all. All she wanted was a hot cup of coffee, a shower, and some food.

She walked through the living and dining room to the kitchen where she made a fresh pot of coffee. Jogging up the stairs, she jumped into a hot shower and tried to scrub the miserable day off her body and out of her mind. Turning off the shower with one hand, Jennifer reached with the other for the baby oil that she smoothed all over her body before she dried off with a thick towel. Her stomach growled as she threw on her bathrobe, letting her know she hadn't had anything to eat since breakfast.

Downstairs Jennifer headed for the kitchen and opened every cabinet to find something to eat. Nothing. She opened her refrigerator. There were two cartons of yogurt that should have been thrown out weeks ago, a jar of olives, a half-gallon of drinking water and a near-empty carton of milk. Damn. When was the last time she got groceries?

Blake took a deep breath, then turned his SUV onto Jennifer's street and parked outside her house. He glanced at her living room window. Her lights were on, which was a good thing and a bad thing. It was a good thing because he hadn't purchased the large sausage and mushroom pizza, hot-from-the-oven, nor the six-pack of Coors in the passenger seat for nothing. It was a bad thing because he shouldn't be within a city block of Jennifer Brennan. Not only was she a detective on his team, but her father was the sheriff, for Christ's sake.

If he had half a brain, he'd turn his vehicle around and head for home. But then, where Jennifer was concerned, he wasn't sure he had even half of a brain. The thing was — he couldn't get Jennifer out of his head. He couldn't stop thinking about her.

Spending all day with Jennifer, interviewing suspects and not being able to touch her, was pure torture. He couldn't look at the woman without wondering what she would be like in bed. Every time he got near her, he felt this buzz of sexual awareness.

The days were tough, but the nights were worse. Each fantasy was more erotic than the last. The dreams started with removing Jennifer's clothing slowly, one piece at a time. They ended with their bodies in a hot, slick dance until they exploded with pleasure. Inevitably, that was the moment he'd awaken on fire, panting and aroused.

He was a bastard coming here tonight. Hours before he'd attended Dick's funeral with Jennifer and watched her grieve for her partner. He was thinking maybe Jennifer didn't want to be alone tonight. Perhaps she needed someone to talk to. If she did, he wanted to be that guy.

Decision made. He was going in. Blake hopped out of the SUV, then reached over to grab the pizza and six-pack. Striding across the street, he jumped onto her front porch, then stopped himself before knocking on her door. He glanced over at Jennifer's porch swing and grinned as an idea sprung to life.

Jennifer's fingers were wrapped around her cell phone as she searched her kitchen for the slip of paper where she'd written the phone number for pizza delivery. Not finding it in the kitchen, she moved to the living room where she searched through a small drawer in her end table.

Jennifer froze. What was that sound? There was a familiar squeaking coming from her porch. Someone was sitting on her swing. Who in the hell swings on someone's porch in the middle of the night? She crept to the front door and opened it to confront whoever was out there.

"Blake, what are you doing here?" Jennifer exclaimed, pulling the belt on her robe a little tighter. "Listen, I'm not really up for company." It took only a second to take in every detail about him—his lean, wide-shouldered build, his dark hair, rugged face and impenetrable eyes. Instead of the dark suit she was used to seeing him in, he wore faded jeans, a black T-shirt and a leather jacket. The words hot, ripped, and sexy came to mind. Something heated inside her. Maybe Blake's company was not such a bad idea after all.

"I'm not here to visit, Jennifer." He began. "When I was growing up, we had a swing on our front porch a lot like this one. I used to swing for hours just to relax. You see, I don't have one at my condo and I was hoping you wouldn't mind if I sat on yours for a while."

Jennifer stared at him for a long moment. Then the mouth-watering scent of Italian spices and sauces reached her nose making her glance longingly at the pizza box next to him on the swing.

"What kind of pizza is that?"

"It's a large sausage and mushroom." Blake replied.

Good God, it was her favorite. "I've changed my mind about company. Come inside."

Blake picked up the pizza and beer then entered the house. Jennifer directed him to the dining room. "There's plates in the cabinet and napkins in the drawer in the kitchen. I'll change clothes and be right down."

As she flew up the stairs to her bedroom, Blake went into the kitchen, opening cabinet doors and drawers until he found the plates and napkins. He placed them on the dining room table and looked around. Even though he'd known Jennifer for five years, this was the first time he'd been in her home.

A brown leather sofa, two side chairs, and a tall bookcase stuffed with books, CDs and a stereo CD player filled the living room. The oak furniture was a mixture of antique and new. A flat-screen television graced one wall. He studied the stack of CDs. It seemed Jennifer's taste in music ran the gamut from Lady Gaga to Blake Shelton. There was a lot he didn't know about her, and he wanted to know everything.

He heard Jennifer coming down the stairs. "I like your house," he said.

"Thanks. Especially, the porch swing, right?" Jennifer

grinned as she headed for the dining room and motioned for him to join her. He opened the pizza box, put a slice on a plate for Jennifer, and grabbed one for himself. She pulled out the six-pack, handed Blake a bottle of Coors, then took one for herself.

"I've always liked old houses. It's Craftsman-style, right?"

"Yes, it was a present my dad surprised my mom with on the day they got married. This old house was renovated with love. They used it as a rental when they bought the pink Victorian house over on Washington Street. They gave it to me when I turned twenty-one." She hoped Blake didn't ask too many questions about the house. Thinking about the day her parents gave it to her dredged up some memories best forgotten.

Jennifer had been seven months pregnant and living with her parents, when they asked if she'd like to join them for a ride. In the car, they drove on country roads through miles of corn fields and forests, stopping only for lunch in a quaint cafe in a small town. At the end of the day, her dad stopped the car in front of the small home where they'd lived when she was a baby. Her dad opened her door and led her inside. The wall of each room wore a fresh coat of paint; the oak wood floors glistened with polish.

"Your mom and I want you to have this house. It's a good house for children to grow up in." The three hugged each other tightly, not knowing that in mere weeks Jennifer would lose the baby.

Blake noticed a flicker of sadness in Jennifer's eyes and took a sip of his beer. There was something about the house she didn't want to talk about. He wanted to know what that was, but not now.

"Where do your parents live?" Jennifer asked, changing the subject.

"We moved to Orlando when I was a child. Mom and Dad bought a lot of property while it was still affordable and built condos."

"Do you visit them often?" Jennifer asked.

"Not really. They divorced when I was fifteen. There was a lot of arguing and fighting over possessions during that time, including their kids. They still argue over who I'm spending time with, so I don't see them as much as I should." Blake glanced at her and noticed pizza sauce at the corner of her mouth. He used his napkin to wipe it off, making her grin and blush.

"I think my parents have been glued at the hip since they met. After all this time, they're still lovebirds."

Blake wanted that kind of marriage someday, the polar opposite of what his parents had. The pizza box empty, Jennifer started cleaning off the table. She picked up her plate and headed to the kitchen, with Blake close behind with his.

Jennifer placed the dishes in the kitchen sink. She froze for a long moment, until Blake touched her arm. She turned around, wiping at tears streaming down her face.

"What's wrong?"

Jennifer picked up a coffee mug with a black-and-white drawing of a woman in a business suit, wearing a cape. "Dick gave me this mug. He said the mug would remind me I could do anything I decided to do. I just needed to believe in myself."

Blake pulled her into his arms.

"I'm going to miss him."

"I know." Blake whispered in her ear.

Jennifer tightened her arms around his waist and pressed her body against him. He felt a pang of longing so strong he couldn't breathe. Lust filled his veins, surging down to his belly. Talk about bad timing. He gently pushed her back, and kissed her forehead, hoping she had not felt his arousal. "You must be tired, Jennifer. I'll leave so you can get some sleep."

Jennifer followed him to the front door. An impulse came over her. Maybe it was the way the man radiated testosterone and she'd been going through some significant withdrawal. Whatever it was, she gave into it, slipped her arms around his neck and kissed him. His kiss tasted like beer, pizza, and man, and she wanted to drink him in. She wove her fingers through his hair and felt him breathing harder now, his chest rising and falling against her breasts. The kiss sent currents of erotic fire surging through her, making her weak in the knees.

At first, Blake stiffened with surprise. But then his pulse spiked as Jennifer slipped her arms around his neck and pressed her breasts against him. Her mouth felt hot and soft and he parted her lips so he could taste her, her tongue tangling with his. He'd imagined kissing her many, many times, but this was a million times better. Blake wanted to pick her up, carry her upstairs to her bedroom and fulfill each of his erotic dreams. He felt her hand slide down to his waist, her fingers lifting his shirt. Damn it. He wanted her badly, but not like this. He was a bastard for coming here tonight — wanting her while knowing she was crazy with grief.

Blake caught her hand, broke off the kiss, and gently pushed her away.

Jennifer fiercely colored and stared at him in shock. What in the hell had she done? What was she thinking?

"I am so sorry. That shouldn't have happened. We

work together."

"Please don't be sorry, I'm not. Working together is not why I stopped the kiss."

"What?"

"Honey, I know you're grieving and I don't want to take advantage." He began. "Besides, it's not like we're partners."

Jennifer thanked God she had plenty to do at her desk the next day. Blake was with the diving team looking for a drowning victim at Bear Lake, which made avoiding him a simple task. She was mortified she'd practically molested him the night before.

Jennifer fired up her computer, ignored her burgeoning email box and started a document. She needed to list everything they had on Catherine's murder. Maybe there was something she'd missed that would pop out at her. She started with their suspect pool which was decidedly emptied when they ruled out Nicholas Connor.

Jennifer knew most homicides were committed by someone known to the victim. Could Catherine have been dating someone that her friends and parents didn't know about? That seemed unlikely for a couple of reasons. Catherine was very personable and many of her friends said she was so open that she had no secrets. In addition,

Catherine knew many people who lived in the community so it's unlikely she was seeing someone other than Nicholas. It would have been reported. That left her work. Could the killer be someone who frequented the Sugar Creek Cafe? She made a mental note to talk to the waitresses again to find out if they'd noticed anyone repeatedly asking to sit in Catherine's area or who hung around to talk to her.

Jennifer then listed more questions. Why did the killer select Catherine? Usually killers choose their victims based on availability, vulnerability and desirability. The victim worked in a high-traffic restaurant. She probably came in contact with a couple of hundred people per day. It wouldn't be that difficult for a killer to stalk a waitress leaving work, at her home, or social activities. It certainly wasn't beyond the scope of reasoning that her killer followed her home that day, and waited outside her house until she left again for Deer Run State Park.

Jennifer heard Blake's voice from across the room. He was talking to a deputy about a floater at the lake. So why was he in the office and not at the lake? It wasn't long before she heard his footfall as he headed toward her cubicle. She aimed her attention at her computer screen.

"Good morning."

Was it her imagination or did his voice sound huskier than usual? She glanced at him, nodded and looked back at her computer.

Blake sat in her guest chair, which in her small cubicle, placed his body a little too close for comfort. "What are you doing?" Soon he'd pushed his chair so he was sitting directly next to her so he could see the screen.

"I'm making a list of what we know about Catherine's murder. I'm hoping something pops out that we may have missed."

"Good idea." He took the opportunity to stretch, and moved his arm across the back of her chair.

Jennifer shot him a look. His hair was damp from a shower. She breathed in his fresh, male scent. "I thought you were supposed to be with your diving team at Bear Lake."

"I was with them earlier. My team doesn't need me to be there to supervise them taking care of a floater." He looked back at the computer. "Let's talk about your list. Anything pop out?"

"Well, yes. A couple of things bother me about the case."

"Like what?"

Jennifer turned in her chair so she was facing him. "There's no concrete evidence, but my intuition tells me that Catherine wasn't killed by anyone she was having a relationship with. I think she was killed by a stranger. Maybe he noticed her at the cafe, started frequenting the place just to see her. She doesn't give him the time of day. It pisses him off so he stalks her until he finds an opportunity to make his move. Like I said, it's only my intuition. Not really any evidence to support it."

"Jennifer, never downplay your intuition." Lightly, he fingered a loose tendril of hair on her cheek. "That's a good theory. What else do you have?"

"There's something else that bothers me. How was Catherine abducted in the first place? Not only was she a candidate for the police academy, she'd completed Frankie's thorough self-defense courses. Catherine knew what to do to fight back and escape. Why didn't she?"

"Maybe he surprised her when her back was turned," offered Blake.

"Maybe. But I'm just not seeing it. Is it safe to assume since Catherine's car was found at Deer Run State Park that it was where she ran that day?"

"Let's say for discussion sake it was. I mean she didn't go to her usual places like the track."

"So if Catherine were abducted from the state park, how did the killer prevent her from screaming for help?" Jennifer asked.

"Good question. Did he use drugs? Maybe we should take another look at the tox report Doc Meade ran."

Jennifer nodded, then continued. "If he subdued her, the killer had to be strong and in excellent condition to get her body out of the park without being noticed. So are we talking about someone who works out a lot, or needs to be in good physical condition for his job? His hands were strong enough to break the hyoid bone in her neck as he strangled her. But do you think he killed her at the park"?"

"No," Blake said. "I don't think Catherine was killed at the park. But if she wasn't, where was she tortured and murdered?"

Jennifer thought for a long moment, then said, "We know he had to prevent Catherine from screaming, so maybe the killer used duct tape across her mouth. Therefore, he could have taken her to a single dwelling like a house or cabin anywhere in the county."

"There's no way the killer lived in an apartment because concealing his activities would be too difficult under the watchful eyes of multiple neighbors," offered Blake.

"I agree."

Then Jennifer turned her thoughts to the killer himself and said, "I think that binding his victim with duct tape satisfied the killer's need for control. He may have felt power or sexual excitement when he killed her. There was evidence of rape."

"Oh, so you're dipping into the behavioral science

bucket," Blake teased.

"Hey, I aced that class." Jennifer slapped his arm playfully, but soon a worried expression crossed her face.

"I can tell there's something else that bothers you about the case. What is it?

"I can't get past the lack of forensic evidence. There was nothing on her laptop that would help us find her killer. It contained the usual emails between friends, Facebook and Twitter exchanges. Nothing that raised a red flag. They returned the laptop to her parents yesterday," said Jennifer.

"What else?"

"We've got a photo with the belt buckle impression on Catherine's neck, but it's useless without a suspect and belt to compare it with." She lowered her voice and leaned closer to Blake. "The killer washed and bleached the body to remove trace evidence and he wiped Catherine's car down so proficiently, there were no fingerprints — not even the car owner's. I think he's killed and covered it up before. He's building his proficiency. He'll kill again, Blake. It's just a matter of time and opportunity."

Nancy, Lane's admin, popped her head in. "Don't you two read your email? Lane wants to meet with both of you in his office."

Jennifer's first thought when she entered Lane's office was that something was up. She was right.

Lane directed Jennifer and Blake to sit in his guest chairs facing him across the desk, then said, "Jennifer, Dick's death leaves you without a partner." Lane began, then turned to Blake.

"Blake, you haven't had a partner since Will's transfer. So it makes sense that I make you two partners."

Jennifer quickly looked down so Lane wouldn't notice the deer-in-the-headlights expression she knew was on her face. Making Jennifer and Blake partners was probably the worse idea Lane Hansen ever came up with and he'd come up with some monumentally bad ideas in the past. Partners? Just the night before, she'd been on her way to reach for Blake's jeans zipper and now they were partners? She frantically searched her mind for a logical reason why they shouldn't be partners, but nothing came to her because in Lane's perspective it made perfect sense. Neither had a partner and they'd been working the same case together for weeks.

"It's a logical move," Lane went on. "I mean you're already working the Catherine Thomas case together."

Blake swallowed hard, clenched his jaw, and made a supreme effort to keep his expression blank. Keeping his focus on Lane, he dared not look at Jennifer. This changed everything. He was able to justify what happened at Jennifer's house by noting that a lot of the deputies were dating or married and no one gave it a second thought. But law enforcement *partners* in a romantic relationship? That was an unspoken cardinal sin. He was in deep trouble for more than one reason.

Blake sat at the bar and ordered another beer in an attempt to wash away a rotten day, as well as the fact that the guy who made it so bad was sitting next to him. The music was loud, each beat hammering his brain, building an eye-crosser of a headache.

"So, you and Jennifer are now partners."

It was Lane's way of easing into a conversation that Blake knew was his goal when Lane asked him out for a drink. Blake kept his mouth clamped shut and his eyes on the flat-screen TV and waited through the moment of silence that ensued.

Then Lane continued, "Listen, I know most guys on the team would prefer *not* to have Jennifer Brennan as a partner, seeing that her dad is sheriff and everything..."

Yeah, that and the fact she's five feet and ten inches of blonde irresistible perfection. Now that they'd kissed, how Blake was going to keep his hands off her was anyone's guess.

"Blake, I'm going to give you some advice that was given to me at one time about partnering with a female."

This was rich. Lane Hansen, of all people, was about to give him partner relationship advice. It wasn't as if most of the staff didn't know about Lane and Frankie getting married shortly after playing undercover roles as husband and wife. No hanky-panky going on there. Right. He glanced at Lane then back at the TV.

"There's this saying, 'You don't screw with your partner and your partner won't screw with you.' Understand?"

"I think I've heard that saying before." Blake responded, praying the conversation would end with the remark.

"I'm not saying anything about Jennifer and you, but just keep things between you professional, *not* personal. There have been too many operations that went to hell in a hand basket because a cop got emotional. Because he or she let it get personal with his or her partner."

Blake's jaw tensed and he continued to pretend he was watching the TV. He wanted to ask Lane how that worked out when he went undercover with Frankie. It was curious how they got married shortly after that operation. Through the long mirror in back of the bar, he saw Jennifer enter and cross the room to where Lane's wife, Frankie, sat in a booth. Why hadn't he noticed Frankie before?

He'd decided after leaving Jennifer's house the night before that he was going to ask her out for a romantic dinner out-of-town. Out-of-town and away from watchful eyes. That plan got drop-kicked the second their boss made them partners. Blake hadn't had a chance to talk to Jennifer alone all day. It wasn't that he was looking forward to discussing partner "rules" with her, but it was unavoidable now.

It was Friday night and the Hoosier Sports Grill was packed with the loud TGIF crowd, just as Jennifer knew it would be, which is why she didn't want to be there. But a promise was a promise — especially if that promise was made to her cousin, Frankie.

Jennifer was an only child and Frankie was the sister she never had. When 'Jennifer was abducted, Frankie — along with Lane and her dad — had rushed to her rescue. The abduction was a time she'd rather not think about in daylight hours, it was enough that her regular nightmares reminded her.

A balloon popped near the bar, and several women screamed in alarm. Jennifer's hand instinctively went to her Glock, which wasn't there because she'd changed into her faded jeans, red tank, and black leather jacket after work. Jennifer couldn't remember the last time she went out after work on a Friday. It was easier to turn on a *Lifetime* movie, have pizza delivered, and settle in for the night on her sofa. But Frankie had insisted that Jennifer join her for drinks, something they hadn't done for a couple of months.

Jennifer scanned the crowd and couldn't find Frankie anywhere. She was starting to think she was the first to arrive when she noticed Frankie standing near a booth, waving her arms like she was on an airfield directing a 747 into a parking spot at the gate. Once she reached the booth, she slid in across from her cousin and noticed a large strawberry margarita in front of Frankie.

"Non-alcoholic, I hope," asked Jennifer, referring to Frankie's allergy to alcohol.

"Of course," replied Frankie as she waved to the waitress, who brought Jennifer the strawberry margarita she'd ordered earlier for her.

"How's Ashley?" Jennifer asked, before she sipped her drink.

"My little girl is moving from her terrible twos right into her terrible threes. Last night she tried to wrap Hunter up with toilet paper. She'd used two rolls before I caught her. I couldn't believe the Giant Schnauzer let her do that."

"Bet Hunter was glad you came to his rescue," said Jennifer as she smiled at the visual. "Speaking of Hunter, I heard Mrs. Smith wandered away from Shady Oaks again. How did you find her?"

"Lane and Sam Brown went up in the copter and searched for her using the thermal imaging camera. I love the thermal imaging technology; it makes objects that emit heat visible in the dark. Anyway, they spotted what they thought was human in that wooded area next to the park on Elm Street. Hunter and I went in and the rest is history."

"What condition was she in?" asked Jennifer.

"Not bad for being missing for eight hours, a little dehydrated. She's eighty-years-old and walked at least five miles. Do you believe it?"

Jennifer shook her head sadly. "She was my first grade teacher."

"Mine, too."

"It makes me sad that a woman who used her intelligence her entire life to help others now has a disease that robs her of the ability of even recalling her name. I hate Alzheimer's disease."

"This is getting depressing; let's change subjects. How's your love life?"

"What love life?" asked Jennifer with a nervous laugh. There was no way Jennifer was telling Frankie how attracted she was to Blake. She'd never hear the end of it.

"What are you doing about getting one?"

"No match-making, Frankie. We've discussed this

before."

"Just observations."

"What?"

"I just happened to notice that when I visit my husband at work, there are some hot and available men there."

"I can't believe you're suggesting I date one of them. Aren't you the one who always told me not to date a cop because they lie too easily?"

"Well, since I married one, I've changed my philosophy." Frankie's eyes scanned across the room and landed on her husband. "Speaking of tall, ripped and hot, there's Lane at the bar."

Jennifer followed Frankie's gaze until she saw Blake. Their gazes locked and a spark of heat flashed between them.

"Isn't that Blake Stone with him?" asked Frankie. "Speaking of smokin' hot and available."

Suddenly, Jennifer felt a desperate urge to leave the bar. Flustered, she grabbed her purse and eased out of the booth.

"Where are you going?"

"I just remembered that I need to feed my cat." With that, Jennifer rushed out of the bar.

Frankie thought for a moment, and then said aloud,

"What cat?"

Dorothy was right when she said, "There's no place like home." And Jennifer couldn't get to hers fast enough. She turned her car onto her street and drove the five blocks it took to slide into her driveway. Clutching her purse, she walked to her front porch, bounded up the steps — then froze. Her front door was ajar. And Jennifer distinctly remembered locking it before she left, along with turning on the porch light. Slowly and silently she eased open the screen door to enter. Her first priority was to find her Glock; then she'd search the house. Unfortunately, she'd left it upstairs in her nightstand.

Jennifer crept into the kitchen, grabbed a steak knife out of the drawer then inched up her stairs.

Blake watched Jennifer leave the bar, then made an excuse to leave himself. Whether he wanted to have that partner conversation with her or not, he needed to talk to her. He pulled his SUV in front of her house and got out. Something was off. It wasn't until he reached the sidewalk that he realized her front door was wide-open. The security-conscious Jennifer he knew would never leave her door open like that. He pulled his gun out of his holster and moved into the house. In the living room, he called for her.

No response.

Gripping his firearm in front of him, Blake moved around the living and dining rooms with his back toward the wall. The rooms were clear, along with the kitchen. Stopping to listen, he heard a soft creaking of a floorboard coming from the second floor so he moved to the staircase landing.

At that moment, Glock in hand, Jennifer bounded out from her bedroom shouting, "Freeze!" Seeing Blake, she lowered her gun and leaned against the wall, her heart beating wildly.

"Damn it, Blake, I could have killed you."

Ignoring her remark, Blake whispered, "Did you clear the upstairs?"

"Yes."

"Then put away your gun. Come down here and tell me what's going on?"

She tucked her gun in the back of her jeans, then followed Blake down the stairs and into the living room. "When I got home, my door was open. I know I locked it when I left, right after I turned on my porch lights. Someone has been in my house."

"Did you check to see if anything was missing?" Blake asked as he eyeballed the room.

"No, I was just clearing the rooms when I saw you."

"Let's do it now. Where do you want to start?" Blake clenched his jaw and focused on remaining calm, which was difficult to do because he wanted to kick the ass belonging to whoever broke into Jennifer's house.

"Nothing looks missing in here," said Jennifer. "It's odd that someone would break into a house and not take a flat-screen TV."

"No kidding."

Blake followed Jennifer into the dining room and almost slammed into her when she came to a standstill at the long table. She pointed at an object sitting in the center of the table. It was an iPhone in a hot pink case, with the name 'Catherine' written in script across the center.

"Catherine Thomas' cell," whispered Jennifer.

Reminded by the crime techs not to touch anything, Jennifer sat on the front porch swing in silence. Blake paced back and forth in front of the living room window as the techs brushed Jennifer's doors and windows for fingerprints. He was livid that the sick bastard who killed Catherine Thomas had been inside Jennifer's home. He'd already called Lane, who was putting a deputy on her house 24/7.

"He knows who I am," said Jennifer softly. "He's

taunting me because I can't catch him."

Blake had come to the same conclusion. To say that he was alarmed that a murderer knew who Jennifer was and where she lived was an understatement. "That's pretty fucking brazen to break into the detective's home who is trying to catch you."

"He thinks he's smarter than we are. He doesn't think there's a slim possibility that we'll catch him," Jennifer replied.

"You can't stay here, Jennifer. Move in with your parents until we catch him."

"Not happening. I'm not running from him." Her home was her oasis and she felt violated the perp was inside her home looking at her things. No one was going to run her out of her own home.

"Jennifer..."

"Drop it," She interrupted.

"You're not safe here."

"If it were your home, Blake, would you let him chase you out of it?"

She watched Blake avert his eyes. "That's what I thought."

The slamming of car doors drew her attention to the street. Lane and her father had arrived. Jennifer sighed. If there was one thing she didn't need, it was her father's concern and her own guilt over having caused the concern.

"Have they found any prints?" Lane directed his question to Blake.

"Not yet. He probably wore gloves."

"What about the cell phone?"

"It looks wiped down but they're going to take it apart to see if they can find prints inside it."

Lane looked at Jennifer. "Are you absolutely sure the cell belongs to Catherine?"

"Yes. Her parents gave it to her for her birthday. They gave me a photo of her holding it up to the camera. It's in her file."

"How are you doing?" He asked with concern in his voice.

Jennifer glanced at Lane, noting the apprehension written all over his face. Lane was acting just like her dad and she didn't appreciate it one bit. "I'm a law enforcement officer. I'm fine." She folded her arms across her chest.

Tim moved closer. "Jennifer, your mother and I want you to move in with us."

Jennifer rolled her eyes and said, "Seriously, Dad. I'm not a kid. I'm not moving home."

"Just until we catch him."

"No, Dad. I'm sorry, but I'm not moving from my house."

Tim gave Lane and Blake a meaningful glance then said, "Fine. We'll move to Plan B."

Jennifer looked at the three of them, afraid to ask, but did. "What's Plan B?"

"Your partner moves in with you." Tim's glare and dare-to-object expression did not go unnoticed. "That's not your father talking, it's your sheriff. Consider it a direct order."

Tiffany Chase had never gone camping in her life, nor had she wanted to. Why anyone would sleep out in the wild with bugs and creatures was beyond her. But that was before she laid eyes on Lance Brody in her college Educational Psych course. He walked in the first day of class, with shoulders a yard wide, tall, hot, and athletic — just her type. And thus began a series of erotic dreams starring Mr. Lance Brody and involving wild, monkey sex in every position.

That Tiffany was already engaged to her community's youth minister evaporated from her brain the instant Lance moved into her presence. Ed. Psych was the only class she'd ever taken that she'd even made an attempt to arrive early.

But every Tuesday and Thursday, Tiffany was one of the first to arrive, because she knew Lance would be there.

Tiffany had never had trouble engaging young men in conversation with her big blue eyes, dark hair, sexy lush lips, wearing her usual tight tees and jeans. But Lance Brody was the exception. Hell, he played football and even that topic didn't seem to interest him. But one day she overheard him talking to another student about camping that weekend. His voice was filled with excitement and she knew she hit pay-dirt. She'd spent that weekend at the library, reading anything she could get her hands on that even remotely had to do with camping.

The following Tuesday, she arrived even earlier than usual and waited for Lance to arrive.

"Hi, Lance. How was your camping trip?" Tiffany leaned toward him, her blue eyes brightened with interest.

"It was great, but how did you know I went camping?"

"Last week, I overheard you talking with John about it. Where did you go?" She spoke in a tone of inquisitive wonder. At least, that's what she wanted Lance to think.

"I pitched a tent over at Bear Lake."

"Oh, I don't think I've camped there, but I've pitched a tent plenty of times over at Deer Run State Park. Do you know it?" She smiled brightly and noted a gleam of interest in his dark eyes.

"Absolutely. I've camped there since I was a little kid. There's nothing like sleeping under the stars, listening to the sounds around you. That's cool you camp, too."

Two weeks later, Tiffany trudged behind Lance, admiring the muscles in his legs and his tight ass as they made their way to his favorite campsite inside Rocky Cliff State Park. The pack on her back felt like it weighed a ton and her feet were killing her. What was she, a pack-mule? The only thing that kept her going was the thought of Lance, naked, sharing a sleeping bag with her under the stars — not that they'd notice the stars much if she had her way.

Finally, after passing about a dozen campers, they reached Lance's favorite camp site. It was away from the others and privately nestled in pine trees near a small stream. Lance pointed out a deer path nearby and promised they'd see a doe or two during their stay.

"We need to take advantage of the daylight. I'll go find wood for the fire and you can go ahead and set up the tent," said Lance over his shoulder as he headed toward the trees.

Set up the tent? Tiffany felt the panic sliver up her spine. She'd never set up a tent in her life, and she didn't recall any instructions in the camping books she checked out. This whole camping thing was way too much work. Tiffany unrolled one of the sleeping bags and sat down as she tried to visualize how a tent might be set up. Before she knew it, she was lying down and fast asleep.

Tiffany felt hands touching her, stroking her, pushing her hair out of her face and away from her neck. Was she dreaming? Had Lance returned? She sighed with pleasure.

"Hey, sleepyhead. What happened with the tent?" Lance asked. He'd started the fire to ward off the chill of the early evening.

She jerked upright. The tent! She scrambled to her feet. "I must have dozed off."

He ruffled her hair with his fingers. "Come on. We'll set it up together."

With Lance taking the lead, they set up the tent and arranged the sleeping bags inside. He opened her bag and took out a package of hotdogs, buns and marshmallows, which Tiffany arranged on a nearby picnic table. As they roasted the hotdogs over the fire, Tiffany began to think that maybe she was wrong about camping. Maybe it was not that bad after all.

As the evening wore on, Lance hadn't made any romantic moves, and secretly, Tiffany was grateful. Every muscle in her body cried out in protest from the four trails Lance made her hike before they set up camp. She felt like she could barely move, let alone muster up the energy for sex. Tiffany reached into her backpack and pulled out a roll of toilet paper. If she didn't go soon, it would be too late. The thought of having to use a public restroom had made her put off this visit for most of the afternoon. Ick. She waved at Lance then made her way to the old log building he'd pointed out earlier. Two little boys scrambled out of the place and ran toward their campsite.

Once inside, she realized the women's side of the restroom was empty and she felt a flicker of apprehension course through her. She'd seen an old horror movie once where the hockey-masked slasher had trapped and hacked his victim in a vacant public restroom. Tiffany rushed into a stall, finished her business, then scrubbed her hands with soap and water at the sink. She shuddered as fearful images of a masked slasher built in her mind, and she wished she were already back at the campsite with Lance. Grabbing the roll of toilet paper, Tiffany rushed out of the building, slamming into what felt like a brick wall. She brushed herself off, then felt embarrassed when she realized who she'd run into.

"Sorry about that. I guess I need to watch where I'm going."

He swept some leaves off her shoulders and pulled something out of his pocket. "Not a problem." His voice was eerily emotionless.

A sharp, piercing pain in her neck caused Tiffany to gasp just prior to slipping into unconsciousness.

6 CHAPTER SIX

Lance Brody threw another log on the fire and checked his watch. Tiffany had been gone an hour. It was close to midnight. He decided to wait a few more minutes then go check on her. For a woman who claimed she was an avid camper, Tiffany certainly seemed out of her element. She had even struggled setting up the tent with him. While on the trails, she had been so out-of-breath, he thought he was going to have to carry her.

Lance lay on his back, gazing at the glittering lights scattered across the night sky, and thought about the first time he'd noticed Tiffany. She was waiting outside the Ed Psych classroom. He'd pegged her as one of the pampered sorority girls on campus, and had steered clear of her. Tiffany was a pretty distraction, but he had no burning desire to become another notch on her bedpost. Lance had heard rumors that her sorority sisters had some kind of a sexual conquest contest going and he wanted no part of it. Besides, he had to keep his grades up or he'd lose his football scholarship. Some of his classes were a bitch this term, so he had no time to toy with women like Tiffany. But all that was before Tiffany shared her vast camping experiences with him.

He glanced at his watch again and noted thirty minutes had passed. He'd lost track of time. He got to his feet and headed down the trail leading to the restroom facility.

Blake pulled his bags out of his SUV, closed the door, and aimed his remote to lock it. He nodded at the deputy parked in front of Jennifer's house. The crime scene techs were long gone, as were Lane and the sheriff.

He'd wanted to spend more time with Jennifer, but not this way. Blake understood why Jennifer was so angry with Lane and her dad. She was a trained and armed law enforcement officer whose job was to protect others. The implication that she couldn't protect herself ran against her grain. But he agreed with them. She needed protection and if they hadn't insisted he move in with her, he would have parked outside her house in his SUV all night. There was no way Jennifer Brennan was getting hurt on his watch.

Most perps didn't have the balls to break into a detective's home. This killer was an anomaly with an ego the size of Mount Rushmore. The bastard obviously thought he could get away with anything. But if he thought he was going to get to Jennifer, he'd better think again.

Jennifer answered her door after his first knock. "Oh, I see my babysitter has arrived." The sarcasm in her voice was hard to miss.

"Let's not make this any harder than it has to be." He moved past her, hung his garment bag in her coat closet and set his duffle bag on the floor. "Look on the bright side, I'm a damn good cook."

"You are?"

He grinned and nodded. "My grandmother is Italian and a retired chef. I spent every summer with her and she taught me how to cook."

Jennifer eyed him carefully. She couldn't remember the last time she had used her kitchen for actual cooking. Italian food? Her mouth watered at the thought. "Interesting. I'll give you a tour of my kitchen tomorrow, but for now I'm beat. Let me show you the guest room."

"I think I'll stay down here on the sofa. I'll cover the first floor while you get some sleep." Once he was sure she was in her bedroom, he checked the house again, testing the locks on each window and door. Peeking through the living room blinds, he saw the deputy was still outside in his car. He made a mental note to make the guy some hot coffee later. He sat on the sofa, removed his shoes, fluffed a pillow, and then lay down. He doubted if he was going to get much sleep with a killer on the loose, and his vivid imagination wandering to Jennifer upstairs in bed.

Jennifer lay awake in bed staring at her ceiling. Insomnia strikes again. Was it insomnia or lust? Okay, lust. Lying on her sofa downstairs was one of the most gorgeous men she'd ever seen. One kiss had sent currents of erotic fire straight to her sexual center. There was no doubt in her mind she was hot for him, but he was now her partner, which made the situation impossible. Add to that, he was living with her. How was she going to be able to keep her hands off him?

Thirty minutes passed and Jennifer was still awake, so she went downstairs to the kitchen to make some Sleepytime tea. She filled her teapot and set it on the stove burner to heat. Jennifer pulled out a jar of honey from the refrigerator and her mug from a cabinet. A movement at the door made her jump.

"Sorry. I heard someone in here and thought I'd check it out. What are you doing?" Blake yawned and leaned against the kitchen doorframe. In only faded jeans, he stood there with his dark looks and rippling muscles looking like a model in a Calvin Klein ad — tantalizingly sexy. The room heated a couple of degrees.

Jennifer's eyes moved upward from his six-pack-abs to his broad chest. Something heated inside her and she averted her eyes. "I couldn't sleep so I'm making some Sleepytime tea. Would you like some?"

Instead of answering, he pulled another mug from the same cabinet Jennifer had just used, making her wonder how he got so familiar with her kitchen so fast. He placed it next to hers and sat down at the kitchen table. She placed a teabag in each mug, poured in hot water, and then brought both mugs to the table. She added a dollop of honey to hers, and passed the jar to Blake.

"Why did the killer target me?" asked Jennifer.

Blake sipped his tea and stared at her for a long moment. "I've been so pissed that he did that I haven't thought about the why."

"I mean, how did he even know I was assigned to his case?"

"Are you still thinking the killer might be one of us? Someone in law enforcement?" His dark eyebrows slanted in a frown.

She nodded and continued. "It all goes back to the way he knew how to wash away trace evidence. Now this. It hasn't been made public who's working Catherine Thomas' murder. So how did he know I was? I don't think we can ignore the fact he could be working for the sheriff's office."

"I just can't wrap my head around that someone we know and work with could do what this killer did to Catherine." Blake said. After a thoughtful pause, he added, "Whoever he is, he's not getting to you, Jennifer. Not on my watch." His voice was firm, final.

There was something in his dark eyes that made her look twice. In that instant, she knew Blake Stone cared about her, and not just as a partner.

Lance searched both the men's and women's restrooms for Tiffany to no avail. Where could she be? He woke up the campers in the six tents down a short trail near the restrooms to find out if anyone had seen her, but no one had. Three of the campers joined him in his search, walking the perimeter of the log building searching for any sign of Tiffany. They met back at their starting point, each reporting he'd found nothing.

Lance walked back to the campsite thinking that she may have returned there, but when he arrived everything was as he left it. No Tiffany. He pulled his cell out of his pocket and called nine-one-one, then dialed another number as he walked toward the park entrance to meet the deputy.

"Blake, this is Lance Brody. I need your help."

By the time Blake and Jennifer arrived at Rocky Cliff

State Park, they'd been notified by dispatch about the missing girl. A deputy securing the front entrance waved them through. Bolting out of the SUV, they reached the trail to the campsites in record time.

"Who's Lance Brody?" Jennifer asked.

"He's a scuba diver who volunteers when we need extra divers. Lance is a college student, so we use him as a volunteer all summer."

"So what's your take on him?"

"Lance is a good guy. He likes the outdoors, camps a lot and just enjoys life. He wants to be a detective someday; majors in Criminal Justice at ISU in Terre Haute."

The main campsites were abuzz with activity, ranging from frightened campers, to crime scene techs combing the area around the restroom facilities inside the crime scene tape. Mobile spotlights illuminated the area. In the distance, deputies could be seen holding large flashlights, searching the woods, undergrowth crackling with each step.

Blake motioned for a young deputy, "Separate the witnesses. Get their names, addresses and statements. Make sure no one leaves until that happens. If anyone saw something suspicious, come find us."

The deputy smiled, seemingly pleased with himself. "Already done, Sir. I've got their names, addresses and statements. Most of the campers were winding down for the evening and getting ready for bed. Two boys in the first tent described a young woman who may have been Tiffany enter the restroom, but no one saw her come out."

Jennifer saw Bob Goldberg, one of her favorite crime scene technicians, just inside the crime scene tape at the restroom. She hurried to talk to him. "Bob, did you find anything?"

"Shit, what a crime scene. The place is like Grand Central Station," Bob complained. "There are more footprints than Advil has pain reliever pills. We did find a pair of footprints that lead to and from the service road. Looks like hiking boots." Bob led Jennifer to the service road and pointed down. See those tire prints? They look fresh. I'm guessing they're from an ATV pulling some kind of cart. I think the park service uses ATVs all the time to pick up trash and debris."

"If she was abducted, he could have gotten her out of the park through the service road," Jennifer said, glancing at Blake, who had joined them.

"Right, *if* the tire prints have anything to do with the girl who's missing." Bob responded.

Holding a small pink purse and a backpack, a young blonde-haired man with a wide-shouldered, rangy body approached them. "Blake, thanks for coming."

"Lance, this is my partner, Jennifer Brennan."

Placing the purse and backpack on the ground, Lance shook Jennifer's outstretched hand and said, "I'm glad you're here to help find Tiffany."

"Lance, I want you to wait for us on that bench over there. Jennifer and I need to check something out," said Blake. "We'll be right back."

"Jennifer, let's check out this service road." Blake and Jennifer carefully made their way around the crime scene tape, careful not to step on anything that might be related to Tiffany's disappearance. Using the embankment, they waded through brush and weeds to follow the service road.

Pointing at the road, Blake said, "See the tire tracks. I think Bob's right when he said the tracks looked like they belong to an ATV pulling some kind of cart."

Blake and Jennifer continued walking about a mile until they came to a three-car garage next to what looked like a maintenance building. Parked next to the building was a red Honda FourTrax Foreman All-Terrain Vehicle. Attached to its hitch was a metal cart, filled with large black plastic bags, presumably stuffed with garbage.

Jennifer pulled her cell phone out of her pocket, "Bob, bring your kit and follow the service road until you come to the maintenance building. We may have found that ATV and cart you were talking about."

Blake held his hand above the motor, careful not to

touch the vehicle. "It's still warm. We need a conservation officer here stat."

"You've got one."

Blake and Jennifer turned around to see an older man in a green uniform approach them. "I'm Sam McGee. I'm the conservation officer in charge of the park. Got a call about all the commotion. Who are you?"

Blake and Jennifer simultaneously pulled out their badges. "We've got a missing girl who may have been transported out of the park using this ATV. Who has access to the keys?"

"My employees. But it's not likely any of my people took out the ATV since the key is locked up inside the maintenance building." Sam moved to the ATV, holding his hand over the motor as Blake had. "I'll be damned, the motor's warm." He rushed to the side door of the maintenance building and found the door unlocked. Jennifer and Blake followed him to a pegboard inside with dozens of hooks with keys attached. "It's missing!" Sam exclaimed. "The key to that ATV is missing."

"Don't touch anything," said Blake. "We've got a crime scene tech coming who will dust for prints."

Frowning, Jennifer said to Blake, "So we have a perp who breaks into this building to steal keys as well as an ATV. For what? To take a joy ride at night in the park? If so, what's with the filled garbage bags?"

"Here's another scenario. Our guy steals the ATV and cart, then rides around the park emptying garbage cans so he doesn't look suspicious. He's trolling for a victim and finds her when Tiffany comes out of that restroom. He subdues her with a stun gun, drugs or something, hides her body under the garbage bags then drives back here to return the ATV." He pointed to the east. "It's then only 100 yards or so to the parking lot where he stashed his vehicle."

When Blake and Jennifer returned to the camping area, they found Lance sitting on the bench where they had left him. As soon as they were close enough, he handed Jennifer the purse and backpack. He seemed distraught. "These belong to Tiffany. I'm so glad you're here. I don't know what to do. I can't believe Tiffany's gone. I've looked for her everywhere."

Placing the backpack on the ground, Jennifer peeked inside the purse, "Not good. Her cell phone is here, in her purse. We won't be able to track Tiffany by her phone." She opened the phone to look for recent calls. "She hasn't made any calls since yesterday."

Blake sat down next to Lance and said, "Let's start from the beginning."

After listening to Lance's story, Jennifer asked, "How

well do you know Tiffany? Is she someone who would leave because she wasn't having a good time?"

Lance leaned forward, put his head in his hands with his elbows braced on his knees. "I don't know her very well at all. This was pretty much a first date."

"How did you meet her?"

Lance scrubbed his hands over his face. "She's in one of my classes. We started talking about our mutual interest in camping a couple of weeks ago. I invited her to join me this weekend."

"Well, if she's an avid camper, she may know her way around the park. Maybe she decided to hike a trail?" Jennifer offered.

Lance shook his head. "No, that's the thing. I don't think she was honest about her camping abilities. She didn't even know how to set up the tent."

Jennifer focused on a long, red scratch on Lance's arm. "How did you get that scratch?"

"Got it while I was looking for wood for our fire. I didn't see the low hanging branch before it cut the hell out of my arm."

Jennifer gave him a skeptical glance and said, "Lance, we need to take you back to the station to get an official statement. You'll need to be photographed, and with your permission, we'd like to get a DNA sample. Do you have anyone you want to call to meet you there?"

Just like taking candy from a baby, capturing this bitch was that easy. Talk about being in the right place at the right time. Too bad, so sad for her. He'd gotten her out of the park in record time. Still unconscious, she lay naked strapped on his wooden kitchen table, her arms and legs restrained by duct tape.

Worrying he'd given her too much tranquilizer, he tapped her arm with his fingers. It had been over an hour. She should have come to by now. He checked her pulse and found it to be a little slow, but that was to be expected. He moved to the living room and threw a couple of logs onto the fire in his fireplace. Sitting in his recliner, his mind wandered to Jennifer Brennan. What he wouldn't have given to see her face when she discovered Catherine Thomas' cell phone lying on her dining room table. He chuckled aloud. He bet that sight sent her heartbeat racing, that is, if the icy bitch had a heart. Leaving the phone was payback for the tongue-lashing she'd given him at Deer Run State Park the day Catherine's body was found. Finding the cell phone must have caused quite a stir, he decided, judging from the number of deputy and crime scene tech vehicles at her house later when he drove by. Amusing. He wasn't through with Jennifer Brennan.

He rubbed his hands together, not from the cold, but from the excitement. The cops were probably combing Rocky Cliff State Park at this very moment, looking for the bitch duct-taped to his kitchen table, but he was confident they'd find nothing. He snickered to himself. He couldn't wait to see the morning news anchor reporting his prey missing.

He'd checked the weather report this time. Rain was predicted before the end of the week. He didn't want to be saddled with the bitch he'd captured tonight as long as he was with Catherine Thomas.

Hearing a muffled scream, he rushed into the kitchen. His prey was awake. Let the fun begin.

If there was anything that Jennifer dreaded, it was delivering bad news to parents. Okay, it wasn't the delivery part; it was their reaction to it. There's no positive spin for the message, "Your daughter is missing."

Blake parked the SUV outside the residence of Vic and Sasha Chase, who lived outside Rockville on a three-acre estate in a gated community. A maid answered the door, and after a glimpse of their badges, quickly summoned Tiffany's mother.

A pretty, dark-haired woman in her forties came to the door, a flash of apprehension in her eyes. "I'm Sasha Chase. How can I help you?"

Jennifer spoke first, "I'm Jennifer Brennan and this is Blake Stone. We're with the sheriff's office. May we talk to you inside?"

Fear raced across the woman's face, and she crossed her arms across her body protectively. "Yes, of course, come in. We can talk in the living room." She motioned for them to follow her. "Mandy, please bring some coffee."

The living room was a study in white, white walls, drapes and fireplace. Several large oil modernistic paintings provided splashes of bold color in red, royal blue and black. Jennifer and Blake sat down on a red sofa in front of the fireplace while Sasha sat in an armchair near them.

The maid who answered the door appeared with a tray of coffee mugs, cream, sugar, and a hot pot of coffee that she laid down on the black coffee table before she rushed out of the room.

"Mrs. Chase..." Jennifer began softly.

"Please call me Sasha. Mrs. Chase is my mother-in-law."

"Sasha, we're here to talk to you about Tiffany."

Sasha gasped as her hand flew to her chest. "Oh, my God! Has something happened to Tiffany?"

"Tiffany was reported missing from Rocky Cliff State Park last night."

"What in the world was she doing there?" The mother seemed incredulous.

"It appears she was camping."

Sasha sighed with relief. "You have the wrong Tiffany. You couldn't pay my Tiffany to camp."

"Mrs. Chase..." Jennifer began.

Sasha held up her hand. "No, I'm serious. If you looked up 'spoiled princess' in the dictionary, you'd find Tiffany's photo. She's an only child and her daddy and I have always pampered her. Tiffany is the *last* person on earth who would be camping. You have the wrong girl."

Jennifer pulled out a small pink leather Coach purse in a plastic bag from behind her and showed it to Sasha. "Does this purse belong to Tiffany?"

Instant tears appeared in Sasha's eyes. "I bought the bag for her for Christmas. Was her driver's license inside?" Reality slammed into her and she choked back a sob.

Blake nodded. "Last night between eleven and midnight, Tiffany left the campsite to use the public restroom facility a short distance away. She hasn't been seen since. The police were called at one-thirty this morning, and have been searching the area for her ever since."

"I can't believe it," Sasha said, but the terror in her eyes revealed she did. "Who was she with? There is no way she would have been at that park alone."

"She was camping with a young man who attends ISU with her by the name of Lance Brody. Is that name familiar to you?"

"What? Lance who? Tiffany is engaged to Evan Hendricks. Why was she with this Lance boy?"

Jennifer jotted Evan's name down in her notebook. "Do you know where we can find Evan?"

"He's the youth minister at the Methodist Church in town."

Blake nodded toward a photo of Tiffany on the fireplace mantel. "May we borrow that photo?"

"Yes, anything you need."

"Does Tiffany have a computer?" asked Blake.

Sasha nodded. "Yes, she has it with her on campus." She began sobbing, rocking back and forth in her chair.

"May we borrow the laptop? There may some information on it that will help us find her."

"Yes, of course."

"Is there anyone we can call for you? Anything we can do?" Blake asked as he and Jennifer stood, ready to leave.

She wiped the tears from her face with her hands. "Yes. You can find my daughter and bring her home to me!"

Jennifer backed the SUV out of the driveway, while Blake opened his laptop to get into Tiffany's bank and credit card information.

"That poor woman was devastated," Jennifer said.

"Now I know what my parents went through when I was missing."

Blake glanced at her and said, "I'd never known your dad to be anything but calm and controlled until the day he called to ask me if I would take the dive team to Monroe Lake to look for your car. I could literally hear the fear in his voice."

"It kind of makes you want to not have kids. How can you ever hope to protect them twenty-four hours a day, seven days a week?"

"Not me. I want kids someday. I want to be the kind of parent to them that my parents never were for me."

Jennifer looked at him thoughtfully and said, "C'mon, Blake, I'm sure your parents love you."

"Not unselfishly, like your parents care about you. I felt more like a bargaining chip during their divorce," Blake said, as he pulled up Tiffany's VISA information. "No luck. Tiffany hasn't used her bank or VISA card in the last forty-eight hours."

"Are you thinking what I'm thinking? I mean, we've got another girl who is taken from a state park. Maybe that's his M.O."

"We need to talk to the boyfriend first. But am I thinking Tiffany may have been taken by the same guy who abducted and killed Catherine Thomas? Yeah, that's what

I'm thinking. If we're right, we don't have much time to catch him. He kept Catherine for five days before he killed her."

Blake put in a call to Lane requesting a deputy get Tiffany's laptop at the ISU campus.

"Let's talk to the boyfriend, Evan Hendricks. Maybe Evan found out Tiffany was hot for another guy and didn't like it."

As soon as he heard Julie back the car out of the garage, Fred Thomas moved into the living room, sat in his favorite chair and grabbed the remote to flick the television on.

Ever since his heart bypass surgery, Julie had been treating him like a ninety-nine-year-old invalid and he was over it. Damn it, he wasn't even in his fifties yet. He was sick of the bland food and tired of Julie walking on eggshells around him. Julie had even gone so far as to choose what television programs he could watch. So what if the doctor told her to not let him get overexcited? What good is life if you can't make your own damn choices?

He flipped channels until he came to the local news. The weather guy predicted rain tomorrow or the next day. Fred was holding the remote, ready to change the channel when suddenly an anchor appeared with a news bulletin.

"Tiffany Chase, an ISU student, went missing from a campsite in Rocky Creek State Park."

Perspiration beaded his forehead and his heart jumped to his throat. Another missing girl? Just like his Catherine, another girl had gone missing!

Fred wondered if Tiffany Chase had been abducted by the same man who killed his daughter. He prayed to God that the police found her before she had the same fate as Catherine. Fred knew what Tiffany's parents were going through and he was sorry for them. But at the same time, he was angry. The damn cops still hadn't found his daughter's murderer, and with this girl missing, they'd take their focus off Catherine and place it on Tiffany.

He pulled out his cell phone and called Detective Stone. Getting his voicemail, Fred left a message, "What the fuck are you doing to find my daughter's killer?"

Fred focused back on the television where the news was now being broadcast live from the state park. Searchers were seen scouring the woods and campgrounds looking for clues for the whereabouts of Tiffany Chase. A photo of the girl appeared along with a phone number for people to call if they'd seen her. Fred remembered the day he and Julie had pleaded on television for the same information about Catherine. No one called. He'd never felt so lost and helpless in his life.

Fear and anger knotted so tightly inside him that his chest began to ache. He flipped to CSN, Crime Story Network, and listened as Grace Cohn discussed the efforts being used to find a missing child in Tennessee. Fred listened as Cohn debated with a local sheriff on whether or not he was using all the resources he had to find the missing child. The next scene was Cohn's interview with the missing child's parents, where she promised she would use all of her broadcasting resources to find their child. A ticker tape at the bottom of the screen listed a phone number for Grace Cohn. Fred reached again for his cell phone.

Later, Fred leaned back in his chair, staring at Catherine's framed photo on the wall. "I haven't forgotten you, honey. Your daddy will never give up the search for your killer. I'll find him, Catherine. Even if it's with the last breath I take, I promise I'll make him pay."

Jennifer pulled into the parking lot next to the red-bricked church where Evan Hendricks worked as the youth minister. She'd called him earlier to make an appointment to talk with him in his office. As instructed, she and Blake entered by using a side door. They walked down a short hall to Evan's office, where he was waiting for them.

Evan stood to greet them when they entered his small office. His eyes were reddened and he was obviously upset.

They'd barely sat down in his guest chairs before he asked, "Are you here to ask about Tiffany?"

"Yes," answered Jennifer. "I apologize that you had to hear about her disappearance from the news media."

Evan shook his head. "It doesn't matter. How can I help you find her?"

"When's the last time you saw Tiffany?" asked Jennifer.

"Last weekend. She helped me with the Red Cross charity event. We saw a movie that night."

"So how did she seem? Did she seem happy?"

"Of course, she seemed happy," he answered abruptly. "We've dated for a long time. We're engaged. She's very happy. Why do you ask?" He averted his eyes from her as he answered, letting Jennifer know he was not being truthful. She began to doubt the pretty picture he was painting about his relationship with the missing girl.

"I ask because she was camping with a guy she met in one of her classes at college." Jennifer paused for a second then added, "Since you were close, you probably already knew that though."

Evan shot her a hostile glare, then put a damper on his emotions. He cleared his throat then answered softly, "No, I did *not* know of her plans last night."

"Now I have to ask this, Evan. Where were you last night between ten and midnight?" Jennifer watched his body language carefully to determine if he would tell her the truth.

"I was home reading my Bible, thinking about my sermon for this Sunday." Again, he didn't meet her eyes when he answered.

Jennifer stared at him for a long moment, then asked, "Do you have anyone who can verify that?"

"I was home alone," answered Evan, gritting the words between his teeth.

Blake had been listening as he studied Evan's office and noticed there were no pictures of the missing girl. There were plenty of photos of Evan hiking and camping, and one trophy for running a marathon. He picked up one of the photos and held it up. "I see you like to hike and camp, Evan. I do, too. Where are some good spots around here?"

"My parents have a cabin at Bear Lake, so I like to go there. Of course, we're lucky we have two state parks in the area. I go to those, too."

"Is that right? What about Rocky Cliff State Park? I hear some of the trails there are pretty rugged."

"Yes, that's right."

"What about Tiffany? Did she like going camping with you?"

"Actually, Tiffany and I have never gone camping. Camping was not her thing." Evan shifted uncomfortably in his chair.

"You know that's the second time we've heard that. Yet, there she was out camping with Lance Brody last night. Odd."

Evan's face reddened and a muscle clenched along his jaw. "If you have no further questions, I have a meeting with a parishioner in five minutes."

"No further questions right now," answered Blake as he stood. "But, Evan, like they say in the movies, don't leave town. We may have some additional questions that only you can answer."

Jennifer and Blake didn't speak until they were in the vehicle. Jennifer said, "He's got no alibi and he tried to hide how angry he was that she was with another guy."

"When I referred to Tiffany camping with Lance, I thought the guy was going to jump out of his chair." Blake opened his laptop and typed up some notes.

"Anger issues, anyone?"

"No kidding," Blake said. "Did you notice that there were no photos of Tiffany in his office? I mean if you're engaged to someone for two years, you would have photos, right?"

"For some reason his name is familiar, but I don't know why." Jennifer pulled out Catherine Thomas's file folder that was tucked next to her car seat. She thumbed through the file until she pulled out a piece of paper. "Here's the list of Catherine's friends, and look who's number ten."

"Evan Hendricks. So there is a connection between this guy and both Tiffany and Catherine. Let's call in for surveillance on him."

Jennifer's cell phone signaled a text had arrived. Soon Blake's did the same. Lane's message was simple. Come back to the office ASAP to meet with the sheriff and him about the Tiffany Chase case.

They were a couple of blocks from the sheriff's office when they noticed a large group of people, some carrying signs, gathered in the front lawn.

"What the hell?" asked Blake.

A woman with a baby carried a sign that read, "Your

daughter could be next." Other signs blasted the police for not finding the missing girl and Catherine Thomas's killer. The group chanted, "Sheriff Brennan, what's going on?"

Jennifer pulled into a side street that led to the back entrance of the building. A deputy was waiting at the door for them. He ushered them in and told them their meeting was in the conference room near Lane's office.

When they entered the room, Lane and Tim were standing near the window facing the front of the building watching the crowd below. Both men joined Jennifer and Blake at the conference table.

Tim looked at the group at the table, his expression reflected a war of emotions he struggled to hide. "I'm going to talk to that crowd in a few minutes. I'm hoping you've learned something I can tell them about Tiffany Chase's disappearance."

Jennifer began. "Here's what we know. Last night between eleven and midnight, Tiffany went missing near the restroom facility at the Rocky Cliff State Park camping area. There were tire prints of an ATV pulling a cart on the service road nearby. We followed it and discovered one of the park's ATV and carts had been stolen. The perp emptied trash cans to avoid suspicion. He disabled Tiffany somehow and probably hid her body under the black garbage bags," she said.

Blake continued the review. "Then, he parks the ATV and cart back at the maintenance building, where he originally stole them. He then transports her body to his own vehicle, about 100 feet away in the parking lot," Blake said, as he tiredly ran his fingers through his hair. "We have no description of him or his vehicle. The campers were the only people inside the park. No one noticed a man emptying trash cans, nor did anyone venture to the parking lot that late at night..."

Lane interrupted. "What about her cell phone? Did you contact the phone company? Do you need a warrant?"

"Tiffany's cell phone was in her purse so we can't track her that way." Jennifer responded.

"Damn it!" Tim pounded the table angrily with his fists. "Do you think this is the same son of a bitch who killed Catherine Thomas?"

Blake spoke up. "We can't be one hundred percent certain. We interviewed the guy Tiffany was engaged to — Evan Hendricks. A couple of his responses were obvious lies. He has no alibi for last night. There may be a connection between Evan and Catherine. We've got him under surveillance."

"What about the kid she was with? Lance Brody?" asked Tim.

ALEXA GRACE

"Took his official statement, photographed his body for suspicious injuries, and took his DNA sample. He's being very cooperative. Seems genuinely concerned about Tiffany. The fiancé has more motive to harm Tiffany than Lance does." Blake glanced at Jennifer who nodded in agreement.

Tim stood up and peered out the window. "Press conference time. I'm going to ask for the community's help to find this girl." He picked up a file folder and a photo of Tiffany Chase from the table, then said, "Don't hesitate to ask if you need any additional resources to find this girl or Catherine's killer." With that, he left the room.

Blake and Jennifer took statements from friends of both Catherine and Tiffany until nightfall, and sleep deprivation set in. They picked up some take out from a local Italian restaurant and headed to Jennifer's house.

Pulling up to her driveway, they waved at Steve Brooks, the deputy assigned to surveillance for the night. As they opened the front door, they both drew their weapons and prepared to search the house. Deputy outside or not, they were dealing with a clever killer and were not taking any chances.

"I'll take the upstairs," said Blake as he headed toward the staircase.

160

Jennifer cleared the living room, dining room and kitchen, and was certain no one had been in these rooms in their absence. She couldn't remember when she was more tired or hungry. Returning to the small table near her front door, she retrieved the food bags and returned to the kitchen. Pulling out eating utensils and plates, she set the table in the dining room. Taking off his suit jacket and rolling up his shirt sleeves, Blake entered the kitchen and washed his hands at the sink. He pulled out a bottle of Chianti, grabbed two wine glasses out of the cabinet, and joined Jennifer at the dining room table. After he opened the bottle, he poured wine in their glasses, and held out Jennifer's chair as she sat down. Then he filled their plates.

"This ravioli looks melt-in-your-mouth amazing. How did you know about this restaurant?" Jennifer asked Blake.

"Seriously? What kind of an Italian would I be if I didn't know where the best Italian food was cooked?" He grinned as he pulled apart the garlic bread and placed a slice on each of their plates.

They dug in and were quiet the rest of the meal, until Jennifer asked, "There's a Lady Gaga concert on TV in thirty minutes. Want to watch it?"

"Sure."

"Great, that gives me time to take a shower, then join

you in the living room." Jennifer bounded up the stairs and before long, Blake could hear the shower running.

He cleared the table, putting the dirty dishes in the kitchen, trying not to imagine what it would be like to join Jennifer in her shower, washing every inch of her sexy body with soap. Working days with her and sleeping at her house on the sofa was playing havoc with his libido. He remembered their only kiss like it had happened an hour before. Beneath her serious work suit was a passionate woman who he wanted more than anything.

It was more than lust, Blake decided. It was her intelligence, warmth and drive that drew him to her, and made him want to spend more time with her. He wanted her in his life. Period.

Going to the living room, he sat on the sofa, pulled out the remote and searched for the concert in the online program guide. He selected the right channel and leaned back. It had been a long, long day.

Jennifer walked into the room, smelling of fresh lilac and wearing a pale pink cami under a pink cardigan with a pair of faded jeans. He'd never seen her wear pink before, and the color suited her. Truth be known, the lilac scent and the outfit turned him on in a big way. He'd never seen her expose so much glowing skin and he ached to touch her.

Jennifer glanced at the television. "Is that the right channel?"

"Yeah, I checked. It starts in five minutes."

For a second, she eyed the easy chair, then the sofa where Blake sat, then decided on the sofa and sat down next to him. He was a big man who filled the space on the sofa, forcing them to sit so close she could feel the warmth of his body as their legs touched. As Blake stretched his arm behind her on the back of the sofa, the closeness of his body felt so good that if she were a cat, she would be purring. Her heart hammered as she felt a heat coursing through her veins. Jennifer settled back, enjoying the feel of Blake's arm around her, his body so close and warm. She cuddled closer and closed her eyes.

Thirty minutes into the concert, Blake asked Jennifer if she'd like more wine. When she didn't answer, he pulled away to look down at her. She was fast asleep so he helped her stretch out, arranged some pillows under her head, then took the quilted throw from the chair and covered her. He sat on the easy chair, watching her sleep. Her facial bones were delicately carved, her mouth full and kissable. She seemed so peaceful, her soft features almost angelic.

Blake turned off the television and the lights. As his eyes adjusted to the darkened room, he could see slivers of light from the street lamp streak across the room. He pulled his jacket across his chest for warmth and leaned back in the easy chair with his feet propped on the ottoman.

Jennifer had the dream again — the one where she was locked in a basement room with windows too high to reach. But this time, she was able to wake herself up before she cried out in terror. Inhaling deeply, Jennifer opened her eyes and was surprised to find she was not in her bedroom. She was lying on the sofa and nearby on the easy chair was Blake, sound asleep. For a moment, she stared with longing at him, listening to the rhythm of his breathing. Finally, wrapping the quilt around her, she rose from the sofa, stopping at his chair to kiss him lightly on the lips before heading upstairs to her room. His eyes fluttered open and he said, "Jennifer?"

His arms reached out to her and in one motion, she was settling into his lap with his heavy arms wrapped snugly around her. Laying her head on his chest, she relaxed and thought, "If you only knew how much I want you, Blake."

Blake's body stiffened as he asked, "What did you say?"

Her hand flew to her mouth as she gasped. Did she say that out loud? She sat up and looked into his eyes, and the smoldering flame she saw there startled her. Blake pulled her hand away from her mouth and hungrily claimed her lips, sending spirals of ecstasy through her. His lips were hard and searching, and she kissed him back with a hunger that surprised her. Jennifer threw her arms around his neck, burying her hands in his thick hair.

Blake crushed her against his body as if he could not get her close enough. He whispered, his hot breath against her ear, "Baby, I want you so much it hurts."

She responded with soft butterfly kisses along his jawline until she reached his mouth. She then kissed him fully, savoring every moment.

As he placed a tantalizing kiss in the hollow of her neck, Jennifer moaned and glided her hands beneath his shirt so she could feel the hard muscles there. Swiftly, she began unbuttoning his shirt. She couldn't wait another second to feel his body against hers. Reaching the last button, she pulled his shirt open and trailed kisses down his chest. She raised her head and pulled off her cardigan sweater, throwing it on the floor. Blake pulled at her cami until he lifted it over her head then crushed her bare breasts to his chest. His body temperature seemed to spike, and the heat coming off him set her already hot blood to boiling.

Suddenly Jennifer was off the chair, lifted into the cradle of his strong arms, and he was carrying her up the stairs to her bedroom. She held on tight, licking and sucking his earlobes until he groaned. Gently, Blake eased her down onto her bed.

"Are you sure about this, Jennifer?"

"Very," she breathlessly responded.

Blake pulled off her faded jeans and panties and threw them on the floor, then removed his own clothing until he was standing naked before her. He reached into his jeans pocket and put something on her nightstand.

Joining her on the bed, he gently outlined the circle of her breasts with his hand. His tongue tantalized her nipples, which had swollen to their fullest. His hand seared a path down her middle and onto her thigh, the gentle massage sending currents of desire through her. Blake kissed his way down her body, skimming either side of her with his hands. Then he cupped her, and Jennifer gasped as a bolt of lust shot through her body like a bullet. Her body ignited as his magic, gentle fingers stroked her, sending waves of ecstasy throbbing through her body until she shattered into a million glowing stars.

Blake moved on top of her, bracing himself with his elbows, as her breasts crushed against the hardness of his chest. She loved the delicious weight of him and wrapped her arms around his neck until he claimed her lips again, his tongue tangling with hers. His kiss deepened until his tongue plunged in and out simulating what another part of his body would soon do — until she arched against him.

"Please, Blake, now," she begged. She'd never wanted anyone like she wanted *this* man.

He reached over her to the bed stand; she then heard the ripping of foil as he covered himself. Passion pounded the blood through her heart, chest, and head as he pushed inside her. She gasped at the force of it. He pulled out and drove inside her again and again.

She rocked against him and he picked up the perfect rhythm that bound their bodies together. He pushed into her in a hot, slick dance she wished would never end, flesh against flesh, man against woman. The heat rippled under her skin as the pressure built and built until she exploded with erotic pleasure. Moments later, he gave a powerful thrust and groaned her name as he found his own release.

Blake rolled over, taking Jennifer with him, planting her head on his chest where she could hear his heart beat erratically. She lay panting, her chest heaving while his hands absently stroked her back. He wanted to tell her so many things, like how he'd wanted her since the first time he saw her at the boat ramp five years ago at Monroe Lake. Blake wanted to tell her he was crazy about her. He stopped himself. It was too much information too soon.

They lay quietly as peace and contentment flowed between them. After a long moment, Jennifer lifted her head to gaze at him and whispered, "You know this is impossible."

Blake rolled over until he was on top of her, braced on his elbows, his dark, eyes burning into hers. "It sure didn't feel impossible to me. I think we need to make love one more time, and then we'll discuss what's impossible."

7 CHAPTER SEVEN

In the morning, down in the living room, Blake pulled a
package of special roasted coffee out of his briefcase,
retrieved the morning paper from the front porch, and then
headed for the kitchen, where he pulled out two cannolis
he'd purchased with the takeout the night before. He loaded
up the coffee filter with fresh grinds then filled the pot with
water. Flipping the switch, he pulled two mugs from the
cabinet — along with a tray — and thought about the night
before.

The gorgeous blonde sleeping upstairs had almost worn
him out. He wouldn't have believed that was possible. And
Blake wouldn't have believed it if he hadn't experienced a
sexual explosion like never before. Jennifer made him
insanely hot. And staying away from her was not going to
happen.

Blake poured steamy coffee into both mugs, placed
them on the tray along with the cannolis, and headed for the

stairs with the newspaper under his arm. In her bedroom, he quietly placed the mugs on the bed stand, pulled back the sheets and slipped back into bed. Jennifer was sleeping on her side toward the window, her hair fanned across the pillow. He planted a soft kiss on her shoulder.

Jennifer stirred, yawned, and stretched and rolled over. She looked beyond him to her alarm clock. "It's five o'clock. You get up at five o'clock?"

Wordlessly, he handed her a mug of coffee and watched her until she propped herself up on one elbow and took her first sip. "Oh, my God. This coffee couldn't have come from my kitchen."

"You like?"

"Oh, yes, I like."

"I bought a bag last night when picked up the Italian take out. I have another surprise for you too. Cannolis." He pointed to the wrapped desserts on the table next to him.

She smiled and kissed him on the shoulder as she wrapped the sheet around her naked body to sit up next to him. Jennifer glanced at the rolled newspaper on his lap, and sipped her coffee again. Delicious. She could get used to this — drinking amazing coffee while curled up next to the hottest man she'd ever seen, let alone slept with.

"I've been getting up an hour earlier than I need to so I can have coffee and read the paper before I start my day."

"Not a bad habit." She whispered.

He opened up the paper and took out the sports section to read first. Jennifer finished off her coffee and laid the mug on the bed stand. She gazed at Blake for a moment, her eyebrows arching mischievously, then peeled off the sheet and got on his lap, straddling him. Hot waves of pleasure heated her thighs as she found the hard bulge beneath his boxer shorts. She moved sensuously against it.

Jennifer ripped the paper out of his hands and threw it across the room. A flash of humor crossed Blake's face, as his large hands gripped her ass and pulled her closer.

"I'm hungry, aren't you?" Jennifer asked as she unwrapped a cannoli. She pulled out the tube-shaped fried pastry dough filled with creamy filling, dipping her finger in the center until it was coated with the sugary mixture. Then she lightly ran her finger across Blake's lower lip. Jennifer bent her head to lick the rich dessert from his lips, then she was kissing him and he was kissing her back with a hunger that had nothing to do with cannolis. His mouth felt hard, hot, and tasted faintly like coffee. Yes, she was pretty sure she could get used to waking up this way every morning.

Much, much later, after they showered, Blake waited downstairs for Jennifer to finish dressing. He read a text from Lane that instructed him to turn on the television to the local news.

Blake lifted the remote and turned on the television, flipping channels until he found the local news. The station was broadcasting live from Rocky Cliff State Park. A male announcer stood next to Evan Hendricks, a large crowd of people behind them. Blake turned up the volume.

"Broadcasting live, I am standing next to Evan Hendricks, the fiancé of Tiffany Chase, the young woman who is missing. Evan, is there something you want to tell our audience?"

Jennifer entered the room and Blake nodded toward the television.

"As Tiffany's fiancé, I want to make sure that everything is being done that can be to find her. With the help of a group of parishioners, I organized this search today of Rocky Cliff State Park where Tiffany was last seen. We have about thirty people here to cover every inch of the park, hiking every trail. Tiffany, if you're watching this, I just want you to know that I'm going to find you, honey. It's just a matter of time."

Blake turned off the television and said, "Do you believe that?"

Jennifer shook her head. "That little jerk is giving the impression that he had to step in because law enforcement wasn't doing enough to find Tiffany. That is so not true."

"Is he trying to make the police look bad or make himself look innocent?"

Outside a sense of heaviness hung in the air. Streaked clouds of gray suggested a spring rain might be coming. Thick, early morning fog made it difficult to see as Jennifer and Blake drove to the Sugar Creek Cafe to ask the waitresses if any of them knew Evan. If there was a connection between Evan Hendricks and Catherine Thomas, they had to find it.

When they entered the cafe, the live broadcast of the search of Rocky Cliff State Park was on every flat-screen television in the place. She saw a booth open in Brianna Hayden's area, so she led Blake in that direction.

As they slid into a booth near a window, Jennifer sensed they were being watched. People had made no secret they were unhappy that Catherine's killer had not been caught, and Tiffany's disappearance just fueled the fire.

Jennifer waved at Brianna, who was watching the television and had not seen them.

Brianna handed them a couple of menus and filled their cups with coffee. "Do you two know what you want this morning?"

Jennifer ordered scrambled eggs and bacon. Blake said, "I'll have the same. What we'd really like is a few minutes to talk to you. Think your boss will let you take a quick break?"

"It's going to have to be a very short break. We're busy this morning. Let me turn in your orders and I'll ask him."

A short time later, she returned, sliding in next to Jennifer. "We've been watching the search on TV all morning. It's a shame about that Tiffany girl going missing."

"We think so too, Brianna," Jennifer began. "Do you know Evan Hendricks?"

"Sure, I've known him for several years." Brianna brushed her bangs out of her face.

"Did Evan know Catherine Thomas?"

She glanced at Jennifer as if her question was the dumbest one she'd ever heard. "Of course, Evan knew Catherine. The two dated for at least a year. But that was before she met Nicholas. Between you and me, I thought Catherine and Evan would get married, but once she met Nicholas, she broke up with Evan. That was that."

Jennifer shot a glance at Blake who nodded, before she asked her next question. "Do you know Evan well?"

"Yes, my parents, my little girl and I attend his church. He's the youth minister so we don't hear his sermon, but we talk to him every Sunday. Truth be told, I wouldn't mind dating him. But I hear he's engaged to that girl that's missing."

A great clap of thunder boomed through the restaurant, so loud it shook the windows. It wasn't long before the wind bent the trees outside and rain slicked down the windows.

Brianna squirmed uncomfortably as she looked back at the kitchen area. "Your order is ready. I'll be right back."

She returned with two plates of scrambled eggs, bacon and some biscuits still hot from the oven. "Listen, if you don't have any more questions, I really need to get back to work."

"Of course. Good to see you, Brianna," said Jennifer. She turned to Blake, "Gee, why didn't Evan mention that he used to date Catherine?" Jennifer wondered aloud.

"We need to pull up his financials and phone records to determine his whereabouts the day Catherine and Tiffany went missing. His alibi, "home alone reading the Bible," is crap if there are no witnesses, phone calls or something to back it up. If we can get a warrant, I also wouldn't mind looking at his computer. But right now, I don't think we have enough solid evidence to get one granted. Even so, Evan Hendricks just jumped to the top of my suspect list," said Blake.

"Mine, too," she agreed.

From Jennifer's seat, she could see Lane enter the cafe. The wind caught the door, letting the rain rush in soaking the floor before he could pull it shut. A waitress ran out with a mop, as Lane tugged his yellow rain slicker off and hung it on the coat rack. He spotted Jennifer and Blake and headed toward their booth. He slid in beside her.

"Glad you two are here," Lane said as he grabbed a menu. Brianna arrived with hot coffee, took his order and rushed back to the kitchen.

Blake turned to make sure Brianna was not within hearing distance, then said, "We're interviewing the waitresses about Evan Hendricks to see if there is a connection between Evan and Catherine Thomas and we just hit pay dirt."

"No shit?" Lane's eyebrows rose inquiringly.

"Catherine and Evan dated and she broke up with him when she met Nicholas," Jennifer offered.

"Sounds like Evan has some more questions to answer." Lane's cell phone sounded and he glanced at the display. "Got to take this. Hope that area over there has better reception. I sure don't want to take the call outside in this weather." He headed toward the coat rack.

Jennifer, chewing on a piece of bacon, noticed Blake steal a biscuit from her plate. He sliced it in two, like he did before, smothered it with apple butter and placed one slice on her plate and the other on his. Then he caught her eye and grinned. The act seemed intimate and touched her heart. If they had been anywhere else, she would have kissed him.

Jennifer glanced at the television. The local news was being broadcast, but now with a weather warning about strong wind and rain on the ticker tape that ran at the bottom of the screen.

Lane returned, "You are not going to believe this." He took a gulp of his coffee then continued, "That search that Evan Hendricks organized out at Rocky Cliff State Park has turned into a clusterfuck of monumental proportions."

"What happened?"

"What didn't? First of all, he recruits a search and rescue team of thirty people. About fifteen of the thirty are some of his senior parishioners who haven't hiked a trail in forty years! The other fifteen are teenagers, ages ranging from fifteen to seventeen, who have no business being on a search team."

"Did anything...."

Lane interrupted, "That idiot, Evan Hendricks, sent all of those people onto the trails, rugged or not, without any of the basic search tools like flashlights, walkie-talkies, maps, water, just to name a few. No one knows which searchers have cell phones, not that they're going to be that helpful because there are widespread areas of the park where there's no reception.

"Someone called nine-one-one because Emma Jo Smith, who is eighty-freaking-years-old, slipped and rolled down a hill near Inspiration Point, landing on a tree root and breaking her hip. Emma Jo weighs over 200 pounds. The EMTs had a helluva time getting her out of the park to the ambulance in the parking lot. Once they got to the hospital, her son, Jack, arrived, exploded and threatened to kick the reverend's ass, or at the least sue him."

Jennifer had never seen Lane so angry. Most of the diners in the cafe seemed focused on him. She placed her hand on Lane's, "You might want to lower your voice; people can hear you."

Lane ignored her and continued, "The organizer of this mess, Evan Hendricks is out somewhere in the park and no one can locate him. There's no command post. Even if there was a command post, none of the searchers have walkie-talkies to communicate back to the post anyway.

Brianna arrived with Lane's breakfast. "I'm sorry, but would you please put that in a to-go box," Lane asked. I'll have to take it with me."

"No problem," she said.

Lane drained his mug of coffee. Shaking his head with

disgust, he said, "I can't believe that no one took into consideration that overtired, hungry or physically exhausted search volunteers are not only liable to miss important clues, but they could also endanger themselves or other volunteers if they are too tired to continue searching, or find themselves alone and unable to get back or call for help."

"Unbelievable," Blake said as he shook his head.

"There's no way to keep track of anyone, so the six deputies I sent out there will probably still be out there looking until tomorrow morning for searchers who haven't returned to their cars. Keep in mind, these six deputies could be out searching for the missing girl, Tiffany Chase.

"What bothers me the most is that no one bothered to contact law enforcement, because if they had, we would have told them that we'd already searched that park with a fine-tooth comb. This whole thing is so fucking needless." With that, he slapped a twenty on the table, grabbed the box of food from Brianna, and left.

Jennifer and Blake worked in their respective offices the rest of the morning and periodically checked the break room television for news about the search effort calamity.

Scanning Evan Hendricks' bank records on her computer screen, Jennifer noticed that on the day that Catherine disappeared, Evan had used his VISA to pay for a delivery of flowers. She made a note to contact the florist to find out to whom he sent flowers. The rest of the purchases made through VISA or his back account were innocuous actions like buying groceries or gas for his car. Nothing else stood out as suspicious for the entire week of Catherine's disappearance.

On the day Tiffany went missing, Evan had used his cell phone to make five calls to Tiffany. He couldn't have been very happy that his calls to his fiancé went unanswered. Later that afternoon, Evan made a call to Allison Wade, and then no calls were made the rest of the evening. So Evan's alibi was still unsubstantiated.

On the day of Tiffany's disappearance, the cell tower report revealed that most of Evan's cell phone calls were made in the vicinity of his church. There were two exceptions. One was a call he made to Allison Wade, which pinged the cell tower closest to his home, five miles away from the church. The other was a call made at eleven o'clock that night to Tiffany; the closest cell tower pinged was the one near Rocky Cliff State Park. "Bingo," Jennifer whispered as she leaped from her chair to tell Blake.

Blake, holding his cell to his ear, glanced up to see Jennifer and winked when he caught her eye. He finished his call and said, "You look as if you've discovered something."

"You could say that. Evan Hendricks made a call on his cell phone at eleven o'clock the night Tiffany disappeared. The cell tower pinged was the one near Rocky Cliff State Park."

"What a coincidence," Blake muttered sarcastically. "Didn't the good reverend say he was at home all night reading his Bible?"

Blake's office phone rang. It was Lane. Blake tapped the speaker button.

"A hiker with a dog just found Tiffany's body in Shawnee Canyon on trail number eight in Rocky Cliff State Park. It's still a fucking mess out here. The rain hasn't stopped and there are five searchers unaccounted for. Don't come out here without proper gear and dress. I'm setting up a command post. Stop there first for walkie-talkies and other supplies you may need." Lane ended the call and Blake slammed the receiver down.

"Jennifer, I need to go to my condo first for my hiking gear, then we'll hit your house before we go to the park."

"No need," Jennifer said. "I put my gear in your SUV the day they made us partners. I don't like surprises."

Jennifer sat in the passenger seat, lacing up her hiking boots as Blake drove toward Rocky Cliff State Park. The rain slapped against the glass as the wipers struggled to keep the windshield clear. Closer to the park, there were cars pulled over to wait out the storm. Jennifer and Blake didn't have that luxury.

Jennifer wrapped her arms around herself and thought about Tiffany Chase. She bit her lower lip and blinked to prevent the pooling tears in her eyes from falling. If only they could have found her sooner.

Blake pulled into the park and flashed his badge at the deputy and conservation officer at the gate house.

"Blake Stone? Sgt. Hansen wants you to stop at the command post before you go to the crime scene. We set up at the picnic shelter near the trail entrance." The deputy pointed to far end of the parking lot where emergency vehicle flashing lights could be seen through the curtain of rain.

Blake parked the SUV. Jennifer threw on her yellow slicker along with her backpack filled with supplies, and jumped out of the vehicle. Rain hammered against her face as she buttoned up the front of the slicker and pulled up its hood to cover her head. She felt Blake walking next to her as she pushed against the wind toward the picnic shelter.

They found Lane giving instructions to a small group of deputies. When he saw Blake and Jennifer, he broke away. "The park service loaned us a couple of ATVs. They're over there." Lane pulled out a map of the park. "I highlighted the service road that runs near Trail #8. It stops near Sugar Creek. Then you'll have to hike the rest of the way to the crime scene, which is about a quarter of a mile away. The crime scene techs are already there and Doc Meade and his team are on their way."

The ATVs plunged through the muddy service road as they made their way to the swinging bridge that crossed Sugar Creek. Below them was a deep canyon nestled on both sides by sandstone cliffs. Jennifer held on tight as she and Blake trekked across the swinging bridge. Each time the bridge moved, her stomach clenched tight. On the other side, they followed the trail through the wooded thicket as the rain continued to pour.

Jennifer's mind was working overtime. How did the killer carry a body through this mess? Even if he had an ATV, he had to hike the remaining quarter mile, just like they were now. The terrain wasn't as rough as it was along Sugar Creek, but it was no cake walk, especially if one was carrying the dead weight of a body.

Jennifer heard voices and knew they were close to the crime scene. Following the bend of the trail, they came to a clearing where she saw crime scene tech, Karen Katz, taking photographs of the nude body of Tiffany Chase. Jennifer and Blake inched closer but stayed on the outside of the yellow tape that circled the perimeter of the crime scene.

Tiffany's body was posed as Catherine's had been, with her arms bent, her hands pressed into a prayer position. Jennifer felt sick and swallowed hard. Blake squeezed her hand. She dared not look at him. The thought of being surrounded by his strong arms was too tempting.

Jennifer circled the body until she could bend to clearly see Tiffany's neck, which had the same deep grooved ligature marks and bruising as Catherine's. Jennifer shivered, more from the visual of the killer straddling this young girl from behind as he choked the life out of her, than the chill caused by the rain that was still falling. If this was the work of Evan Hendricks, she would make him pay. That Tiffany's body was posed as if in prayer did not escape Jennifer. Is this the youth minister's way of communicating something about the girls?

Doc Meade arrived with two assistants. He immediately had the assistants roll Tiffany over on her side. "Damn it," he mumbled. "That sick son of a bitch has done it again. Look at these lacerations. He tortured this poor girl, just like he did Catherine Thomas."

Jennifer and Blake returned to the command post to talk to Lane. He was standing next to the sheriff, deep in a conversation Jennifer could not hear. Her father's fisted hands told her how angry he was.

"We still have two missing searchers," Lane said as they approached. "Have no clue which trail they took so the deputies are hiking each one until they find them."

Tim cut in, "What's your take on the crime scene?"

Blake began with an accounting of Tiffany's injuries, "It

appears she was tortured and killed in the same manner as Catherine Thomas. There are deep ligature marks around her neck and lacerations across her buttocks and thighs. She was probably tortured before he killed her and dumped her here."

Repulsed, Tim shook his head. "I want to review the map of Deer Run State Park to see where the service road is in respect to where we found Catherine's body. If that's how he abducted Tiffany and got her out of the park, I don't doubt he's done it before."

"I'll bet my next paycheck it's close, and that there is an ATV and cart involved. Although, how could we prove it? The roads that day were as wet and muddy as they are today," offered Lane.

Jennifer said, "Once again, this is not the primary crime scene. He did not kill Tiffany or Catherine in the parks. Where is he taking them? He has to have a house or cabin in this general vicinity between both parks."

Lane reached for his cell phone, "I think it's time our deputies did a house-to-house to ask questions and report anything or anyone that looks suspicious."

Tiffany's autopsy the next day bore no new revelations. The cause of death was strangulation with a ligature, most likely a leather belt. Her hyoid bone was broken and there was residue of duct tape on her mouth, wrists and ankles where she had been restrained. Her body had been scrubbed with bath soap and household bleach. Like Catherine, Tiffany had been raped, and the killer had used a condom to prevent DNA analysis of his semen.

Later, as Jennifer prepared interview questions for Evan Hendricks, she got a text from Blake for her to meet him in the break room. When she entered the room, both Lane and Blake were looking at the television. On the screen was Evan Hendricks being interviewed by Grace Cohn of CSN, Crime Story Network.

"Just what we need," Jennifer said with a sigh. Grace Cohn was a nationally known crime commenter and television host known for her outbursts and often vicious treatment of guests on her program. She often bashed efforts made by law enforcement to solve crimes.

"Mr. Hendricks, please tell us who you are in relation to the murdered girl, Tiffany Chase?" Grace Cohn asked Evan, who appeared to be sitting in his desk chair at his small office in the church.

"Ms. Cohn, Tiffany and I were engaged," Evan began, wiping at his eyes with a tissue.

"Tears? Are you kidding me?" asked Blake as Jennifer rolled her eyes.

"Just yesterday," Evan stated. "*I* organized a search to

find her."

"Yeah, Evan, let's talk about the search from hell. I've got a couple of things to add to that discussion," said Lane.

Grace Cohn let Evan get out a couple more sentences before she interrupted him. "What I want to know, Evan, is why you organized a search."

"The local law enforcement did not appear to be giving Tiffany's disappearance the focus it needed. She should have been found before she was murdered."

"That son of a bitch!" exclaimed Tim as he entered the room and stood next to Jennifer.

"Let's talk about you, Evan," Grace Cohn began. "My producer tells me Tiffany had gone camping with another man the night she disappeared. If you were engaged to her, that must have made you pretty angry."

Evan looked at someone adjacent to the camera with confusion, then back at the camera, "I didn't find out until much later that Tiffany was camping with someone else."

Cohn smirked and said, "Well, I know if I found out my fiancé was with someone else, I'd be hopping mad."

Evan's face visibly reddened and a muscle twitched at his jaw. "I told you I didn't know about it until after she disappeared."

Cohn didn't skip a beat. "By the way, where were you

the night Tiffany Chase disappeared? Maybe you can answer that question after the commercial break."

The camera shot back to Grace Cohn. "For our viewing audience," Cohn began. "We were unable to get anyone from the county sheriff's office to respond to our calls. If the law enforcement agencies that are assigned the Tiffany Chase murder would please call in, we would like to hear their explanations about this investigation. Our telephone number is listed at the bottom of your screen."

"When hell freezes over," said Tim as he left for his office.

A commercial soon appeared and Lane turned to Jennifer and Blake, "Are you two ready to interview this prick?"

"We're headed to his house now."

Wordlessly, Fred and Julie Thomas focused on Grace Cohn's interview with Evan Hendricks until the commercial break.

"Why does that guy look so familiar?" asked Fred.

"Honey, Catherine dated Evan before she met Nicholas. Don't you remember him coming to the house to talk to her? He was very upset that she broke up with him. He thought they were getting married."

Fred froze. Evan Hendricks was engaged to Tiffany Chase who was abducted and murdered much like his Catherine. Until Julie had brought it up, he had not remembered Evan dating Catherine, it was so long ago. But one thing that was clear was that Evan had had a relationship with both murder victims. This was way too coincidental. How likely was it? In Fred's mind, it was only too clear now that Evan murdered both young women. He'd made a promise to Catherine and he intended to keep it.

"Julie, I just remembered that I'm out of my heart medicine," Fred said as calmly as he could. "Would you please run to the drug store and get the prescription refilled?"

"Sure, honey. Let me put on some lipstick and get my purse."

He waited for her by the door that led to the garage. As she approached him with her purse slung over her shoulder, he grabbed her and kissed her hard. "I love you, Julie. Always remember that."

As soon as Fred heard the car pull out of the driveway, he went to his bedroom closet and pulled out his rifle, Smith & Wesson pistol, and a black duffle bag. Then he pulled out his laptop to look up Evan's address.

Fred raced to Evan's house. When he arrived, he

noticed a news van parked in front, so he drove down the street, did a U-turn, and then parked under a huge oak tree a block away to watch the house.

When Blake and Jennifer pulled up outside Evan Hendricks' home, a white news van with the Crime Story Network logo on the side was parked outside. A man was loading up camera equipment into the back while a female reporter talked to Evan on his porch.

Blake and Jennifer waited in their SUV for the conversation to wrap up. They got out of the vehicle when they saw the reporter get into the van.

Evan spotted them walking up his sidewalk and slammed the front door in their faces. Blake pounded on the door. "Evan, open up. We need to talk to you."

Evan flung open the door and glared at them with burning, reproachful eyes. "I know what you're doing. You're getting a lot of pressure to solve Tiffany's disappearance and murder so you think you're going to pin it on me. Well, you're wrong!"

"Evan, we just want to talk to you. That's all. There's no reason for you to be so upset," Jennifer said as she inched closer to the door.

The news van hadn't moved and both occupants were listening to the conversation on the porch.

Jennifer didn't see Evan's fist until it slammed into her cheekbone, sending her stumbling backward until she fell off the porch, pounding her head painfully onto the hard ground. Starbursts appeared behind her eyelids before she blacked out.

Fred Thomas witnessed the assault, started his car, then sped past the house. He knew where they would be taking Evan Hendricks, and he wanted to be there first.

Blake grabbed Evan's thumb, bending back his wrist until Evan screamed with pain. He then jerked Evan's arm behind his back and dropped him to the porch floor. "Evan Hendricks, you are under arrest for assaulting a police officer. You have the right to remain silent... "

As his Miranda rights were stated, Blake shoved his knee into Evan's back to hold him in place while he grabbed his handcuffs from his back pocket. Once he had each wrist cuffed, he jumped off the porch and helped Jennifer to her feet.

"Honey, are you okay?" Blake lifted her chin to check her injuries. A raw abrasion streaked across her cheek, her right eye was swelling shut and blood dripped from her nose.

Jennifer clenched her jaw as pain radiated across her face and she wiped the blood from her nose with the back of her hand. She fought the waves of nausea that ensued. Her legs felt wobbly so she leaned on Blake for support.

"I'm fine. Just pissed he got the drop on me."

With his arm around her waist, Blake helped her to the SUV and into the passenger seat. "Give me a minute to get the asshole into the back seat. Then I'll find the first aid kit."

Camera mounted on his shoulder, the man from CSN filmed as the female reporter talked in low tones into a microphone. They followed Blake back to the porch.

Blake jerked Evan Hendricks to his feet then led him to the SUV where he locked him in the back seat. Once in the driver seat, he pulled a small first aid kit from the glove box. Opening the kit, he took out some alcohol pads, ointment and some Band-Aids.

"Jennifer, let me see your face."

She leaned toward him, saw the alcohol pads and moved back. "That alcohol is going to sting."

"Honey, come here. I have to clean out your cuts or you'll get an infection."

Jennifer grimaced but leaned back toward him. He gently cleaned each cut, and then applied some antibiotic ointment. Jennifer drew the line when it came to putting Band-Aids on her face, so he put them away.

Suddenly, Blake put his hand at the back of her neck,

pulled her close and kissed her gently on the lips.

"Oh, why don't you two get a room?" Evan said.

"Shut up!" Blake and Jennifer shouted in unison.

Once they were on the road, Blake looked in the rear-view mirror and saw the CSN news van behind them. Great. Just great. He called ahead to let Lane know they were bringing Evan Hendricks in, as well as a reporter from Crime Story Network.

By the time Fred Thomas reached town, it was past six o'clock and the bank and stores were closed, which suited his purposes just fine. He parked in the back parking lot of the Glory Days Hotel. He walked to the front of the building, entered the lobby and asked for a room on the third floor facing the street. After he received his room key card, he headed back outside through the rear exit to his car for his things.

Settling in his room, he opened the drapes and stepped out onto the balcony to take in his perfect view of the front entrance to the sheriff's building. He sat on a plastic chair at a small table for a moment, waiting for his heart rate to slow. Once it did, he went back inside and pulled out his loaded rifle. He pulled a soft cloth from inside the case, and polished the gun as he sat on the balcony.

Fred remembered the day Catherine was born. She was the prettiest baby he'd ever seen, with rosy cheeks and a cloud of brown hair. He'd handed out cigars to anyone in the hospital who would take one. Fred had loved watching her grow up: coaching her through her first home run, teaching her to fish until she caught one, watching her as she entered the living room all dressed up for her first prom. She was close to Julie, but Catherine had always been a daddy's girl.

He had never let her down. And he wasn't about to start now.

Blake drove into town, relieved that things seemed quiet. As he got closer to the sheriff's building, he was grateful there wasn't a crowd on the front lawn, with people chanting and holding signs. He pulled the SUV in front of the building, got out with Jennifer, and prepared to get Evan Hendricks out of the vehicle, ignoring the white CSN van parking behind them.

Evan refused to get out. Blake yanked him out by his arm and pressed him against the SUV as Evan struggled to get his balance. Jennifer came around the other side to take one of Evan's arm to walk him in while Blake took the other.

Blake noticed the appearance of the CSN cameraman and shouted, "Get back in your van."

The cameraman stopped momentarily but followed

them with his camera as he filmed, now with the female reporter at his side.

A deputy appeared at the front glass-door and waited for them. They were about five feet from the door when a shot rang out and Evan Hendricks' body slumped heavily to the ground, dragging Jennifer and Blake down with him. Blake whipped his Glock out of his holster and looked toward the direction of the shot, but saw only the orange setting sun reflected in the old hotel's windows.

The cameraman shoved the reporter to the ground and dived on top of her to protect her with his body.

Another shot blasted through the air and the back of Evan's head blew off, showering Jennifer with his blood. Blake checked Evan's pulse. He was dead. Blake thought Jennifer had also been shot. Staying low to the ground, he dragged her toward the building to the deputy who helped them inside. Blake picked Jennifer up and sat in a chair in the lobby, cradling her body with his arms. He wiped blood from her face and looked into her dilated eyes. She was in shock.

"It came from the hotel!" The deputy shouted. "Third floor, last room!"

"Get the EMTs here, stat!" barked Blake to the deputy as he lay Jennifer on a sofa. "Don't leave her for a second."

Blake joined Tim and Lane as they ran to the door with

AK-47 rifles with scopes to cover the four deputies who ran into the Glory Days Hotel. A shot sounded from within the hotel.

Blake raced across the street and into the hotel. He took the stairs two at a time until he reached the third floor. At the end of the hall, the deputies kicked in the door of the last room facing the street. Blake waited until they cleared the room, then entered.

Fred Thomas was stretched across a bed, still holding the pistol that enabled him to take his own life. The rifle he used to kill Evan Hendricks lay across a small table on the balcony.

Blake opened an envelope lying on the bed, which was addressed to Julie, and pulled out the note inside.

Julie, I want you to know how much I love you and that this had nothing to do with you. I made a promise to myself and to Catherine to take the life of the killer who took hers. I've kept the promise. I don't want to live in a world without Catherine. I'm sorry.

8 CHAPTER EIGHT

Banned to the emergency room waiting area, Blake got up to pace again. The nurses wouldn't let him stay with Jennifer while the doctor examined her. He wanted to stay with her. No, it was more than that. Blake *needed* to be with her. This waiting and not knowing if anything was wrong was the worst kind of torture. Twenty minutes had already passed and he, Lane and Tim had heard nothing. He glanced at the other two men. Tim was talking quietly on his cell phone while Lane hovered over his laptop.

Blake walked to the end of the room and stood before a wide window that overlooked the hospital parking lot. What if something was seriously wrong with Jennifer? When Evan Hendricks hit her, she'd tumbled off the porch, slamming to the ground. How hard had she hit her head? Jennifer said she was fine, but he should have realized her injuries were worse than she admitted. If anyone knew how stoic Jennifer was, he did. Should he have gotten her medical care then, before he brought Evan to the sheriff's office?

Blake's mind drifted back to the shooting and replayed the scene in slow motion. Who in the hell would have guessed that Fred Thomas would flip out and shoot Evan Hendricks? How did Fred even know they were bringing Evan to the sheriff's office? He had to have been watching Evan's house. And if he was, why hadn't Blake seen him?

If he'd had any inkling of what Fred planned to do, he would have called ahead for back-up and delivered Evan to the back entrance of the building. He'd been such a fucking easy target from Fred's room at the hotel. Blake raked his fingers through his hair. His stomach clenched as he visualized Jennifer covered with Evan's blood, as she lay next to his lifeless body. Christ. Could he have prevented this clusterfuck?

Blake heard a woman's voice, turned, and noticed Frankie enter the waiting room, along with Jennifer's mother, Megan. Turning back to the window, he let their husbands explain what had happened. He didn't feel like talking to anyone, unless it was to Jennifer's doctor. All he wanted to hear was that she was going to be fine, and then he wanted to take her in his arms and never let her go.

Blake began pacing again. He couldn't just sit still and think about it. He had to do something. He checked his watch. Ten minutes had flown by and he realized they'd heard nothing about Jennifer for thirty minutes. Blake rushed out of the room, down the hall to the nurses' station and cornered the first nurse he saw.

"Any news about Jennifer Brennan's condition?"

"I'm sorry. I can't give out any information about her unless you're family. Are you?"

"Yes, I will be soon enough. I'm her fiancé," he lied.

The nurse eyed him skeptically, then said, "The doctor's with her now. He should be out with some news soon. Just be patient and wait."

Blake returned to the waiting area, nearly colliding with Frankie, who looked as apprehensive as he felt.

"How is she? Did you learn anything?"

Rubbing the back of his neck, Blake shook his head. "Not really. The doctor's with her and we should hear something soon."

Frankie returned to her chair next to Lane, who pulled her to him, gently kissing her cheek. Megan and Tim were huddled together talking quietly.

Blake walked back to the window, looking out but not really seeing anything. He remembered the first time he and Jennifer had made love. As he lay with Jennifer's head on his chest, his arm at her waist, holding her close, he'd vowed to never let her go. He couldn't lose her. Not now. Not ever.

An E.R. doctor in green scrubs with an aluminum

clipboard tucked under his arm entered the waiting room and asked for Jennifer Brennan's family. Blake couldn't get to the man fast enough as the group huddled around him.

"The blow to Jennifer's head when she fell from the porch caused a concussion," the doctor began. "She has the typical symptoms: headache, nausea and dizziness. I think she'll be fine as long as she gets some rest the next couple of days. I gave her a mild sedative and Jennifer is resting now, but she's asking for Blake."

He stepped forward, ignoring the curious glances of the others. "I'm Blake."

"You can go in, but only stay for ten minutes, then the rest of you can visit her. But don't stay too long, she needs her rest. I want to keep her here for the night. We'll see how she's doing in the morning before I decide whether or not to release her."

Jennifer's eyes were closed when Blake entered the room. He sat quietly in the chair next to her bed and held her hand, weaving his fingers between hers. Except for the dark purple bruising splashed across her cheek, she looked pale, even against the starched white of the sheets. Kissing her hand, Blake watched as her dark eyes opened and a weak smile stretched across her face.

"Hi, Blake," she whispered.

He moved to the side of the bed, sat down next to her and pulled her in his arms. "You really gave me a scare, honey."

"Oh, I'm fine. You know you can't always believe what doctors tell you."

"Don't even start. He's prescribing rest for a couple of days, and I'm the guy who's going to make sure you do it." Blake kissed her, his large hand at the back of her head, gently holding her in place.

"How am I supposed to think clearly to debate with you kissing me like that?"

"That's the goal. I'll keep kissing you until you promise me that you'll take it easy for a couple of days." Blake ran his thumb along her jaw line where even darker bruising had set in.

Jennifer flinched, and said, "I can't lie around doing nothing. Not going to happen. What if Evan is innocent? If Evan didn't kill those girls, there's a killer out there abducting and killing young women. I don't think he'll stop with two."

"Okay," Blake sighed. "Let's agree to discuss it later. How's that?" Yeah, they would discuss it, and then he would make sure she rested.

"Guess it will have to do." She pulled him by his shirt and kissed him fully on the lips. "Your kisses could be therapeutic."

"Your mom, dad, Frankie and Lane are waiting to see you. Plus, you're supposed to be resting, so I'll come back in a couple of hours." Blake pulled her close, gently kissing her until she wrapped her arms around his neck to pull him closer for more. He reluctantly broke off the kiss and left the room.

Frankie, Lane, Megan and Tim filed into Jennifer's room to find tears streaming down her face as she focused on the television. A film of Evan's shooting was being featured on Grace Cohn's program on CSN.

As soon as Tim realized what she was watching, he grabbed the remote control from Jennifer's bed and flipped off the television.

"Dad, is Evan dead?" asked Jennifer as her mother moved beside her to squeeze her hand.

"Yes. There was nothing anyone could do for him." Tim hated to give her the news, but he refused to lie to her.

"How are we going to know whether or not he killed Catherine and Tiffany?"

"I've got a team at his office and home right now looking for evidence."

Frankie moved behind Jennifer to fluff her pillow.

"Okay, that's enough crime talk. Remember the doc said our girl needs her rest."

"Yeah, and along those lines," added Lane. "Don't count on coming in to work for a couple of days. Enjoy some time off."

"Take the time off, Jennifer." Frankie hugged her, then headed for the door with Lane. "We need to go now to pick up Ashley. She had a play date with Melissa and Michael Brandt Jr. today. I'll call you tomorrow morning to see how you're doing. Get some sleep, okay?"

Megan glanced at Tim, then hugged Jennifer, too. "Your father has that look he has when he wants to talk to you alone. I'll see you tomorrow, sweetheart. Get some rest."

Before Megan left, she pointed at her husband, "You, I'll see at home." She kissed him and then left the room.

"Okay, Dad, what's up?" Jennifer began. "Mom's right, you've got that look."

Tim ran his fingers through his hair and moved closer to her bed. "Is there any chance you'll agree to be taken off this case?"

Jennifer shot him a glare. "Absolutely not. Please, Dad, don't take me off the case!"

"Okay, don't get upset. I had to ask," Tim began as he

sat down. "I'm a dad who hates it when his girl gets hurt."

"I know, Dad. But I'm a trained professional. Evan got the drop on me. I won't let it happen again."

Tim nodded and pulled her hand into his and held it tight. A long moment passed before he asked, "Is there anything you want to tell me about you and Blake?"

Tensing, she asked, "What are you talking about?"

"I watched him pace for an hour in the waiting room before they let us see you. He was sick with worry. Blake's feelings for you go way beyond that of a partner. What about you, Jennifer? What do you feel for Blake?"

Jennifer looked down at her hand held by her father, their fingers intertwined. This was dangerous territory. He was her sheriff as well as her father. He could insist she be assigned a new partner and the thought of being away from Blake was more painful than her injuries. The only time she'd ever lied to her father was five years ago when she tried to hide her pregnancy from him. Jennifer had been in college and the thought of disappointing him had terrified her. The lie had led to her abduction and the stress had nearly killed her parents.

Jennifer couldn't lie to him again. "Dad, I think I'm in love with Blake."

Blake and Lane were waiting for Tim when he left Jennifer's room.

"We need to talk about the case," said Lane as Tim nodded in agreement. "Let's get a table at the Pizza King. We can talk while we eat."

Tim arrived at the Pizza King first, ordered a large sausage and mushroom pizza and then waited for Lane and Blake to arrive. He tried to absorb that his daughter was in love with one of his detectives. His first response was relief. It had been five years since she'd broken it off with that idiot Paul Vance. Tim was beginning to think his daughter was filled with so much distrust for men that she'd never allow herself to get close to a man again. Within the last thirty minutes, all that had changed big-time.

Jennifer was in love with Blake Stone. Tim found he wasn't all that upset about the pairing. Blake was a good man. Early on when Blake had joined the department, Tim had his doubts about him. He was good-looking and buff and had the female deputies panting for him like he was a rock star. Tim's fear was he'd become a player and would lose focus on the job. That didn't happen. Blake kept his personal life private, and his analytical skills and single-mindedness had helped his department solve some important cases. Tim trusted him enough to assign him to protect his daughter because he had no doubt Blake would lay down his life for her — without hesitation.

Jennifer was in love with Blake, but how did Blake feel about her? At the hospital, Blake seemed genuinely concerned that Jennifer had been hurt. More than concerned — the guy was crazy with worry. But did that mean he loved her? Tim had no idea what he would do if Blake Stone hurt his little girl, but he knew it wouldn't be good.

Lane and Blake joined him at the table just as the waitress delivered three cold bottles of Coors.

"Good choice on the brews, boss," said Lane as he took a gulp. "Stress makes me hungry. Did you order?"

"Large sausage and mushroom."

"Excellent."

Tim looked long and hard at Blake, who was peeling the paper from his beer bottle and seemed distracted. "Blake, I talked to Karen Katz on the way over here. So far they haven't found anything in Evan's office or home that could link him to the murders."

His jaw clenched, Blake just looked at the sheriff.

"So tell me again, what do you have on Evan Hendricks?" Tim asked.

"He was engaged to Tiffany Chase and it's unlikely he was too happy she was doing some overnight camping with another guy."

"Do you have a witness who can collaborate he knew

they were camping together and he was angry?"

"No, sir," Blake admitted.

"That information wouldn't have helped your case without a witness. What else do you have?"

"We were bringing him in to discuss his relationship with Catherine Thomas. A witness told us Evan was angry when she dumped him for Nicholas Connor a couple of years ago." Blake paused for a second as he searched his memory, then continued. "He didn't say a word about Catherine when we questioned him before. We thought he was hiding the connection between Catherine and him."

"Anything else?"

"He had no alibi for the night Tiffany Chase went missing. In addition, his cell phone pinged at the tower near Rocky Cliff State Park around the same time we estimate she was abducted."

Ripping the price tag off the new blue scrubs he wore, he took the stairs up to the fourth floor instead of the elevator. Too many people rode the elevator. No witnesses were the best witnesses. When he'd called earlier, pretending to be a relative of Jennifer Brennan, a nurse had given him her room number. Finally reaching the fourth floor, he slowly opened the door and stepped into the hall. Jennifer was in Room 410, just past the waiting room. He was within six feet from her room, when Sheriff Tim Brennan stepped out. Startled, he dove into a patient room that luckily was empty.

Waiting until the sheriff walked by, he composed himself and strode to Jennifer's room, closing the door behind him. He stood over her as she slept, confident that even if she awoke, Jennifer would not recognize him in scrubs, with a fake mustache and black-rimmed glasses.

He brushed Jennifer's hair away from her cheek so he could see her injuries. They weren't as bad as he'd liked. Too bad. He'd seen the CSN video several times when Jennifer fell off Evan Hendricks' porch in slow motion after he slugged her. She was a lucky bitch. Anyone else would have broken an arm or at least a wrist, but not this one. In the next CSN video, there's Jennifer in the midst of chaos as Fred Thomas takes his best shot and blows Evan Hendricks away. It was more exciting than some of the scenes in his favorite Quentin Tarantino movies. He'd remembered cheering in front of his television.

All in all, he'd had a damn good week. He'd whisked Tiffany Chase out of the park without even one witness, had his fun with her at his cabin, and then — miracle of all miracles — it rains! And it was a toad-strangler. He'd gotten Tiffany to her final resting place when the sky opened up and rain gushed down her body like a river dam had broken, efficiently washing away any trace evidence that might have been left after her bath and bleaching.

Then the week got even better when he'd learned that Evan Hendricks was the person of interest for both Tiffany's and Catherine's murder. He almost chuckled aloud at the thought. The police actually thought that Evan Hendricks was responsible for the brilliant abductions and murders he'd achieved. They couldn't be serious. And that TV bitch Grace Cohn couldn't shut her trap about how Evan lived in the community as a quiet youth minister when in reality he could be a sociopathic serial killer. Seriously? Did people really think that Evan Hendricks had the brainpower to plan abductions and no-evidence murders? It was fucking ridiculous. He'd honed his skills for years.

He stared at Jennifer Brennan as he fingered the hypodermic needle he had in his pocket. He was in a quandary here — the idea too last-minute. He'd wanted her dead since the day at Deer Run State Park when she'd screamed at him. The days when he'd stand still for being humiliated in public ended with the death of his mother. Jennifer Brennan needed to die, but was this the right time and place?

Since the hunting and securing of his prey were always well-planned, the immediacy of this idea was unnerving because it was too impulsive and risky. Was he slipping? Was he at the point where he had no control over his urges? He reviewed his options.

If he disabled her with the drug, Plan A was to wheel her out of the room on a gurney, get her to a stairwell, carry her down the stairs fireman-style, then use the wheelchair he'd stashed near the first floor stairway door to whisk her to his vehicle. There were a lot of things that could go wrong with Plan A. Now that he thought about it, it was one of the dumbest plans he'd ever had. Plan B was a lot less risky, but definitely not as much fun because the strategy was simply killing her with an overdose. One injection and good-bye Jennifer Brennan.

Blake couldn't shake the voice at back of his brain that was telling him something was off. Call it his gut instinct or intuition, whatever it was, it was now screaming at him that something was very wrong. He raced back to the hospital and plunged into the first parking space in the lot. Sprinting into the lobby, he flashed his badge at the security guard and darted toward the elevator.

On the fourth floor, it was too quiet, as if all the patients slept simultaneously. No chatter from a hospital room television or from patients' guests broke the silence. Christ, it was only nine at night. The hallway was devoid of people except for a nurse in pink-print scrubs at the nurses' station, who was glued to her computer screen and didn't seem to notice Blake as he passed by.

When Blake reached Jennifer's room, the door was closed and he quietly opened it so he didn't disturb her if she was sleeping. Inside, a tall, dark-haired man in scrubs bent over Jennifer. Blake cleared his throat, obviously startling him because he jumped and whipped around to face him. Blake checked his name tag — "Barry."

"Hey," said Blake. "Didn't mean to scare you, Barry. How's she doing?"

"Good," Barry mumbled, as he peeled off his latex gloves and slipped them in his pocket. "Just taking her pulse.

It's fine. Nothing to worry about." He brushed past Blake and hurriedly left the room, closing the door behind him.

The tingling at the back of Blake's brain turned into a throbbing, earsplitting declaration, telling him something was off with the male nurse. But what? Blake's mind did an instant-replay, starting from the moment he entered the room. Why did the man say he was taking Jennifer's pulse? His hands were near her neck not her wrist. He ripped open the door and stepped into the hallway, his right hand resting on his gun. Seeing Barry, he headed down the hall to follow him.

Blake eyeballed him from head-to-toe, noting that Barry was wearing hiking boots. What kind of a nurse, or doctor for that matter, wears hiking boots to work? Just as Blake started to run toward him, the man glanced back at him and picked up speed. Not stopping at the nurses' station as Blake predicted, the guy made a beeline for the stairwell door. Suddenly Barry blasted through the heavy door, slamming it against the wall, then flew down the stairs. He was already at the third-floor landing when Blake entered the stairwell, racing down the stairs by taking the steps two-at-a-time. By the time Blake reached the third floor, he heard the second floor stairwell door open, then close.

Blake raced down the stairs to the second floor and charged into the hallway. The second floor was as quiet as the fourth floor when he'd entered earlier. No one was in the hall. Drawing his gun, he held it at his side as he peeked into each patient room looking for Barry. There was no sign of the man in the blue scrubs.

Blake yanked out his cell to call hospital security. He provided a description of Barry, then gave orders to search for him and to detain him if he tried to leave the hospital.

He briefed Lane and asked for backup to search the hospital for Barry and to cover Jennifer's room. He then hurtled back up the stairs to the fourth floor. What if the man in the scrubs had hurt Jennifer? He assumed she was sleeping, but what if she wasn't?

He raced down the fourth floor hallway until he reached the nurses' station. He slammed his fist on the counter to get the nurse's attention. Flashing his badge, he said, "Page a doctor to Jennifer Brennan's room, then follow me!"

The nurse, her face now flushed with anxiety, asked, "What's going on?"

"I just found a man dressed in blue scrubs in her room. Do you have a doctor or nurse on duty tonight wearing blue scrubs and hiking boots?"

"Sherry Simpson and I are the only ones working the night shift and I assure you, neither of us would be caught dead wearing hiking boots."

They reached Jennifer's room and Blake ushered the

nurse through the door. "Check everything to make sure she's all right."

The nurse rushed to Jennifer's side, immediately grasping her wrist to take her pulse. "Pulse is a little slow."

Something caught her attention, and she moved blanket near Jennifer's neck. "Oh, my God."

Blake moved beside the nurse to see a hypodermic needle hanging precariously from a tiny fold in Jennifer's neck. The nurse made a movement to remove the needle, and Blake grabbed her hand. "Don't touch it!"

Blake pulled a pair of latex gloves out of one pocket and a small evidence bag out of the other. Once he donned the gloves, he gently pulled the hypodermic needle out and then held it up to the light to see how much of the liquid inside could have been injected into Jennifer's body. It looked like three fourths of the drug was still in the hypodermic. They needed to identify what was in the syringe and fast. Blake slipped it into the evidence bag and sat on the bed.

"Jennifer, wake up!" Her body limp, Blake pulled her against his chest, supporting her back with his arm. She began talking, but her speech was so slurred he couldn't understand what she was saying.

He looked at the nurse, who was pressing her hand against her chest, her expression wide-eyed and terrified.

"Who's your lab director?"

"Clifford Jones, but he's gone for the day. Left work hours ago."

"Where's he live?"

"Over on Elm Street, near the golf course."

Pulling out his cell phone again, Blake called dispatch. "Get a deputy over to Clifford Jones' house on Elm Street near the golf course. He's the lab director for the hospital and he's needed in his lab for an emergency. It's Jennifer Brennan. Tell the deputy to get him here *now*."

Blake glanced at the nurse who was now in a huddle with the E.R. doctor and said, "We need to find out what's been injected into Jennifer Brennan's body." For a moment, they both stared at him. "Stop standing around and draw some blood or whatever else you need to do!"

The doctor took action first, focusing on the nurse. "Get the phlebotomy kit and get some blood drawn. Get a urine sample too. Run the samples down to the lab and tell them we need the results stat!"

He then motioned to Blake, "Help me get this bed down to the E.R."

Hands on his hips, Blake stood with Tim and Lane outside the Emergency Room, each too tense to sit in the waiting room. Finally, the E.R. doctor appeared along with the lab's director, Clifford Jones.

Jones spoke first. "Jennifer was injected with a small dosage of Rohypnol. Since you're law enforcement officers, you know that this date rape drug is often used to incapacitate victims with its potent sedative effects."

He glanced at Blake. "She's lucky you walked into her room when you did, because if she had received the full dosage we found in the syringe, she would have overdosed or died."

Tim spoke to the doctor, "What can you do for her?"

The doctor responded, "To be safe, we're giving her oxygen because the drug can impact breathing. We're also treating her with activated charcoal to soak up the drug from her stomach and intestinal tract. I also conducted an examination to confirm whether a sexual assault had taken place. It's standard hospital practice when we find a woman has been given this drug."

The men stiffened noticeably.

The doctor shook his head. "No sexual assault." He paused for a moment, then continued. "The effects of the drug may last from eight to twelve hours. I predict she will sleep throughout this time, but we will monitor her closely. I'm keeping her down here in the E.R."

"I'm putting a deputy in a chair next to her bed," said

Lane. "I'm also assigning an officer to work with hospital security to secure all entrances and exits. This was a direct attempt to take out a law enforcement officer, and we'll pull out all stops to prevent it from happening again."

The doctor nodded, then said, "By the way, we've had to calm Jennifer down a couple of times. Her speech is slurred, but we think she is afraid of being locked in a blue room. Do you know what she's talking about?"

"I do," said Tim sadly. "Five years ago she was kidnapped and kept in a basement room lined with sound-proofing foam. It was royal blue."

Once a deputy was in place at Jennifer's bedside, Tim, Lane and Blake gathered to talk confidentially in a corner of the hospital's dining room.

Tim sipped his hot coffee then asked, "Blake, did you get a good look at the guy in Jennifer's room?"

Running his fingers through his hair, Blake tried to visualize the man in Jennifer's room. "He was about six feet tall, brown hair, brown mustache and black-rimmed glasses. The mustache didn't look right and may have been part of a disguise."

"Anything else?" asked Tim.

"He wore brown leather hiking boots that looked well-used, like he'd worn them for a long period of time."

"Why would this guy target Jennifer?" Lane wondered.

"I think he may be the same guy who left Catherine's cell phone in Jennifer's house." Blake began. "He killed Catherine, and maybe he thinks Jennifer knows something that would connect him to the murders."

"Guess that leaves Evan off the hook," said Lane.

"Evan Hendricks no more killed those girls than I won the lottery last week," said Tim. "We've got a serial killer on our hands and he's still out there planning his next move."

Looking confused, Lane said, "I thought you had to have three or more murders to determine serial killings."

"I personally don't give a damn what the definition is, we've got two girls dead, both tortured and murdered the same way by the same offender. We've got an organized and intelligent killer who knows enough about forensics to cover his tracks. I'm not waiting until we have a third murder until I call it the way I see it. I'm also not too proud to call out for help. The FBI has resources and experiences with this kind of thing. We need help."

"I have a direct contact with the FBI who has experience with serial murders," offered Blake.

"Who is it?"

"My sister, Carly, is a special agent in the Criminal

Investigation Division of the FBI division office in Tampa. She's dealt with serial murders. She's on leave now. I could ask her to fly here to help us."

"Why was she put on leave?" asked Tim.

"She's just coming off a sex trafficking case where her partner was killed." Blake explained.

"What happened?"

"The traffickers made Carly's partner as an agent and beheaded her before Carly and backup got there. Carly discovered her body. Her backup had secured the others, but the leader drew a gun on Carly and she shot him in the face. He died at the scene."

"But why was she put on leave?" Lane wondered aloud.

"Carly and her partner had worked together several years and were close. She took her murder hard, so her supervisor put her on leave."

"Do you think she'll be up for helping us?"

"The time off is driving her nuts. Carly needs something to do, something that requires her specialized talents. If I ask her, she'll be on the next flight to Indiana."

"Ask her."

Blake relieved the deputy at Jennifer's bedside and watched her sleep, the clear plastic oxygen mask covering her face. He picked up her hand to kiss it.

"Honey, I am so sorry I left your room," Blake whispered, his voice cracking. "I was supposed to protect you and I let you down. I promise you I won't do that again."

Jennifer whimpered softly in her sleep, so Blake lifted the mask. "No, don't lock me in the blue room." She wrapped her arms protectively around her body. "Don't hurt my baby."

"Can you hear me, Jennifer?"

Though she didn't open her eyes, she nodded fearfully.

"Honey, I'm here and I promise you that no one is going to lock you anywhere. They won't get past me. Don't you worry. Just sleep. Everything's going to be okay. I'll be right here."

Two days later, Blake opened Jennifer's front door to find a petite woman with a slender build waiting on the porch.

"Hello, my name is Allison Wade. I need to talk to Jennifer."

"I'm sorry, but Jennifer is resting."

"Blake, I'm not an invalid. Let Allison in." Jennifer called out.

Reluctantly, Blake stood aside and directed Allison to the living room, where Jennifer sat on the sofa.

"Hi, Allison. Is everything okay? What brings you here?" Jennifer recognized the woman as the cashier at the 7-Eleven where she filled her car with gas each week. They'd exchanged short friendly conversation for the past year.

Blake headed to the kitchen to make some coffee while the two women talked.

Allison sat near Jennifer, looking down at her clenched hands as tears streamed down her cheeks. She said, "It's my fault that Evan Hendricks is dead."

Confused, Jennifer responded, "Fred Thomas killed Evan, not you, Allison. Why would you think it was your fault?"

"I didn't come forward." She began. "It was more important for me to keep the family secret than to help Evan. It's just that I thought, he's innocent, so there's no way anyone could prove he did anything wrong the night Tiffany was abducted.

"Start from the beginning, Allison."

"My boy, Danny, got involved in the youth activities

that Evan ran at the church. He trusted Evan, and one day after Evan questioned Danny about a new set of bruises on his arms, Danny told him about his father's drinking. It took a lot of courage for Danny to tell the family secret. We were so ashamed; we didn't want anyone to know about Wayne's problem. I feared his employer would find out and he'd lose his job. Then what would happen to us?" She paused for a long moment, looking out the front window.

"My husband, Wayne, is a good man with an evil addiction to alcohol. When Wayne's drunk, he becomes a different person — one who is angry and violent. Though he's been drinking a long time, it's only been the past year that he hit us. I used to be able to protect Danny by sending him to his room, but the older he gets, the more he wants to protect his mom. He puts himself right in front of me and he bears the bruises to show for it."

Allison glanced at Jennifer, her brow furrowed. "Danny came home the day he talked to Evan and begged me to meet with the youth minister, too. So we started family counseling. I begged Wayne to go with us, and at first he refused. When he saw how much it meant to Danny, he joined us.

"Evan talked to us about getting Wayne into rehab. Easy thing for folks with money, but that's not us. Wayne drives a truck for Holden Dairy, and as you know, I'm a cashier at the 7-Eleven. We make enough for the essentials, but the costs of rehab were beyond our reach. But Evan found a place that would take Wayne and worked out payments based on our income." She paused, visibly trembling with intensity.

"Jennifer, that's what we were discussing the night Tiffany Chase went missing. Danny, Wayne and I were with Evan until after ten that night. Because Wayne had been drinking and I'd just worked two shifts, Evan was worried about us driving home, so he followed us in his car. Evan couldn't have abducted Tiffany — he was with us. So you see, Fred Thomas may have killed Evan, but it was my fault. If I had come forward sooner, he would have never been considered a suspect."

From the window, Jennifer stood watching Allison walk to her car; the woman's shoulders slumped as if the weight of the world rested on them. No matter what Jennifer said, Allison remained convinced she caused Evan's death. Jennifer felt guilt of her own. She turned to see Blake standing near her.

"Blake, is there anything we could have done differently to prevent Evan's shooting?"

"I've thought a lot about that. In a perfect world, we could have prevented the media from discussing and speculating on Evan's guilt or innocence, thus preventing

Fred Thomas from knowing about Evan's involvement in the case. Grace Cohn may market her program as informative, but when she uses talking heads to speculate on an active investigation, she seriously jeopardizes the case and puts viewers, like Fred Thomas, at great risk."

"But what would our country be without freedom of speech?"

"It's a question of professional ethics," Blake said, glancing at Jennifer, and noticing the dark circles under her eyes. "Honey, sit on the sofa or go upstairs for a nap. The doctor told you to rest."

"I'll take a nap upstairs if you take one with me." Jennifer's eyes glittered mischievously.

"Not a good idea. We both know if I go up there with you, we won't be napping."

"Okay, you're right. I am a little tired," Jennifer said as she headed for the stairs.

"Good, get some rest. There is someone I want you to meet later."

She stopped in her tracks, and turned to face him. "Who?"

"You'll see. Just get some rest."

He pulled his Jeep in front of the empty house for sale, which sat about a block from Jennifer Brennan's house. He surmised she must be home from the hospital since a police cruiser was parked in front. The lucky bitch was like a cat with nine lives. If that damn detective hadn't barged in, he would have unloaded the syringe in her neck. As it was, it was sheer luck that any of the Rohypnol was injected. Not that he knew, since he'd panicked and left the syringe in the bitch's neck.

Finding an empty patient's room when Blake Stone was chasing him was a godsend. He'd locked himself in the bathroom, stripped off the scrubs and dumped them in the waste can. Then he removed the fake mustache and glasses, depositing them in his pocket. By the time he reached the hospital lobby, the place was crawling with cops. He stayed calm, walking right past them and out the door. Once he reached his Jeep, he nearly vomited from the tension.

He looked in the rearview mirror and brushed his fingers through his hair, then opened a bottle of water and took a gulp. The whole hospital escapade was a joke; he shouldn't have attempted in the first place. He had to do a better job of tapping his behavioral controls, or his next impulsive act could be his last.

Behavioral control. That's what his old-bag fifth grade teacher, Miss Sing, had told his Mama after she caught him beating up Jerry Groden, then taking his new bike. "Your son has poor behavioral controls," she'd said. "He doesn't accept responsibility for his actions. Instead, he blames others."

He'd gotten the crap beat out of him when Mama returned from school later. He hated Mrs. Sing after that, and kept a close eye on her house, which was one of those white houses with a manicured lawn and white picket fence that other people lived in — certainly not he and Mama. He discovered that the teacher loved cats and fed all the stray cats in the neighborhood. That's when he'd taken the box of liquid ant killer in Mama's cupboard and laced any cat food he found on Miss Sing's porch. She must have found two dozen dead cats littering her lawn before she wised up and stopped feeding them. She called the police, too, not that they ever found anything.

Miss Sing had gotten off easy. If he'd been older, she'd have gotten a taste of a leather belt across her bare ass. He would have taught her a thing or two about behavioral controls, and she wouldn't have lived to tell about it.

9 CHAPTER NINE

While Jennifer napped, Blake made a pan of homemade lasagna. Now it was in the oven, garlic bread ready to go in next, and a fresh vegetable salad waiting in the refrigerator. He'd sent a deputy to pick up his sister at the airport an hour ago, so Carly was due to arrive any minute.

Jennifer awoke to the most delicious aroma that had ever filled her home — spicy and Italian, just like the gorgeous man downstairs in the kitchen. He'd obviously whipped up something amazing. She couldn't wait to get downstairs to thank him.

In her bathroom, Jennifer showered, dried her hair, applied fresh makeup and finished with a swipe of rose gloss across her lips. She changed into a sexy black knit shift she'd never worn, and obeying doctor's orders, slipped on a pair of ballerina flats instead of the sky-high heels she liked to wear. As she brushed her hair, she heard the doorbell and remembered that Blake had mentioned a surprise guest.

Blake answered the door and pulled his sister into a hug, while the deputy who had driven her stood awkwardly on the porch holding the handle of her rolling suitcase.

Once the deputy left, Blake pulled her inside the living room and looked at her. Carly was five feet and ten inches, like Jennifer, but she was too thin and lacked Jennifer's curves. She'd always been slender, but Carly looked like she'd lost weight she couldn't afford to lose.

Like Blake's, her eyes were the color of espresso, and filled with intelligence, but today there were glints of sadness. Her tanned skin was more the result of her rich Italian lineage than the hot Florida sun. She was only twenty-seven-years-old, but the worry lines across her forehead suggested she'd already known more trouble than people twice her age.

"Are you hungry? I made lasagna. Gram's recipe."

"It smells delicious. Thank goodness, one of us learned how to cook like Gram."

Blake led her to the kitchen, where he pulled the lasagna out of the oven and pushed in the cookie pan of garlic bread slices.

Jennifer burst into the kitchen ready to launch herself into Blake's arms, but stopped short, rooted to a spot on the tile floor. There were two people in her kitchen and the second one was female with long ebony hair and a body that was runway model thin. The woman was laughing, as if she and Blake had just shared a private joke and Jennifer's other-woman radar went on alert. Her mind raced. What if Blake's special guest was a fiancé he'd neglected to tell her about or worse a pregnant ex-lover, carrying his baby?

She cleared her throat to get their attention and stiffly accepted Blake's hug.

"Hello, Jennifer. I'm so glad to meet you. Blake's told me a lot about you." The woman said as she extended her hand.

Blake spoke next, "Jennifer, this is my sister, Carly."

Sister? Blake has a sister? "Hi, Carly," she said weakly as she grasped her hand and squeezed.

"Dinner's ready and we have a lot to talk about," said Blake as he cut the lasagna into squares. He pulled the garlic bread out of the oven. "Why don't you ladies sit in the dining room and I'll serve dinner?"

"I never pass up a chance to be served by a man," joked Carly as she smiled at Jennifer.

"In the kitchen, you thought I was Blake's girlfriend," Carly stated, staring at Jennifer with impenetrable dark eyes.

Jennifer just stared back, struggling to keep her expression blank.

"Yeah, you did. I could tell by your deer-in-the-headlights expression."

Blushing, Jennifer looked down at her lap as she unfolded her napkin. When she looked up she met Carly's wide smile.

"Don't look so embarrassed. I'm delighted you care about my brother. He's a pretty amazing guy."

With a sheepish expression, Jennifer replied, "Sorry about that."

"No problem. Blake's dated a lot of women. With his looks, he could have any woman he wanted. But you're the first woman he's ever talked about to me, so I knew you were special."

Jennifer glanced at Carly and wondered why Blake had never confided to her about having a sister.

"Blake never mentioned me, did he?"

Jennifer squirmed in her seat, then answered, "No."

"Not surprised. He's always been ultra-private about his family. Did he tell you about our parents' divorce?"

Jennifer nodded in the affirmative.

"Then you know it was a hard time for us as children. Mom and Dad argued all the time, using us as bargaining chips. All we had was each other, so we became close. After the divorce, we lived with Mom, but she and Dad continued their war. It changes your perspective about relationships. I think it's the reason Blake has, until now, avoided a serious relationship with a woman. It's hard for him to trust."

Jennifer secretly smiled. Blake was serious about her. Not that she didn't already know that, but it was nice to have it confirmed. He hadn't left her side since the hospital.

Blake walked in with a loaded plate for Carly and one for Jennifer. He returned with a plate for himself, as well as a bottle of red wine that he poured into each glass.

Tearing her garlic bread into pieces, Carly said, "Blake, remember the time when we told Mom and Dad we were both going into law enforcement. I thought Dad was going to have a coronary."

"Really?" asked Jennifer. Her father had reacted the same.

"Dad assumed we'd work the family business. Can't blame the guy," said Blake. "He'd worked hard over the years to build a couple dozen condo and apartment complexes. I think Dad had planned from the day we were born that we would someday take over."

Jennifer looked at Carly. "So you're in law enforcement, too?"

"Yes, I'm a special agent in the Criminal Investigation Division of the FBI division office in Tampa. Right now I'm on leave, so I'm available to help you and Blake with your case."

Clearly surprised, Jennifer looked at Blake. "What?"

"Your dad, Lane and I talked at the hospital. We think we have a serial killer on our hands and we need help. I knew Carly was on leave so I got your dad's permission to bring her in on a consultant basis. She has experience with serials and has a good profiling background."

"Why didn't you tell me?" She glared at him with burning, reproachful eyes.

"Because your health is more important than this case, Jennifer. Your doctor said no stress." He met her glare head-on, expecting her reaction, but he stood by his decision. How could she not realize how important she was to him? That she was much more than just a partner.

At that moment, Jennifer said nothing. She didn't want to make Carly uncomfortable with a disagreement between Blake and her right then. As soon as she and Blake were alone, she'd have plenty to say, including the fact she was his partner and had a right to be clued in — concussion or not.

It had been another shit day at work. They'd had a department picnic and the whole boring gang of assholes was there. He suffered through it and couldn't wait until quitting time.

Inside his cabin, he pulled two cans of beer out of the refrigerator then plopped in his favorite chair. He gulped the beer and crushed the can with his hand when it was empty. Picking up the remote control from the end table, he aimed it at the television and clicked the on button.

The Grace Cohn Program was on CSN and the bitch was blowing her mouth like usual, "This Indiana community can rest now that the serial killer in its midst is dead."

Nice. Thanks to her the whole world thinks Evan Hendricks pulled off the unsolved murders of the century, as if the little prick had his cunning and forethought. It'd be a joke if it wasn't so damn stupid. He may have to visit Grace Cohn after he took care of Jennifer Brennan.

He picked up the other can of beer and flushed it down his throat, not really enjoying the taste, but liking the buzz it gave him. Crushing this can, too, he tossed it on the table with the other one.

Restless, he wandered around his cabin until he reached the kitchen. The room was dismal with outdated appliances, Army-green painted cabinets, stained Formica countertops, and linoleum floor that had seen better days — maybe a century ago. What a dump. But it was free rent, so what the hell.

He did an inventory of his tools and lined them up on the kitchen counter: duct tape to secure prey to the table, leather belt, bath soap and towels. Opening the cabinet under the sink, he saw several gallons of bleach he'd need to wash down the table, the prey, and the room. He opened a drawer to reveal his stash of Rohypnol tablets and syringes. All items accounted for; he was ready for the next time he had one of his urges to troll for prey.

Going back to the living room, he sat back down in his chair and stared at the television. Grace Kohn had moved on to a story about a missing child in Louisiana. His mind wandered. He was almost sick to his stomach about his failure to kill Jennifer Brennan. But soon it would be a distant memory, he consoled himself, that would not be repeated. He was back on his game. Hell, when it came to his particular game, he was the master.

He wanted to kick it up a notch next time, and considered using one of Ted Bundy's ruses. Good old Ted had some great ones, like the times he wore a cast on his arm. Bundy had looked so pathetic when he asked for help, those smart-ass college girls must have thought they were bestowing a random act of kindness on the poor guy — not knowing it would be their last random act of any kind.

He considered this trick, but discarded it. The cast on the arm could be cumbersome if the prey fought back. Maybe he'd use the disabled vehicle ruse on a country road. He'd used it successfully before. That might be fun.

The thoughts he was having about stalking and capturing prey resulted in some physical reactions that were all too familiar. His jaw clenched and he ground his teeth until pain radiated through his ears. Sweat trickled down his back, while a vein throbbed in his neck as he worked himself into a frenzy. The demons were back, clawing at his insides until the urges to kill emerged — relentless and overpowering.

Deep inside, the urge was so powerful that the thought of resisting didn't enter his mind. He knew the longer he tried to ignore it, the stronger it got. He would track his prey soon, capture and torture her until she begged for mercy.

After her shift ended at the Sugar Creek Cafe, Brianna Hayden did what she did every day: she took her two Labrador Retrievers, Salt and Pepper, for a walk down the country road that ran in front of her parent's home. Only two-years-old, the dogs were energetic and delighted to begin their daily adventure.

Brianna's two-year-old daughter, Mandy, was taking a nap while Brianna's mother fixed dinner, so it was the perfect time to get some exercise and still be back before dinner was served. What a day she'd had. It hadn't slowed down since breakfast at the restaurant where she waitressed. There were a lot of reporters in town since Fred Thomas shot Evan Hendricks. The whole thing was horrible and made her sick. People were so wrapped up in the shooting drama that they seemed to have forgotten that two young women were tortured and murdered in their midst. Didn't anyone care about the victims? All people could talk about was Evan's shooting and how glad they were that the serial-killing bastard was dead.

Brianna inhaled deeply, enjoying the cool country air, and laughed when she noticed that Pepper had picked up a stick and was prancing proudly with it wedged in his mouth.

It wasn't that long ago that Catherine Thomas had followed her home from work when they were on the same shift, so that she could join Brianna on a walk. They'd discussed their day, their love lives, and their world in general. Catherine had been one of her few single friends, who seemed to enjoy hearing about the antics of her two-year-old. She missed Catherine, and there wasn't a day that went by that she didn't think of her, trying hard to remember the Catherine who giggled at her jokes, and not the Catherine who spent the final hours of her life in a tortured hell.

Cal Fisher's house was in her vision so she knew she'd completed a mile. Once they reached his property, Cal's Jack Russell Terrier, Liz, let out a series of ear-piercing barks to protest the two Labradors that were encroaching upon her territory. Cal appeared at the picture window, waved at Brianna, then tried to distract Liz with a dog treat.

Brianna and her two dogs walked further until she could see what looked like a disabled Jeep at the side of the road. As they grew closer, she recognized the driver as the good-looking man she'd seen at the diner. He pulled a rag out of the back and then disappeared under the hood of the vehicle. Brianna's dad was a whiz at car repair and had taught her at an early age how to fix anything that could go wrong under the hood. That's why she decided to make this guy's day and help him get his car back on the road. That he was tall, dark and handsome had nothing to do with it. Right.

Blake and Jennifer watched as a deputy helped Carly get into the front seat of his vehicle. He'd already put her suitcase in the trunk, and she was holding the thick double-murder case file in her arms. Carly had refused Jennifer's offer to stay in her extra bedroom, explaining she was eager to dive into the case to start her analysis and she could do that better in the quiet of Blake's empty condo.

Blake followed Jennifer into the dining room, where she stacked dirty plates, then took them into the kitchen. She opened the dishwasher door just as Blake came in with the wine glasses.

Jennifer cut him a glare and said, "You should have told me."

"You were pretty much unconscious when the decision was made, so that would have been a little difficult."

"Blake, I've been home for two days," she accused.

"I've been trying to keep your world as stress-free as

possible, just like the doctor ordered."

"You're not my nursemaid, you're my partner!" Jennifer exclaimed.

"Oh, really? I thought I meant a little more to you than that." Blake shot back.

"You do. I didn't mean..."

Blake cut her off by yanking her against his chest and kissing her hard, like he'd wanted to for days. He tightened his arms around Jennifer, feeling her soft curves molding to the contours of his hard body. Raising his mouth from hers, he gazed into her eyes and saw a burning need matching his own. He kissed the pulsing hollow at the base of her throat as she moaned with pleasure, then moved to nibble at her earlobe. "Honey, are you sure you're up for this?"

Jennifer slid her hand down to the obvious evidence of his desire and whispered, "Just as much as you are."

Blake was breathing hard as he pressed her against the refrigerator. He was turned on, hot and hard, kissing her until her senses reeled, as if short-circuited. One hand slid down her taut stomach to the swell of her hips, then her thighs, where he snagged the hem of her dress and pulled it off, throwing it across the kitchen. He eased the lacy cup of her bra aside so his lips could tease a hard pink nipple, then his tongue made a path down her ribs to her stomach, his fingers diving beneath her panties to search for her pleasure points. Jennifer gasped as he found her sensitive nub and began a sensual massage she wished would last forever. Instead of stopping, it went on and on, as she pulled at him and wrapped a long leg around him to pull him closer. Moaning softly, she closed her eyes, pressing her fingers into the muscles of his back. Finally, her body quaked, exploding in a downpour of fiery sensations. Jennifer's knees gave. If his arms hadn't been tightened around her she would have melted to the floor. She wanted him. God, how she wanted him, naked and inside her.

Blake reached around her to unfasten her bra, letting it fall to the floor. She pulled at his shirt until he ripped it off. She licked and flicked his nipples with her tongue, then ran her tongue down his hard abs as her fingers explored the firmness of his body.

"Honey, are you okay?" His voice was low and hoarse.

"Better than okay," She responded breathlessly.

"Good to know," Blake said as he scooped her into his arms and headed for the stairs leading to her bedroom.

Tori Hayden stirred the green beans and bacon simmering on the stove as she listened to her granddaughter, Amanda, cooing on the baby monitor nearby. Wearing her hot-pad gloves, she pulled out a pan of baked macaroni and cheese, Brianna's favorite. On her way to the baby's room to pick up Amanda, she stopped in the living room where her husband, Steve sat watching the evening news.

"Honey, call Brianna. Dinner's ready."

Steve rose from his chair and moved to the window to scan the yard for Brianna as he fished his cell phone from his jeans pocket. His daughter and her dogs were nowhere in sight, so he dialed her cell phone number. Suddenly, Brianna's black Lab, Pepper, ran into the yard, his leash trailing behind him. Salt was close behind. Something was wrong. Brianna had a fear of losing her dogs and would never have let them off their leashes.

Tori, holding Amanda in her arms, entered the room and noticed Steve at the window. She moved next to him. "What are you looking at?"

"Brianna's dogs are in the yard, dragging their leashes behind them."

"What?" she asked, alarm singing through her voice. "Where's Brianna?"

Tori followed her husband to the kitchen door. As soon as he opened it, both dogs rushed in and headed toward their water bowl on the kitchen floor.

Steve looked at his wife, struggling to keep concern from his expression, as he grabbed a set of keys from a hook on the wall. "Tori, I'm going to take the truck and find

Brianna."

Carly Stone emptied the first case file on Blake's dining room table, making organized stacks of photos and evidence collected for the Catherine Thomas murder. Then she did the same for Tiffany Chase. Carly pored over the evidence, focusing on every detail and accepting nothing at face value. Using a yellow highlighter, she marked important information to consider in her analysis. Once she finished studying Catherine's and Tiffany's files, she pulled two rolled sheets of flip chart paper from her suitcase and taped them to the wall. Picking up a black marker from the table, she wrote Catherine's name at the top of one sheet and Tiffany's on the other. It was important for Carly to look closely at each victim before doing an analysis of their killer.

Both women were in their twenties and considered low-risk, meaning they lived fairly normal lives — Catherine as a waitress, and Tiffany a student. Neither woman was a known substance abuser, nor were they prostitutes, as was common in high-risk lifestyles. Both women were physically fit, and appeared to have been abducted from local state parks. Two questions ran through Carly's mind. Were the women stalked? Or were they randomly selected because they were at the wrong place at the wrong time, and crossed the killer's path? She was unsure the evidence would help answer either question.

When comparing the two murders, Carly noted that both women were restrained and tortured by prolonged beatings with a folded leather belt at the primary crime scene. The beatings troubled Carly and she made a note to reconsider them when she created a more in-depth analysis of the killer's psychological makeup.

An additional similarity between victims was that each appeared to have been raped prior to dying. In each case, the killer had used a condom that was not found at the secondary crime scene. Both women were returned nude to the state park and posed in a way that suggested the victim was praying.

Rubbing the tightness in the back of her neck, Carly placed the black marker on the table and headed for the kitchen to make coffee. It was going to be a long night.

Blake moaned when he heard his cell phone vibrating on the table next to his side of the bed. Jennifer's arms and legs were wrapped around him like a grapevine as she slept soundly on his chest.

"Stone."

"Blake, we have another missing girl. Brianna Hayden. Went for a walk and didn't return." Lane spit out the words like bullets, his voice laced with anxiety.

"Oh, shit," Blake groaned.

"You know her?"

"We interviewed her at the Sugar Creek Cafe. She's a waitress there and was friends with Catherine Thomas."

"I'm running her cell phone records now on my laptop. Wait a minute. God damn it. The last ping on Brianna's cell phone occurred around six-thirty, then the signal stopped completely. Her cell has either been turned off or had its battery removed."

"Remember, the same thing happened with Catherine's cell."

"Yeah, I know," Lane said tiredly. "I sent deputies and the copter. They're searching now. Get out to her parent's place on Route 27 and take the missing person report. Parents' names are Stephen and Tori Hayden. She's got a two-year-old daughter named Amanda."

Blake disconnected the call and sighed. There was a child involved; that made the case that much harder. He prayed they found Brianna, and this whole thing had no connection to their killer.

Jennifer lifted her head. "I'm going with you. This is my case, too."

"No argument from me. But if you start feeling dizzy or anything, you need to tell me."

"Deal."

They were several miles from the Hayden house but could see the glittering top lights of police cars and light beams from the helicopter looming overhead. Cars of curious onlookers, neighbors and the media clotted the road, so Blake flicked on the emergency dashboard lights and siren, forcing drivers to pull over. Soon electric blue flashes of light filled the SUV as Blake pressed the accelerator to pick up speed to maneuver past the cars.

Blake and Jennifer parked alongside the road and approached the house on foot. On the Hayden's front porch stood Lane, Frankie and their search and rescue dog, Hunter. Lane motioned to Blake and pulled him into quiet conversation.

Frankie spotted her and said, "Jennifer, what in the hell are you doing out here with a concussion?"

Firing her best drop-it glare, Jennifer hugged her and patted Hunter on the head. "Why are *you* here, Frankie?"

"Mrs. Hayden is inside searching the dirty laundry for an unwashed shirt that belongs to Brianna. We're giving it to Hunter for the scent, then we're going to see if we can track Brianna."

"Good idea. We're going in to interview the parents and take the missing person report. Maybe by the time we finish, you'll have some news for us."

Jennifer followed Blake inside the house to the living room where Steve Hayden sat in a rocking chair holding a fussy two-year-old who had to be Brianna's daughter. The child tucked her head inside his arms and alternated between sucking her thumb and crying out loud. Jennifer's heart squeezed.

Sitting on the sofa, she pulled out a small notepad and a pen. "Mr. Hayden, I'm Detective Jennifer Brennan and this is my partner, Blake Stone. We need to ask you some questions that will help us find Brianna."

With a long, anxious sigh, Steve nodded and continued rocking Amanda.

"We know Brianna took the dogs for a walk tonight. Is that something she did on a regular basis?"

"Every night. Soon as she gets home from work. She said the walks with the dogs helped her unwind, clearing her thoughts."

"Is there a particular route that she takes for her walks?"

"Yes, she takes the same route everyday so her mom and I could find her if Amanda needed her. She turns left at the end of the drive, walks past Cal Fisher's home as her one-mile marker, and then walks another mile until she's past the Isaac house and pasture. Then she turns around to head home." Wrinkling his brow, Steve cleared his throat and said, "When the dogs came home without her, I knew something was very wrong. I drove her route in my truck and couldn't find any sign of her. It was like she disappeared into thin air."

"Has Brianna confided in you that she's experiencing problems with anyone who would want to hurt her?" Blake asked.

"Naw, she gripes a lot about John Isaac, her boss at the cafe, but all the waitresses do. He's an asshole who thinks he's a tough guy because he can boss the women around at work. I can't think of anyone who'd want to hurt her. She's a good girl." Steve paused thoughtfully then added, "Ever since Catherine Thomas was murdered, she's been grieving. They were friends and Brianna misses her."

"I understand. What about Amanda's father? Is he in the picture? If so, do he and Brianna get along?"

"We haven't heard from that bastard since the day Brianna told him she was pregnant. Skipped town. Tried to find him for child support, but his family is keeping their mouths closed about his whereabouts."

Outside, Tori Hayden sat crying alone on a wicker sofa on the porch, still clutching a couple of Brianna's shirts to her chest. Jennifer sat down beside her and patted her arm.

"Mrs. Hayden, I'm Detective Jennifer Brennan. We

need you to join your husband in the kitchen to complete the paperwork we'll file for the missing person report."

Brianna's mother wiped at her eyes, moved toward the door, and turned to face Jennifer. "You'll find her, won't you? You'll bring her back to us?"

Jennifer nodded, giving the woman an unspoken promise she knew she may not be able to keep. But hope was something she could never allow herself to deny loved ones of the missing.

She joined Blake at the end of the driveway. He was talking to Frankie who had returned with Hunter and Lane.

"We got to a spot past Cal Fisher's house and Hunter just stopped. He'd lost the scent. We looked closer and found fresh tire tracks on the side of the road where a vehicle had pulled off and parked."

Blake shook his head with disgust. "Like someone knew she took this route for her walks and was waiting for her."

Frankie continued, "There were drag marks in the dirt. My theory is that he disabled her somehow, dragged her to his car and stuffed her inside."

Lane offered, "The crime scene techs are photographing and casting the shoe and tire prints now. My money is on them to link the tire prints to a specific tire so we have a ballpark idea of what kind of vehicle he's driving."

"I used to have a Jeep in high school. Those tire tracks looked just like the tracks my Jeep left," added Frankie.

Jennifer pulled into Cal Fisher's driveway and saw him walking toward the them before she and Blake even got out of the SUV.

"What's going on? Never seen so many deputies driving around in this area in my life. Hell, there's even a copter. Who are they looking for?"

"Mr. Fisher?"

Cal nodded and motioned for Jennifer and Blake to join him on the screened porch where he picked up his yapping Jack Russell and held her on his lap.

"We're looking for Brianna Hayden. Do you know her?" Jennifer began.

"Course I know Brianna. Her parents are my closest neighbors. Watched her grow up."

"Did you see her earlier this evening?"

"Sure did. She was walking her dogs like she always does around six o'clock. I know that, because my Liz here barked up a storm to let me know Brianna's Labs were encroaching on her territory. I waved at Brianna from my picture window in front."

"Which direction was she headed?" asked Blake.

"North, toward town. A long time ago, Brianna told me my house is her one mile marker. She usually walks a second mile ending up by John Isaac's place where she turns around and goes back home."

"John Isaac? Is this the same John Isaac that owns the Sugar Creek Cafe?" asked Blake.

"That's the one. I imagine you've heard about John's run-ins with the law. He's got a bad habit of beating up his wife and little boy."

In the vehicle, Jennifer opened up her laptop and ran John Isaac's name. In the past three years, he'd been arrested five times for domestic violence against his wife, Eve, and twice for suspected child abuse. Pulling up the child protection records, Jennifer noticed that Isaac had beaten his five-year-old son with a belt. His kindergarten teacher noticed the bruising and welts when the child refused to sit down because it was painful.

"The child abuse was done with a belt, Blake. Just like the way Catherine and Tiffany were beaten."

Blake considered the information and added, "Catherine and Brianna waitressed for him at the cafe. Tiffany was local; I bet she ate there with Evan. That's three connections. Could he be our killer?"

John Isaac's place was the opposite of Cal Fisher's or

the Hayden's clean, manicured lawns and painted homes that reflected owner pride. The grass stood about a foot tall, long overdue for a mowing. There were children's toys scattered in front and a bicycle thrown across the back stoop. The house itself was a two-story farmhouse with peeling white paint. Plastic still covered the windows to ward off winter winds.

Blake pounded on a side door until a small woman appeared. She wore a faded pair of jeans with a soiled T-shirt and a cardigan sweater that she was buttoning as she joined him on the porch. A cut on her lip was bleeding, and large purple bruises darkened on each side of her neck. A thin boy hovered behind her as she glanced at their SUV where the blue lights were still flashing.

"Cops? Where were you a couple of hours ago when I was getting the crap beat out me? What took you so long to get here?"

Jennifer moved forward. "Mrs. Isaac, may we come in so you can tell us what happened."

"It's Eve. My name is Eve."

As Jennifer followed the woman into the house, Blake winked at the little boy and pointed to his bicycle. "Nice bike. I had one like it when I was your age."

The little boy puffed up with pride, picked up the bicycle, did a couple of spins in the driveway then parked it near the house when he noticed Blake had pulled out a package of gum. He slowly moved near Blake, eyeing the stick of gum being offered to him. Snatching it from Blake's hand, he folded it a couple of times, stuffed it in his mouth then sat next to Blake on the porch step.

"So you're a real policeman? Can I see your badge?"

Blake handed it to him and said, "My name's Blake. What's yours?"

"I'm Shawn Isaac. I'm five-years-old," he said holding up five fingers.

Blake gently ran his thumb over a mark on the boy's face. "This red mark on your cheek. Did you dad do that?"

"My teacher said that you're never supposed to tell a lie to a policeman," he said, his wide eyes searching Blake's face.

"That's true, Shawn."

"I'm supposed to say that I fell off my bike."

"But that's not what happened, is it?"

"No, sir," Shawn said shaking his head. "My daddy hit me and knocked me down. When I started crying he called me names and said boys don't cry."

A muscle angrily flicked at his jaw as Blake imagined John Isaac hitting his five-year-old son, and then lashing out at him when the pain made him cry. At that moment, he wanted to kick John Isaac's ass.

"Tell me what happened, Shawn."

"Daddy came home from work and got mad because Mommy didn't have dinner ready. He called Mommy a lazy, worthless cow. Then Mommy told Daddy to go to hell. That's when he got really mad. He threw the kitchen chair and shoved Mommy so hard against the wall that she hit her head hard. She tried to push him away but he got her by the neck and pushed her back against the wall. Mommy was making sounds like I do when I'm choked, so I tried to push Daddy away from her. That's when he hit me. He told Mommy he was going to the liquor store in town and he left."

The squeak of the screen door hinges drew Blake's attention. He turned to see Shawn's mother dragging a large suitcase and Jennifer carrying some boxes that he pulled from her arms.

"Eve and Shawn are going to stay at a women's shelter tonight. I've arranged for a counselor to talk to Eve tomorrow and find living arrangements for them."

As they headed toward Eve's car, they were startled by the scream of tires as a green Toyota whipped into the driveway spitting gravel and nearly hitting Shawn.

"What the hell are you doing?" shouted John Isaac to

his wife as he popped out of the vehicle and staggered toward her.

Blake ignored him as he placed the two boxes in Eve's car trunk.

"I'm leaving your ass." Eve returned as she shoved the heavy suitcase into the trunk. "You drunk again, John? What a surprise."

"You bitch!" John shouted as he pulled back his arm to strike his wife but Blake caught it in mid-swing, pushing John off balance so he fell to the ground.

John scrambled to his feet and swung his arm, hitting Blake across the cheek. Pain exploded in his ear and jaw. Jerking John's arm behind his back, Blake dropped him to the ground. Still gripping his arm, he pushed his knee into his back to hold him in place as he snapped a pair of handcuffs on his wrists.

Jennifer helped Eve and Shawn get into the car, and stood watching as Eve pulled the car around and drove down the driveway to the road into town. She then pulled out her cell phone and dialed dispatch for backup.

Blake yanked John to his feet then walked him to their SUV where he pressed him against the side.

"Where have you been tonight, John?" asked Blake as he kept his hand pressed to John's chest to keep him steady.

"Anywhere but here, asshole."

"Want to be a little more specific?" The guy was getting on Blake's last nerve. If he didn't get more cooperative, he'd take this little talk down to the sheriff's office.

"I was at the bar next to the liquor store on Main Street. What's it to you?"

"Was anyone there who can verify your story?" asked Jennifer.

"Yeah, the little bartender with the nice ass. Why do you want to know?"

Ignoring his crude remark, Jennifer continued, "Have you seen Brianna Hayden this evening?"

"Not since work. Why?"

"She's missing and I think you might be able to help us find her."

Isaac exploded. "What the fuck are you talking about? I don't know where she is. I already told you, I haven't seen her since work today."

Blake shoved him against the vehicle, "Calm down and watch your language."

"What about when you left for the liquor store? Did you see Brianna walking her dogs?" asked Jennifer.

"No. I didn't see anyone." John spit on the ground, then reconsidered. "Wait a minute. I saw a guy having truck trouble on the highway across from my barn. Didn't stop to help him 'cause he looked like he was in better shape than I am. Let him fix his own damn truck."

With raised eyebrows, Jennifer tilted her head to the side, looked pointedly at Blake, then asked John, "How about a description of the man as well as his truck?"

"It was a Jeep, maybe 2009 or 2010. I know because I've been looking for one for sale. It was brown and tan with some kind of lettering on the side; I was going too fast to read it."

Jennifer jotted down the description, ignoring the deputy who just pulled his cruiser into the driveway. "What about the man? What did he look like?"

"I don't know. I don't make a habit of checking out men."

"Give it a try, John," she urged.

"Okay, he was tall, maybe six foot one or two. He had a thin build, but not skinny. Muscular. He had on a short-sleeved shirt and I noticed his arms and legs were tan like he'd been outside a lot. Couldn't see his face because he was wearing a brown ball cap and was bent down under the hood looking at the motor."

"Anything else?"

"Now that I think about it, that may have been a uniform he was wearing. It was brown and tan like his Jeep."

The deputy slid in on the other side of John and grabbed his arm. "Take him to the jail and book him," Blake said. You can start out with domestic violence, slugging a law enforcement officer and child abuse. You can get a statement from his wife tomorrow. I'll email mine to you."

Jennifer waited until the deputy backed out of the driveway before she leaned against him, running her fingers along Blake's jaw. "I can't believe he hit you. Besides being an officer, you're twice his size."

Blake took the opportunity to snake his arm around her waist to pull her close to kiss her.

"Do you believe him?" asked Jennifer.

"You mean about the disabled Jeep? Yeah, I do."

"So do I. It matches what Frankie said about the tire prints and her guess for the vehicle."

"I'm calling in a BOLO with the perp and vehicle description. See what we come up with." He pulled out his cell phone and noticed he'd received a couple of calls. "Crap, Carly's been trying to reach me."

It was two in the morning, but not one of them objected to the time of the meeting. Tim, Lane, Blake and Jennifer filed into the sheriff's conference room one-by-one, poured a cup of hot coffee, and then took a seat. At the end of the room, the wall was covered with flip charts, post-it notes and area maps. With her back to them, Carly was still jotting notes. When she realized they'd arrived, she started the meeting without fanfare.

"I apologize for the hour, but after I spoke to Blake and learned you have another missing girl, I thought it critical for you to hear my analysis." Carly began pointing to the sheets of flip-chart papers lining the wall.

"On these wall charts are some similarities between the victims: they were both in their twenties, physically fit, and abducted from a local state park. Neither of them had a high-risk lifestyle such as excessive drug use or prostitution. Both women were tortured and raped prior to their deaths, then their bodies were returned to the same state park in which they were abducted, and posed nude to look as if they were praying. In addition, the killer painstakingly removed valuable trace evidence we could have used to solve this case." Carly paused for a moment, sipped some water, then continued. "None of this is news to any of you. I am sure you've considered it many times. This is a very distinctive M.O."

"What about Brianna Hayden? She was abducted from

a country road not far from her house, not a park," asked Blake.

"Brianna fits his preference for physically fit women in their twenties. Like Catherine Thomas, she worked at the Sugar Creek Cafe where he could have noticed her, and followed her home after work. He may have watched her house until he learned her routines."

Jennifer spoke up. "Do you think the killer is stalking his victims or choosing them at random based on availability?"

"I don't have a good grasp on that yet, but I do have some ideas on who your killer is and isn't." Carly began, noticing the flicker of doubt in Tim's eyes. Doubt from law enforcement officers was not a new thing for Carly. Many felt that profiling was hocus-pocus. She was determined that by the time Tim left the meeting, he would see the value in her analysis, and use it to catch a killer before more young women died.

"Your killer is very familiar with the area parks and outdoor recreation," she continued. "To return the victims back to the public areas where he abducted them indicates he is familiar and comfortable with the area."

"You mean he's a local?" asked Blake as he ran his fingers through his thick hair.

"Absolutely. He lives here, works here, or has a reason

to frequent the area. Serial killers typically do not travel far to commit crimes, preferring instead, areas they are familiar with and which they can move around without raising suspicion."

Lane fired a question, "Are you saying we may know him?"

"Perhaps, but if you do know him it's because this type of killer likes to stay in the know about the case. You probably don't suspect his involvement," said Carly, as she walked to the hot pot of coffee on the warmer, tipped the pot to refill her mug and returned to her seat. "It's feasible that your killer leads a normal life and functions well in society, but he has this other dark side to his personality."

"How is he so easily abducting such physical fit women?" Jennifer wanted to know.

"Simple. He's physically fit, as well. I also think he's a lot like Ted Bundy, in that he's good looking, charming and persuasive. He seems normal and unthreatening. How else would he be able to convince even the most cautious young woman to drop her guard, trust him and go off with him?"

"Could he be disabling them with a drug?" asked Jennifer.

Carly added, "Since he tried to inject you with Rohypnol in the hospital, there's a chance he's also using it to disable his victims. Rohypnol comes in tablet form, so he must be mixing them with water in order to get the drug in the syringe."

"Carly, what about the beatings with the belt? Any thoughts about that?" Tim leaned forward in his chair, eager to hear her response.

"Your killer has a fantasy about torturing women with this particular type of beating. I think he's re-enacting something he experienced in childhood. Typically, serial killers have dysfunctional family lives. Your guy had a parent who was domineering and aggressive. Since he chooses only women as victims, my guess is it was his mother who beat him with a belt while he was restrained to something, like he's restraining his victims. He may have fantasized since childhood about repaying his mother's cruelty by beating and killing women, starting with her. There's a good chance he was sexually abused."

Lane asked, "What about the way he poses the bodies?"

Jennifer interrupted before Carly could answer. "Connected to that, there is something that's always bothered me about the call Julie Thomas got from the killer, besides the fact he was calling from her dead daughter's phone." Jennifer began. "He told her that 'good girls don't always go straight to heaven. Sometimes they get to visit hell first. I made sure of that with your Catherine.' I wonder if he believes this, and that's why he posed his victims in prayer?"

"The posing is a part of his fantasy," Carly explained. "Perhaps his mother was a religious zealot who hated men and convinced her son that only females entered heaven. Another explanation is that he tortures to inflict enough pain so his victims pray for mercy."

"What else can you tell us that will help us catch him?" inquired Tim.

"Judging by his behavior and M.O., he appears to be an organized killer who plans methodically, and is probably above average intelligence. It appears he abducts his victims in one place, but kills them in another, and then disposes the bodies in the original abduction site." Carly paused.

"The guy knows a thing or two about trace evidence too," added Tim.

"He's likely a man who watches forensics programming because he displays a basic knowledge of investigative tools and how to avoid detection," said Carly.

"Carly, I have a theory about the timing of the body dumps. On the days when the bodies of both Catherine and Tiffany were found, it was raining. Thus, washing away any trace evidence he may have missed when washing and bleaching the victims," said Jennifer.

Carly thought for a moment. "Interesting. He may be thinking the rain further helps him to avoid detection. That's another thing that supports how methodical he is.

There is little your killer does without planning."

"If he abducted Brianna like we think he did, that means we have until it rains to find her," Jennifer declared as the others nodded in agreement.

"Any ideas on his occupation?" asked Lane.

"He could be anyone who's familiar with local outdoor recreation areas. He could be a cop, fireman, a hunter or even someone connected to the state parks. He's a man who spends a lot of time enjoying outside recreation."

"To think our killer may be a cop on my team makes me physically ill," said Tim.

Blake spoke up. "I've been thinking about that disabled tan and brown Jeep on Brianna's walking route that our witness saw. The park service provides this type of vehicle to their conservation officers. Each of the conservation officers in area parks is also provided a cabin by the park service. We woke up the human resources director, got the conservation officers' addresses, and sent deputies to visit each one to ask a few questions and check on the Jeeps."

Carly continued, "One more thing I've learned from the research of Louis Schlesinger is that the number-one way serial killers are apprehended is by a surviving victim. Especially early on, your killer made mistakes because he had not perfected his techniques. I think your guy has been doing this for years. There may be a victim out there who survived his attack who can lead you straight to your murderer." Carly downed the last bit of her coffee before she continued.

"One of my friends is an FBI Analyst at ViCAP. I've sent her the particulars of your case, including the distinctive M.O. of this killer. She owes me a favor, so she's already started to delve deeper into the case, looking for similar homicides, searching ViCAP and other FBI and non-FBI databases. She'll prepare a report for us that will offer fresh investigative leads. If your guy's M.O. matches other murders, no matter where or when they occurred, she will let us know."

"When do you think we'll hear from her?" asked Tim.

"She's working this as we speak. My bet is we'll get the report tomorrow."

10 CHAPTER TEN

From the front window of the cabin, he watched the two deputies climb back into their cruiser and back out of his driveway.

He'd been duct-taping Brianna's wrists to his kitchen table when he heard a car motor. Dashing to the window, he'd seen a sheriff's car parked in the driveway. Two deputies headed toward his front door. His heart had slammed against his chest and he'd almost pissed himself. What the fuck was the law doing at his cabin? Hell, most people couldn't even find it, nestled in the woods, separate from the cabins of the other conservation officers.

He'd glanced back at Brianna, still unconscious on the table, then opened the front door to join the deputies on his porch.

"Evening, officers. How can I help you?" He'd plastered on his friendliest smile and aimed it toward the female deputy who'd blushed, just like he'd wanted her to.

Not impressed, the male deputy sidled up to him on the front porch and said, "We're looking for a missing girl and wondered if you'd seen her."

"Naw, came straight home after work."

Annoyed, the male deputy pulled out a folded photo from his back pocket. "How do you know if you've seen her or not if you don't know what she looks like?"

The officer's tone made him bristle. He clenched his jaw and took the photo of Brianna Hayden and pretended to study it.

"Nope. Haven't seen her. But if I do, I'll call."

The deputy took the photo from him, folded it and returned it to his back pocket. The officer stood glaring at him for a long moment, then pointedly glanced toward the door. Panic rushed through him like river rapids. If they got inside the cabin and discovered Brianna, he was a dead man. It had all happened so fast, he hadn't had time to slip his service revolver in the back of his pants. He was unarmed, two against one and he didn't like the odds. He thought he heard moaning coming from within the cabin and he realized he'd forgotten to tape the prey's mouth shut. Shit!

"Hey, do you two know of any job openings with the sheriff's department?" He kept his voice friendly, just like he was talking to two friends.

"There might be a deputy job open soon. I know Eddie Shelton is getting ready to retire," offered the female deputy.

The male deputy eyeballed him. "Why are you asking? Tired of the conservation officer gig?"

"Yeah, I've been doing it too long. Besides, I hear deputies make more money."

Both deputies snickered. "Yeah, we're practically millionaires," muttered the male deputy, as both officers headed back to the cruiser.

Though the deputies were gone, he remained at the window, paranoia clawing at his brain. Never before had the law come to his door. Why now? Why had they stopped at his cabin?

He turned to pace in front of the fireplace. Had they pinpointed him because they'd found some evidence he missed when he dumped Catherine and Tiffany? Had someone seen him with Brianna near his Jeep?

Hearing a moan from the kitchen, he realized his prey was regaining consciousness. "Shut up, bitch! I'm trying to think," he shouted.

Flipping the television on, he surfed to the weather channel and discovered no rain was predicted for the next seven days. Damn it. Sure, he'd love to play with the prey for another seven days, but could he risk it? He turned the TV off and continued pacing. Maybe he'd grabbed Brianna too soon after going for Detective Bitch at the hospital? Had he made mistakes? Left evidence behind?

Hell, Jennifer's dad was the sheriff. What did he think was going to happen when he went after his daughter? He decided he didn't care who her father was, the bitch was going down. It was Jennifer's fault the law was coming to his door. She thought she was so damn smart, treating him like a moron that day in the park next to Catherine's body, in front of his father. Not that he ever gave a shit for what the old man did or didn't think of him.

Hearing the whop-whop-whop of a helicopter in the distance, he wiped the beads of sweat off his brow. He couldn't believe he was sweating over this, or anything for that manner. Was he slipping? No, he couldn't be. He was the guy known for his no-evidence murders. There was no way they could be on to him. Could they?

The wailing and whimpering in the kitchen turned into an ear-piercing scream that echoed throughout the room. He grabbed his belt and raced to the kitchen, giving his prey a punishing lash of the belt. He then reached for the duct tape on the counter.

Charlie Barnett had fished in Bear Lake since he was six-years-old , when he'd listened to his dad proclaim time and again the lake was the best fishing spot in the county. Though his dad had passed away years ago, Charlie still agreed.

Dawn, with the sun an orange orb rising in the lightening sky, was his favorite time for fishing. He knew the closer it got to noon, the more pleasure boats and jet skiers would be racing back and forth in the deep water of the lake, ripping into the peace he'd looked forward to all week. He sucked in a lung-full of fresh air and listened to the water gently lapping against the shore, as he watched a doe and her fawn drinking at the water's edge.

With one more wet slice of his oar, Charlie slipped the anchor into the water, watching until it disappeared in the deep, inky darkness of the lake. Laying his oar in the boat, he pulled out his fishing rod, carefully hooked a worm, and then tossed it toward the reeds that lined the inlet. Holding onto the rod with one hand, Charlie used the other to dig into his ice chest for a bottle of water. He'd twisted open the bottle and lifted it to his lips when he felt the pull of the first nibble. Slowly and carefully, he lifted his rod and flicked the line to tease the fish until it nabbed the bait, and Charlie pulled it in. Although catfish was one of Charlie's favorite catches, this one was on the small side. But he removed the hook from its mouth and threw the fish in his bucket anyway. There was plenty of time to catch bigger ones.

He re-baited the hook and threw the line back toward the reeds. It wasn't long before the line yanked so hard, he almost dropped the fishing rod. Charlie glanced toward the reeds and spotted the biggest catfish he'd ever seen thrashing near the surface. Shit, if only his dad could see this whopper! He jumped to his feet, gripping the rod, winding the reel and tightening the line as he fought with the fish. Lifting one foot to the boat seat, he braced himself and pulled hard on the line.

Charlie leaned forward, too far, and the boat flipped over. Suddenly he was in the shockingly cold water, thrashing to free himself from the fishing line as his body sank. A sharp pain surged through his back as he landed on a sharp rock on the sandy bottom of the lake. He freed himself from the line and kicked his legs to propel to the top. But something stopped him.

Frantic, he looked down at his ankle and noticed a thick chain looped around his shoe. What the hell? Something touched his him. That's when he found himself staring face-to-face with a beautiful young woman, her face frozen in death, floating eerily in the water next to him. Her dark hair wafted about his face, one of her long fingers caught in his buttoned shirt. Panic like he'd never known before welled in his throat, but he couldn't scream, though God knew he wanted to.

Charlie kicked himself free, swam to the water's surface, and gulped in air to fill his aching lungs. He struggled with the boat but finally flipped it upright and climbed in. After he pulled up the anchor, Charlie grabbed an oar and gasped, panting in terror as a fresh wave of panic swept through him. Piercing the water with the oars, he pushed toward shore. He had to get to his truck where he'd left his cell phone. Jesus Christ, had he really just found a body?

The minutes it took for him to reach shore seemed like hours. Charlie jumped out of the boat and pulled it onto the boat ramp, then raced toward his truck. Pressing his hand against his front right jeans pocket, fresh alarm flipped a switch and sent his heart racing anew. Where were his keys? He patted the left-front, then the right, thankfully finding his keys. He whipped them out, opened the truck, fished for his cell phone in the glove box, and called nine-one-one.

With his scuba diving search team mobilized, Blake and team was in the water with Charlie Barnett onboard within sixty minutes. Jennifer sat near a table set up with containers of hot coffee and pastries for the searchers as she watched the sheriff's boat propelling in the water, aiming toward an area of the lake where Charlie fished. Lane stood nearby with his cell phone, briefing Tim.

A wave of apprehension surprised her. Where did that come from? Blake was a trained scuba diver and had five years of experience behind him. But that didn't stop her from considering worst-case scenarios where

Blake dived into the lake and never came back up. She shivered and crossed her arms protectively around her waist, cursing herself for being such a damn coward. What was it about telling the man she loved him that scared the crap out of her?

The coroner's van arrived and Doc Meade headed toward the table as his assistants unloaded a gurney from the van. He plopped down in a chair next to Jennifer and snagged a donut from the open box on the table.

"They find anything yet?" asked the coroner as he munched on his donut.

"No, they just left." Jennifer responded. "The fisherman isn't sure about the exact location, but he knows it's close to some reeds near the North shoreline of the lake."

"You realize, Jennifer, that the girl he saw in the water may not be connected to our killer. Could have been a skinny dipper who swam too far from shore. Hell, it could be anybody."

"You're right. It doesn't fit our killer's M.O. He has a propensity for posing the nude bodies of his victims at the site where he abducted them. So if he's killed Brianna, we should find her body in a ditch near John Isaac's place."

Doc Meade nodded in agreement. He accepted the thermos Jennifer handed him and poured hot coffee into a paper cup.

"Besides," Jennifer added as she searched the blue sky for clouds. "It's not raining."

Propped up on pillows in his bed, Tim ended his call with Lane and placed his cell phone back on the table. He leaned back against the pillows and thought he should get out to Bear Lake, but couldn't muster the energy. He listened to the sound of running water, as his wife, Megan entered the shower.

Tim always hated it when anything interrupted his Saturday morning ritual with Megan. They'd made a pledge during their honeymoon years ago that Saturday mornings belonged to the two of them, to have breakfast in bed, and then make love for hours. With his demanding career and caring for a small daughter, there had been a couple of Saturday mornings they'd missed. But they were few and far between.

He imagined Megan naked in the shower and felt a hot jolt of lust surging through his veins. Tim pulled a box of matches out of a drawer, got out of bed and quietly crept to the bathroom where he lit every candle. He then flipped the light switch off, removed his boxer shorts and pulled back the shower curtain.

"Well, hello, big boy," Megan said. "What took you so long?"

Tim crushed her to him and hungrily kissed her as he angled their bodies under the water, until it sluiced over them. He kissed her over and over until heat flowed in his veins, straight to his erection.

Megan's hands began a slow massage with lemony shower gel that started with his shoulders, moving down until her fingers caressed the hard muscles in his back, as her breasts moved against him, driving him wild with desire. Pushing him against the shower wall, her hands went to work on his chest and pecs; her fingers making gentle circular motions with the gel. She slid her hand down and grinned at the very male moan that came from the deep of his chest when she touched him. His senses reeled as if short-circuited. Turning off the water with one hand, he reached for towels with the other. As quickly as he could manage it, the two were on the bed and he was exploring and worshiping every part of his wife's body, trying to communicate he loved her as much today as the day they got married.

Jennifer leaned against a tree, impatiently tapping her foot. They'd been at the boat ramp for close to three hours, and they hadn't found a body. She was beginning to suspect Charlie Barnett was either senile, or had never seen a woman's body in the lake in the first place. This had better not be a wild goose chase, or Charlie could find himself on a personal tour of a jail cell. Jennifer looked across the lake to the boat's latest stop and glanced at her watch. Suddenly, Jennifer's cell phone vibrated in her jacket pocket.

"Brennan."

Lance Brody's voice sounded through the phone. "We just found her. Blake's bringing her up now. She'd been thrown in with a thick logger chain wound around her body, and got stuck to the branches of a fallen tree at the bottom."

"Is it Brianna Hayden?" Jennifer wanted to know.

"Won't be able to tell until we get her onboard."

Jennifer disconnected the call, and shoved the cell back in her pocket. She called out to Doc Meade, as Karen Katz joined him. "They found the body. They're coming back as soon as they have her onboard."

Doc Meade and Karen Katz got up and walked to the boat ramp to wait. Jennifer pulled a stack of towels from the back of the SUV and joined them.

As soon as they were close enough, Blake and Lance jumped off the boat, then pulled it onto the boat ramp while a deputy ran to get the trailer. Charlie Barnett jumped out of the boat and ran to the nearest tree, where he braced himself as he vomited.

Doc Meade's two assistants scurried next to the boat with a gurney, lined with an open body bag.

"Blake, is it Brianna?" asked Jennifer.

Blake nodded with disappointment. He took a towel from her and rubbed his hair and face with it.

The coroner assistants wheeled Brianna's body up the ramp, then Doc Meade bent over her. "Her body hasn't been in that lake any more than a few hours. It's in a relatively good condition, not like the swollen messes we usually find after the victim's been in the water for days or weeks."

He arranged the body on its side. "Take a look at this. Same ligature marks on her neck."

Blake and Jennifer rushed to his side.

"See her back and bottom. There are only one or two lacerations where he hit her with the belt. He'd beaten the other victims so much their behinds looked like raw hamburger. What made him change his M.O.?
"

Hands gripped on the steering wheel, Blake rushed

back to the house so he could shower, change, and take Jennifer to the hospital for her follow-up appointment at one o'clock. Lane had threatened to put her on leave until she brought him a release from her doctor.

The waiting room was packed with anxious people clicking the keys on their laptops, rustling through magazines, or playing games on their cell phones. Blake nearly groaned out loud when someone turned the channel of the large flat-screen on the wall to CSN. What he didn't need today was to hear from armchair experts and talking heads about Brianna going missing, and how the sheriff's department could do a better job.

Itching with anxiety, he moved to the window to look outside. He'd always disliked hospitals, but since Jennifer's recent stay, he'd begun to detest them. Checking his watch, he noted that Jennifer had been with the doctor for fifteen minutes. Someone tapped him on the shoulder and he whipped around.

"Down boy, it's only your sister," Carly said. "Guess Jennifer's still with the doctor and that's what has you so tense."

"You must be psychic, Carly." Blake grumbled.

"Come buy me a cup of bitter coffee and a stale sandwich in the cafeteria. We need to talk."

The cafeteria Saturday special was baked chicken,

mashed potatoes and green beans. Blake carried two plates, along with two Cherry Cokes, to the table where Carly waited. "Sorry, they were all out of stale sandwiches. Hope this will do," he said. She was shuffling through a folder stuffed with papers and barely noticed him.

"Earth to Carly."

"What? Hey, that looks good for hospital food. I'm starving." She watched as he set the plates, cans, and napkin-rolled silverware on the table. She unrolled her silverware and dug in. "Cherry Coke? I haven't had one of these since high school."

"I figured you needed the sugar for energy. Did you get any sleep at all last night?"

"Nope. I'm used to it. FBI agents never sleep," she responded with a mouth full of food.

"Something's off," said Blake aloud. It had been bothering him since Doc Meade pointed it out on the boat ramp. "The killer deviated from his M.O. with Brianna."

"What do you mean?"

"He killed her, but without the tortuous belt beatings the others suffered. In addition, he dumped her body in a lake, whereas he'd posed the naked bodies of his first two victims in the park where he had abducted them."

"Those are some definite changes from his usual preferences. Anything else?"

"Yes, he didn't wait for rain."

"The only thing I can think of that would make him change his M.O. is that something freaked him out. All of his preferences for the way he abducts, tortures, murders and dumps his victims are very comfortable for him because he's successfully used them for years without getting caught." She stared at him for a moment then continued, "Blake, keep a close eye on Jennifer. He'll try to get to her again. Is there any way you can move her into a safe house?"

"You've met Jennifer. What do you think?"

"I can't criticize her. I'd probably react the same way," admitted Carly. "Listen, I have some news for you. We got some hits in ViCAP."

"Really?" asked Blake. "Got to tell you how mad I am at myself for not running the M.O. through myself. We kept coming up with local suspects. Not a good excuse though, and it sure won't happen again."

"No one's blaming you, Blake. Let it go," said Carly. "In the past five years, there have been five murders with your killer's M.O. in Ohio. All victims were women in their twenties, tortured over a period of time with belt beatings, then murdered and dumped nude in state parks posed in a praying position."

"You've got to be fucking kidding me. Five?"

"Five. Like your case, there was no trace evidence and no witnesses. I tracked down a detective in Columbus who worked two of the cases. He said he always thought the killer worked in some capacity in one of the state parks, but could never find enough evidence to arrest anyone."

Blake shook his head with disgust. "With our three victims, that makes eight women who have lost their lives to this sick bastard. It's got to end."

Carly reached over and lightly patted his arm. "You'll catch him, Blake. I know you will." She paused. "There's something else. I got a call from my supervisor in Tampa. He's assigning me a new case — an abduction of a four-year-old boy. My plane leaves in a couple of hours.

"Damn it, Carly. It seems like you just got here."

"I know, but duty calls. Tell Jennifer I said good-bye, and I want to hear from you the minute you nab your killer."

"Promise."

Blake hugged his sister and walked her to the

elevator where they said good-bye in the lobby. After finding out from the desk nurse that Jennifer was still with the doctor, Blake headed back to the waiting area.

His cell phone buzzed.

"Blake Stone."

"Blake, this is Karen Katz. I meant to tell you something at the boat ramp, but I forgot."

"What's that?"

"There was a latent print on that syringe you gave me that was filled with Rohypnol."

"Are you sure? The perp was wearing latex gloves."

"He must not have been wearing them when he filled the syringe," Karen reasoned.

"I hope you're not kidding me, because that's the best news I've gotten in a while."

"Nope, I never kid about forensics. I just sent it to IAFIS and should have results within the hour."

"Excellent. Jennifer and I are headed to the office soon. See you there."

He'd barely gotten his cell phone back in his pocket when Jennifer appeared in the waiting room, waving a doctor's release form in the air.

Megan Brennan played an old disco CD and danced around her kitchen. She opened the refrigerator and pulled out a quart of milk, a bowl of potato salad, mayonnaise, and slices of turkey, laying each item on the counter. She snagged the loaf of bread and began making turkey sandwiches.

It was Saturday and her husband had made mad, crazy love to her a few hours before. Tim had just called to say he'd be home for lunch, and she intended to feed him a delicious meal, then seduce him until he dragged her back to their bedroom.

Megan heard the doorbell, so she wiped her hands on a dishcloth and walked through the living room to the front door.

Opening the door, she stood face-to-face with a young man whose ruggedly handsome face was vaguely familiar.

"Good morning, Mrs. Brennan. From the look on your face, I'm guessing you don't remember me."

"I'm sorry," she apologized.

"I'm Damon Mason. Remember, you came to my dad's funeral."

Dick Mason's son? How could she have forgotten?

"I'm so sorry, Damon. Of course, I remember you."

"If I could just have a minute of your time," he began, nervously glancing at a truck that sped down the street.

Before Megan could respond, he pushed past her standing in the foyer, and walked into the living room. She'd intended to tell him she was too busy this morning to chat, but as long as he was here, she decided to sit with him in the living room to listen to what he had to say. Maybe the poor guy was still upset about his father's death. Megan closed the front door and entered what was now a darkened living room. Why had Damon closed her window blinds?

Once her eyes adjusted to the change in light, she noticed he stood near the sofa, smiling from ear-to-ear. There was something about his smile that conflicted with the evil glint in his eyes, and sent a shiver up her spine. He pulled his hand from behind his back to reveal a long hypodermic needle. Before Megan could scream, he plunged it into her neck, her vision pixeling before going solid black as she slumped to the floor.

Back at the office, Jennifer fired up her computer, went to her email, and groaned at the number of messages she'd received after missing two days of work.

It took her an hour to read and respond to each one.

Though she didn't think she'd find anything, Jennifer checked Brianna's bank records for any withdrawals after she went missing, but found no activity at all. She would have been surprised if she'd found anything. Brianna's killer didn't want her money; he wanted her to suffer, for some sick reason known only to himself.

Then Jennifer crossed her fingers and checked for cell phone activity. If Brianna's cell phone had been turned back on, they could track her through her phone's GPS. No such luck. There had been no use of the phone since around the time Brianna disappeared. The frustration tore a hole in her stomach. How many more women would die before they caught their killer?

Jennifer sent Blake a text, asking for Carly's phone number. She couldn't let Carly leave town without talking to her. Jennifer doodled on a piece of paper as she waited for Blake to text her Carly's phone number. Previously, he had briefed her on Carly's ViCAP findings. There was something about the murders in Ohio that tugged at her brain. A beep sounded to announce Blake's text with Carly's number.

Jennifer reached Carly on her first try. "Carly, I'm sorry you have to leave so soon."

"Hey, I'm happy to be off administrative leave. Not having a case was making me a little crazy."

"Carly, thank you for all the work you did on our case."

"All I want is for the information to help you find your killer," Carly responded. "Jennifer, Blake told me about how your killer deviated from his usual behaviors with Brianna's murder."

"Yes, he mentioned that."

"Your killer didn't take time with Brianna to torture her, as was his preference. Therefore, it's unlikely he got his usual sexual satisfaction from her killing. That concerns me, as does the fact he dumped her body in a lake, as opposed to posing her at the site where she was abducted. He may be losing control."

"What does that mean?" Jennifer asked.

"It means something happened to knock him out of his comfort zone. Something freaked him out, and I fear he'll take risks he wouldn't ordinarily take. He'll become more dangerous."

"Good. I want him to make some mistakes that will help us catch him."

"Jennifer, why do you think he focused on you? He broke into your home to leave Catherine's cell phone. And at great risk, he tried to get to you in the hospital," said Carly.

"I don't know, and believe me, I've thought about it. Until Evan Hendricks' shooting, the media did not connect my name with the case. So how could he know I was assigned to it?"

After a moment, Carly said, "Please take extra precautions for your safety. He will come for you again, sooner than later."

"Don't worry about me. Despite what my dad and Blake may think, I can take care of myself."

"If I were you, I wouldn't take any walks by myself in your area parks anytime soon," joked Carly half-heartedly. She didn't want to think about anything happening to Jennifer. It would destroy her brother.

"Wish you could stay longer so we could spend more time together," Jennifer lamented.

"That makes two of us. Maybe you and Blake could fly to Florida when all this is over."

"Sounds like a plan."

"Before we hang up, Jennifer, I have to ask you to promise to do something."

"What?"

"Tell my brother you're in love with him. He

needs to know."

Tim got out of his car and had his keys out to open the back door when he realized it was standing ajar. That's odd. But he dismissed the tingling in the back of his neck by reasoning Megan may have gone to the garage for something, and thought she'd closed and locked the door. Tim slipped into the kitchen and called out for Megan. He noticed the food on the counter, rolled up a piece of turkey, and bit off a chunk. Wandering into the front of the house, he noticed the darkened living room.

"Megan, I'm home. Hey, what's going on in the living room? We never have the blinds closed." His wife loved sunlight. As soon as she woke up in the morning, she opened the blinds and draperies on every window in the house. The only time they were closed was at night, and that time she was in the hospital with her heart attack.

He stepped into the foyer where he noticed the front door was unlocked. Hell, Megan was more security-conscious than he was. First the back door, now the front? There was no way she'd leave either door unlocked. He froze. The alarm slammed into his stomach like a gut-punch. Something was very, very wrong. He pulled out his service weapon.

"Megan! Where are you?" he shouted as he raced up the stairs to the second level. He continued to shout Megan's name as he checked each bedroom and bathroom without finding her.

Tim sprinted down the stairs to the first floor, to the den, then the family room where the flat-screen TV above the fireplace was on, but no Megan. He ran back to the kitchen, glancing at the items lining the counter.

Dashing out the back door, he went to the garage and hoisted up the door. Megan's car was still inside. After searching the back yard, Tim went to the front, looking up and down the sidewalk.

He moved to Don and Nicole French's house next door and pounded on the door. When Don answered, he asked, "Have you seen Megan?"

"No, but I've been working in the basement on a new bookcase all morning." He called out for his wife who came to the door.

Nicole smiled when she saw who was at the front door. "Hi, Tim. Good to see you."

Her husband slipped his arm around her. "Honey, have you seen Megan this morning? Tim's looking for her."

"I haven't seen Megan, but I noticed you had a visitor earlier," Nicole began.

"Visitor?" asked Tim.

"Yes, I was doing the dishes and looking out my back window when I saw a truck pull in your driveway," she said. "I only noticed it because I wondered why he backed so far up in your driveway, almost up to the garage door. It may have been nothing, but usually visitors to either of our houses park in front. The only people who park that close to the garage are Jennifer and you. Like I said, it was probably nothing."

"What kind of vehicle was it?" asked Tim, his heart in his throat.

"Now I'm not good with cars," Nicole paused, looking at her husband. "But I think it looked like the same thing Buck drives."

"My brother, Buck, drives a Jeep," offered Don.

A quick and disturbing thought hit Tim. "What color was it?"

"It was brown and tan."

Tim flew to his car, his heart racing as he punched Lane's number into his cell.

"The killer has Megan!"

Upstairs in Forensics, Blake impatiently drummed his fingers on Karen Katz's desk while he waited for her phone conversation to end. Once it did, she reached for a file on her desk.

"Hey, Blake. I know why *you're* here." Karen said as she brushed her long bangs out of her eyes.

"Did you get results on the latent print on the hypodermic?"

"Sure did."

His heart in his throat, Blake asked, "Past offender?" With the number of murders under his belt, this guy had to have been arrested for something in his past.

"Nope. This guy's prints were only in the system because he works for the Indiana Department of National Resources in the Division of State Parks and Reservoirs."

"Shit! Who is he?"

"Damon Mason," Karen declared.

"Dick Mason's son? Are you sure?" Blake asked in disbelief. Even as Karen nodded, his mind raced. How could a twenty-year detective on the force have a son who would commit these heinous acts? He searched his memory to the day of Dick's funeral, which was the last time he saw Damon. He seemed cold and stoic, but Damon never left his father's casket. Blake remembered telling Damon how sorry he was about his loss and that his dad was a good man.

Just then, Karen's supervisor called her to his office. Still stunned, Blake sat in Karen's guest chair, thinking about Carly's profile of the killer, and how she'd said he'd be very familiar with the area parks. Well, Damon Mason worked in them every day. The son of a bitch used the local parks, meant for recreation, as a hunting ground for young women. He was everything Carly described: good-looking, athletic, normal, and unthreatening.

But was he jumping to conclusions? That Damon was the man who attacked Jennifer in the hospital didn't mean he was a serial killer. Did it?

Blake pulled out his cell phone and dialed the State Parks and Reservoirs human resources director he'd talked to the night before.

"Barry, this is Blake Stone. We talked last night. I need your help, and please don't make me get a subpoena to get it. Time is of the essence."

"I heard you found Brianna's body," Barry murmured sympathetically. "Do we agree the information we discuss didn't come from me?"

"Agreed. You employ a conservation officer by the name of Damon Mason. What can you tell me about him?"

"Hold on a second while I find his file." Blake heard some papers rustling, then Barry returned to the phone. "Here it is. What do you want to know?"

"How long has he worked for you?"

"Looks like about six months."

A muscle flicked in his jaw as Blake gripped his cell and asked, "Does he drive tan and brown Jeep?"

"Sure. All the conservation officers have them."

"What about ATVs? Does he have access to them?"

"Sure. Of course he does."

Sickened, Blake shook his head as he thought about how easy it was for Damon to get the bodies back into the park using an ATV with a cart, driving the service roads. Even if he had been seen, people wouldn't give a conservation officer on an ATV a second thought. Just like the night he used one when he abducted Tiffany Chase.

"Do you have his resume in the file to see where he worked before coming here?"

After a moment, Barry said, "His resume lists his last job in a state park in Ohio where he worked for five years."

"Where he murdered five women..."

Ending the call, Blake flew out of the room and bounded down the stairs so he could tell Lane that Damon Mason was their killer. He got to Lane's office but the door was closed and his admin wasn't at her desk. This couldn't wait, he thought as he burst through the door. Lane and Tim sat at Lane's small conference table. Fatigue was settling in pockets under Tim's eyes and he looked upset.

"What's going on?" Blake asked Tim.

"The killer has Megan and I don't even know where to start looking since we don't know who the bastard is."

"Yes, we do," blurted Blake.

11 CHAPTER ELEVEN

Jennifer poured hot coffee into her mug then snagged a homemade chocolate-chip cookie baked by one of the deputy's wives. She chatted with Joey Fields, one of the new recruits, who also nabbed a cookie, declaring there were absolutely no calories in it.

As Jennifer got closer to her cubicle, she realized her desk phone was ringing so she hastened to get it.

"Jennifer Brennan."

"Jennifer, this is Damon Mason."

Jennifer rolled her eyes. She still hadn't shaken her initial negative impression of Damon. And she'd tried because she'd cared so much about his father. She picked up her pen to doodle on a notepad, which she usually did when she was on the phone.

"What can I do for you?" she asked.

"I just found something my father left for you." His

voice sounded breathless like he had run into the room to call her.

"Your dad left something for me?" That was odd. Why was she just now hearing about it?

"Yes, I just found it while I was looking through his things," Damon explained. "I think you'll want to see it right away."

"See what? What did Dick leave for me?"

"It's a letter addressed to you. I found it taped under one of his dresser drawers. The outside of the envelope says that you must read the letter inside immediately following his death."

"Oh, my God," Jennifer exclaimed. Thinking of her old partner made tears well up in her eyes. She still missed him terribly. "Where are you, Damon?"

"I'm at Dad's house. His attorney told me this morning that Dad left it to me. I was going through his things when I found the letter. You'll come to read it, won't you? I have this feeling it's important."

"Yes, I'll be there soon." Jennifer hung up the phone, grabbed her purse and walked around the corner to tell Blake. He wasn't at his desk. She looked toward Lane's office and noticed the door was closed. Maybe Blake was with him.

Blake was going to have a fit when he found out she went out alone, but damn it, she was a trained officer. She could take care of herself.

Finding a pen on his desk, Jennifer wrote him a short note saying she had an errand to run, and would be back soon.

Tim, Lane, and Blake studied a map of Deer Run State Park. Blake used a marker to circle the cabin where Barry said Damon Mason lived.

"It will take up to sixty minutes to deploy the on-duty and off-duty officers on the SWAT team. Depending on the traffic, and factoring in the curves in the road, it should take the SWAT team a maximum of twenty additional minutes to reach Damon's cabin," said Lane.

"Deploy them! And tell Andy to get the copter ready." said Tim. If Damon Mason had Megan, Tim needed to get her checked out at the hospital as soon as he could. With her heart condition, he could take no chances. And if the son of a bitch hurt her, he'd pay.

Adrenalin rushing through them, Tim and Blake raced from Lane's office to put on their Kevlar vests and grab their protective helmets, while Lane did the same. They'd go up in the copter while Lane directed the SWAT team from the ground.

In his cubicle, Blake ripped off his jacket and put on the Kevlar vest. He was about to call out for Jennifer when he noticed a post-it note stuck to his phone. He pulled it off and saw it was a message from Jennifer. Gone to do an errand? She couldn't be serious. What was it about laying low did she not understand? That's just what the killer wanted, for Jennifer to be out-and-about alone. Damn it.

Blake fished his cell phone out of his pants' pocket and dialed her number. As he listened, he heard a ringing sound from the other side of the cubicles. He walked to the other side and stopped when he got to Jennifer's office. Her cell phone was ringing from where it was lying on top of her desk.

Blake called dispatch to page Jennifer. "If she doesn't respond, send out a BOLO for her. Tell deputies to stop her car and get in contact with me immediately. Her life may be in danger."

Blake headed for the stairwell and he raced up to the roof to the helicopter pad.

Jennifer turned onto County Road 47, slowing down to adjust to driving on the gravel road. She couldn't imagine what Dick would have wanted to tell her in a letter. He wasn't a letter-writing kind of guy. Most of the time, she couldn't even get him to use email to communicate at work.

The last time she'd traveled this gravel road was the day they'd found Dick Mason, dead, his house filled with carbon monoxide fumes. The thought of Dick feeling so lost that he'd taken his own life filled Jennifer with sadness, and her eyes welled with unshed tears.

Jennifer pulled into Dick's driveway and thought she saw someone standing in the living room picture window. But when she looked again, there was no one there. As she drove closer, she noticed a tan and brown vehicle parked in Dick's open garage. The word "Jeep" was written in large letters in the center of the black spare tire cover. A dark, ominous thought flashed in her brain. A tan and brown Jeep was the vehicle John Isaac saw parked along the road by his property the night Brianna Hayden disappeared.

Her heart skipped a beat as she remembered Carly's profile. The killer was very familiar with the areas parks and recreation areas. Who would be more familiar than a conservation officer? Her hand resting on her holstered Glock, Jennifer quietly opened her driver's side door and crept into the garage. Painted on the Jeep's door was a logo for the Division of State Parks and Reservoirs. Oh, my God. The killer couldn't be Damon, could it? Not Dick's son.

She had to call Blake and get back-up. Jennifer patted each of her pockets. Where was her cell phone? She swung around to search for it in the SUV and slammed into the hard wall of Damon Mason's chest.

"What are you doing out here?" asked Damon.

"Oh, nothing. Just wondering where Dick's car was."

He responded quickly. "Sold it at auction about a month ago."

"Oh, that explains it."

"Does it?" He eyeballed her suspiciously as he pulled his service revolver out of his holster, pointing it at her. "I'll take your gun, Jennifer."

Jennifer hesitated, weighing her options.

"Now!" he shouted. "Pull it out slowly, place it on the ground, then gently slide it over to me with your foot."

Jennifer bit her lip, slid her Glock out of her holster, and did what he asked. What choice did she have?

"So what's going on, Damon?"

"You'll find out soon enough. Go into the house." Holding his gun against her back, he pushed her up the porch steps and through the open front door. He closed and locked the door behind him. "Oh, I nearly forgot. We have another guest that I'm sure you'll want to see."

Jennifer arched her eyebrow questioningly. "Who?"

Instead of answering he shoved her toward the kitchen. In the center of the room, on a long oaken table, lay her mother, fully clothed, but unconscious and restrained with duct tape.

"Mom!" she screamed. She ran to her mother's side, pulling at the duct tape so she could get to her wrist to check her pulse. "You fucking monster, what have you done to her?!"

"Better watch yourself, Jennifer. You don't want to get me angry."

"Why is she unconscious? What did you do to her?" she demanded as tears shot from her eyes.

He just smirked and shrugged his shoulders.

"You injected her with Rohypnol, didn't you? How much did you give her? She has a heart condition." Jennifer ripped at the duct tape on her mother's wrist with her long fingernails until she could free one arm. She pressed her fingers on Megan's wrist to find a pulse. She found one but it was very slow.

Jennifer glared at Damon and said, "We need to get her to a hospital. She's had a heart attack before, and I don't know how the drug is affecting her."

"Sounds like you have a problem, Jennifer," Damon said. "Now get your ass to the living room so we can have a talk. Then later, I'll see if a good beating with a belt will wake Mommy. You can watch."

Blake and Tim watched from the police helicopter overhead as Lane reviewed Damon Mason's background and suspected offenses — as well as the layout of the area surrounding his cabin — with his SWAT team. He also laid out two contingency plans to capture Damon Mason, one with hostages, and one without. Equipped with their weaponry, they got into a black van and headed toward Deer Run State Park.

Flying ahead, the police helicopter was approaching Deer Run State Park when Blake's cell phone vibrated.

"Blake, this is Ginny from Dispatch with an update on your BOLO request. We have not been able to locate Jennifer Brennan."

"Thanks, Ginny. Tell them to keep looking."

"What's that all about?" asked Tim.

"Jennifer left me a note at the office, telling me she'd gone out for an errand. I tried calling her, but she'd forgotten her cell phone at the office. I put a BOLO on her, but no one has found her yet."

"So you're telling me that my wife *and* only daughter are missing?" Tim raked his fingers through his hair. The women he held most dear were gone — both at risk from a serial killer who would not think twice about snuffing out their lives.

Following them from the air, Blake and Tim watched as the van carrying the SWAT team parked off the road about a half-mile from the cabin. The officers jumped from the van and crept through surrounding wooded area until they were able to form a perimeter around the cabin.

Blake's heart was racing when he pointed at Damon's cabin, as they hovered overhead. There were no cars in the driveway, but that didn't mean the suspect wasn't hiding inside.

From the ground, Lane swept the length of the cabin with a pair of high-powered binoculars, but saw no movement inside or out. From the helicopter, Tim used the thermal imaging camera to make visible any objects that emit heat. Like Lane, he found nothing.

Using a bull-horn, Lane urged Damon to come out because he was surrounded. When there was no answer, Lane signaled the team, which formed a single-file line, each person poised low-to-the-ground while approaching the cabin.

On the porch, the point man breached the door and threw in a flash bang. The grenade exploded in a flash of light and a loud boom to disorient any suspect inside the cabin. As each team member entered the cabin, he or she quickly dropped into position in the area of responsibility Lane had discussed with them earlier. Soon they had cleared each room of the cabin. Damon Mason was not there.

Blake's cell phone vibrated again. Filled with frustration about not finding Damon, he yanked it out of his pocket and barked, "Blake Stone."

"Detective Stone, this is Carl Freeman. Do you remember me? I was Dick Mason's neighbor."

"Listen, Mr. Freeman, this is not a good time."

"I understand. I guess I should have called nine-one-one," Carl apologized.

Blake's curiosity kicked in. "What's going on, Mr. Freeman?"

"It could be nothing, but I just drove past Dick Mason's place and there are cars in the driveway. I'm worried someone is breaking into the place."

Blake pushed the cell's speaker button so Tim could hear the conversation.

"Did you say there are vehicles at Dick Mason's house?"

"Yes, sir. There's an SUV in the driveway and some sort of vehicle in the open garage that I didn't get a good look at," he explained. "Do you want me to go back and check it out?"

"No!" Blake shouted. "We're on our way. Don't leave your house, Mr. Freeman."

Jennifer glared at Damon from the sofa in the living room, and cursed herself for the hundredth time for not waiting for Blake. How could she have been such an idiot! Now she was trapped by a sociopathic serial killer, and her mother may lie dying in the other room. She had to think of a way disarm him.

Damon was pacing, going to the window to look out, then coming back. Then doing it again. He was showing signs of paranoia, which could work for her, or against her.

"I know about your mother, Damon," Jennifer said.

"You don't know shit," he exclaimed.

Jennifer spoke softly as if she sympathized with him. "I know she abused you. She beat you with a belt when you were just a child and couldn't defend yourself."

"Shut up!" He swung around from his stance by the window.

"It must have been horrible for you, with no one to protect you from her," said Jennifer. "I know your dad felt terrible about leaving you behind."

"You've got to be kidding me. My father knew he was

leaving me with a monster, but he left anyway. He cared only for himself."

"You're wrong, Damon, he told me..."

He cut her off. "So the old man felt a little guilt. So what? He abandoned me and didn't give a flip about how I suffered in her hands. But he paid. I made sure he did. Once he sucked down that cup of valium-laced coffee and passed out, I turned his car on in the garage. Good-bye Daddy."

"You murdered Dick? You killed your own father?" Jennifer's accusing voice stabbed the air.

Tim talked to Lane from the copter. "We think Mason is at his father's home on Route 47. Jennifer may be there, too. It's at least thirty minutes driving the SWAT van, but we can cut that time in half by flying."

"We're right behind you," said Lane as he and his team ran back into the van.

Tim turned to the pilot, "How many body harnesses do you have onboard?"

"I mean no disrespect, sir," Andy began. "But when was the last time either of you rappelled out of a helicopter?"

"Not a concern, officer. How many?" Tim's voice was gruff and demanding.

"There are two special ops harnesses and two rescue vests in the back," Andy replied.

Tim searched until he found the two special ops harnesses and threw one to Blake.

"I know the house," said Blake. "Dick has a huge front yard, but it's pretty open. Stretching from the small backyard, there's about a mile of woods, then a clearing with a small pasture for horses. We can rappel there."

Tim nodded and Andy aimed the copter toward Route 47.

"Your partner was a worthless piece of crap," Damon exclaimed. "And so are you. I had you pegged the first time I saw you. You've been nothing but trouble to me. Do you think I don't know it was you who sent those deputies to my cabin?

"I don't know what you're talking about."

He moved closer to her until his finger was wagging inches from her face. "You're a lying bitch, just like the others."

Jennifer used the opportunity to swiftly extend one of her long legs to kick the gun out of Damon's other hand. It sailed across the room and they both rushed toward it. Her hand was within an inch of reaching the gun when Damon grabbed her left arm. She swung her right fist up, then crashed it down to deliver a hard blow to the bridge of his nose. Blood sprayed, and he staggered backward as she dived for the gun.

Damon pulled at her feet, flipping her on her back. Big mistake. As she scooted away from him, he followed and she delivered a vicious kick to his groin. As he bent down, she chambered her fist, slamming it down to the cluster of nerves half-way between the side and the front of his neck.

As he slumped to the floor, she grabbed his service revolver and ran to the kitchen to help her mother.

Terrifying the two horses in the pasture, Andy lowered the helicopter so both Blake and Tim could safely rappel to the ground. Then he circled the area as they had asked.

Once they jumped the pasture fence, the men entered the woods, wading through thick grasses, bushes, weeds and debris as they headed toward Dick Mason's house. At the edge of the trees, Blake aimed the thermal imaging camera toward the house.

"There are two people in the kitchen," he whispered to Tim as he aimed the camera to the front of the house. "There's one in the front room."

Tim pointed to the front of the house to communicate he was going in that direction. Low-to-the-ground, Blake moved to the back of the house. He angled himself to peer into a back window, but the curtains were closed. As he crept to the back stoop, he could hear Jennifer crying out. He kicked in the back door and came face-to-face with a revolver Jennifer pointed instinctively. She lowered the gun and he pulled her into his arms. That's when he saw Megan Brennan restrained on the kitchen table.

"Where's Damon?"

"In the living room, unconscious."

Blake rushed to the table to help Jennifer remove the remaining duct tape from Megan's wrists and ankles. When Blake tried to pull her into a sitting position, she slumped back to the table.

"He's injected her with Rohypnol," Jennifer said, as she placed her ear near her mother's face. "Her breathing has slowed. She needs medical treatment, Blake. Mom has a heart condition."

They both heard a commotion in the living room, but before they could respond, Damon appeared in the doorway with his arm tightened around Tim's neck, and a gun pointed at the sheriff's head.

Both Jennifer and Blake stiffened, but refused to lower the guns they pointed at Damon.

"Let my father go," Jennifer demanded. "Let him go now!"

"Go to hell, Jennifer. I don't take orders from a bitch," Damon growled in return. "Put your guns down on the floor, or Daddy gets it. Then Mommy."

With her finger on the trigger guard, Jennifer held her weapon in the firing position. She moved into the firing stance, with her feet shoulder-width apart and her left foot a step past her right, her dominant eye focused on Damon's head. "Not going to happen, Damon. My gun stays where it is. Let go of my father."

At an impasse, Damon's eyes darted from Jennifer to Blake and then back.

Just as Jennifer inserted her trigger finger into the trigger guard, Tim delivered a punishing elbow jab into Damon's rib cage, then he dropped to the floor. Recovering quickly, Damon aimed his gun at Tim, but before he could pull the trigger, a bullet from Jennifer's gun slammed into Damon's head.

Tim pushed Damon's body off him, and checked his pulse. "He's dead."

Blake took the gun from Jennifer's shaking hands and slipped it in the back of his waistband. He then pulled Jennifer into his arms and held her until she stopped trembling.

Tim whipped out his cell phone. "Andy, get that copter back here! My wife needs to be taken to the hospital."

 Frankie and Lane had a "Thank-God-Its-Over" cookout on a beautiful spring day. Anne and Michael Brandt were already there, as well as Tim and Megan Brennan, when Blake and Jennifer parked in the driveway. In the backyard, Lane hovered over his top-of-the-line gas grill that Frankie surprised him with on his last birthday, as Tim supervised the grilling of the steaks. Frankie pointed to a huge cooler filled with ice, beer, wine coolers, and sodas, telling Blake and Jennifer to help themselves.

 Michael and Anne sat in patio chairs on the lawn, watching the kids play with the dogs. Little Ashley scrambled after a ball thrown for the Giant Schnauzers, Harley and Hunter, to chase, inspiring five-year-old Michael Brandt, Jr. to lecture her on the fine arts of playing catch with dogs. When Ashley's face puckered up and tears filled her eyes, Michael Jr.'s twin, Melissa, hugged the little girl and told her she could chase the ball if she wanted to. Michael Jr. shrugged his shoulders to demonstrate his frustration, then joined his dad to debate the subject.

 Frankie asked Megan about her hospital stay.

 "The Rohypnol slowed down my breathing, so they gave me some oxygen and treated me with activated charcoal. I hate hospitals. I couldn't wait to go home. I don't know what all the fuss was about. I'm fine."

"Is it true about Rohypnol? That it causes you to forget what's happened?"

"I can't remember a thing that happened after Damon Mason entered our home," Megan replied. "I'm disappointed I missed all the exciting parts, like the ride in the helicopter to the hospital."

Tim joined them and said, "Personally, I could have lived without remembering all the exciting parts."

"Yeah, me, too," said Blake. He glanced at Jennifer and wondered why she'd been so quiet all day. He put his arm around the back of her chair and stroked her arm gently with his fingers.

Lane looked at the couple and asked, "So you two both have a week's vacation. What are you going to do with it?"

"We're flying to Florida to see Carly, and I want to introduce Jennifer to my parents," Blake said.

Jennifer added, "I can't wait to see Carly and get some sun. Florida beaches are beautiful."

"Is your counseling finished?" Tim asked Jennifer. Per policy, all officers involved in a shooting were required to attend counseling sessions.

"Yes, Dad," she answered.

"How'd it go?"

"I'll tell you what I told Dr. Shields. I don't for a minute regret shooting that vicious killer."

Tim hugged his daughter and said, "You saved our lives that day."

"Dad, there's something I want to do for Brianna's little girl, Amanda."

"What's that?"

"I want the money in the trust fund that Paul Vance left me to go to her," Jennifer said. "I want Amanda to grow up, go to college, and do all the wonderful things in life that I'm sure Brianna wanted for her."

Michael spoke up. "If that's what you want to do, I'll help you make it happen."

After an impromptu softball game, where Jennifer skidded into home base for a home run, the party broke up and everyone headed home. Blake parked the SUV in front of Jennifer's house and followed her inside. He noticed her scraped knee was bleeding, so he bounded up the stairs for the first aid kit.

Blake found the first aid kit in her bathroom medicine cabinet where she said it would be. He pulled it from the shelf, and then closed the cabinet door. Somehow the kit slipped from his fingers and plopped into the small waste basket next to the sink. He plucked the kit from the waste basket. That's when he noticed something and froze. There was a small plastic tube with the words "pregnancy test" written on its side. Pregnancy test? Slowly, he reached back into the can and held the plastic tube up so he could read the results.

Jennifer heard him walk into the room, his footsteps heavy and slow. She turned to see if he had the first aid kit and what she saw sucked the air out of her lungs, as if she'd been punched in the chest.

Blake stood in the doorway holding her plastic pregnancy test tube between his index finger and his thumb. His eyes were glistening and his expression bore a seriousness she'd never seen before.

"I'm not going to ask you why you didn't tell me. I'm not even going to ask you how long you've known. But I am going to answer the questions you haven't asked." He tossed the plastic container onto the end table and moved a step toward her.

"Yes, I want this baby," he continued. "Yes. I can't think of anything I want more than our little boy or girl."

"Blake, I..."

"There's more that I want. I want you, this baby and me to be a real family. I want a house with a picket fence and a swing-set in the backyard. I want a front porch with a swing so we can sit out there and talk about our days, and make plans for our future." His large hand took her face and held it gently. "I want to spend my days knowing that I will spend my nights with you and our kids."

"I love you so much, Blake."

"Honey, I'm crazy about you. I want to marry you, Jennifer. I want us to make that lifetime commitment and keep it." Blake paused for a second. "Will you marry me? Will you trust me to be the man who will always be there for you?"

In one forward motion, Jennifer was in his arms where he held her snugly, kissing her hard.

"I'll take that as a 'Yes'."

Dear Reader:

If you liked *Deadly Relations*, I would appreciate it if you would help others enjoy this book, too, by recommending it to your friends, family and book clubs, and/or by writing a positive review on Amazon, Barnes and Noble, Goodreads or Smashwords.

If you do write a review, please send me an email at **alexagrace@cfl.rr.com**. I'd like to add you to my e-newsletter list so that you can get updates about upcoming releases first, be eligible for drawings for prizes, and get free ebook alerts.

Thank you.

Alexa Grace

P.S. If you should find a mistake: I always strive to write the best book possible and use a team of beta readers, as well as an editor, prior to publication. But goofs slip through. If something slipped past us, please let me know by writing to me at **alexagrace@cfl.rr.com**. Thank you.

Turn the page for more sizzling romantic suspense

from

Alexa Grace

Deadly Offerings

Book One of the Deadly Trilogy

Available Now

Deadly Offerings

Book One of the Deadly Trilogy

He may offer her only chance at survival.
But will she survive the passion that rages between
them?

Anne Mason thinks she'll be safe living in the Midwest building a wind farm. She may be dead wrong. Someone is dumping bodies in her corn field and telling Anne they are gifts—for her!

As the body count rises, Anne realizes a cold-blooded serial killer is patiently waiting and watching her every move. And he won't stop until he ends her life. It is clear there are no limits to this killer's thirst for revenge or how far he will go to get it.

Anne is not at all pleased to learn that her new next-door neighbor is county prosecutor Michael Brandt — the same man who represented her ex in her divorce proceedings. He is the last person Anne can trust, but may offer her only chance at survival from a psychopathic killer. But will she survive the passion that rages between them?

Excerpt from *Deadly Offerings*

Anne peered into her refrigerator. Not a piece of junk food in sight. She opened the freezer. How could she be out of ice cream at a time like this?

She had to get out of the house. Tonight bad memories hung over her like a thundercloud. She relived the humiliating divorce hearing over and over, becoming angrier each time.

She tried to sleep. No success. She got out of bed and pulled on a pair of jean shorts, a black glittery Lady Gaga tank top and her Reeboks. She'd go for a drive to clear her head. It was close to midnight but with any luck, she'd find someplace open to stock up on junk food.

She backed her SUV out of the garage, shoved the gear to drive and moved down the street, windows down, the breeze whipping her ponytail about her face. She drove down Route 40 until she reached a section of fast food restaurants, bars and a mini-mart. The mini-mart didn't look busy so she parked in front.

She grabbed a shopping basket and strode down an aisle of the store picking up Reese's Peanut Butter Cups, Butterfinger candy bars, tortilla chips, a jar of salsa, and a quart of soda as she went. She moved to the refrigerator case and eyed the selection of ice cream. She pulled out a couple of cartons of Ben & Jerry's Red Velvet Cake then headed to the teenaged cashier whose eyes were plastered on her long legs.

She paid for the items, whirled around and slammed into the hard chest of a tall man entering the store. Her items tumbled from the bag. The salsa jar rolled across the store as did the bottle of soda. The man uttered "sorry" as he bent to help her pick up the items. He picked up the salsa and put it in her bag. He moved down the aisle to get the soda that had rolled under a freezer then turned toward her. In a black leather jacket and snug faded jeans, he was one of those men that radiated testosterone. And wasn't it just her luck, or lack of, that Michael Brandt, her jerk ex-husband's attorney was heading toward her holding her soda, sending her a dazzling smile that sent her stupid heart racing. She yanked the soda bottle out of his hand, thanked him and resisted the childish urge to kick him in the shin. Instead, she rushed out of the store.

She opened the back of the car to place the groceries inside. She pulled a Butterfinger bar out of one of the bags and got into the front seat. As she opened the candy bar, she glanced at Michael Brandt, still inside the store, who was now staring at her with an odd expression on his face, hands on his hips.

She heard movement in the back seat then felt something hard slam against her face. The candy bar flew out of her hand and landed on the floorboard.

"Drive."

She looked in the rearview mirror and gasped; a sliver of panic cut through her. A man in a black ski mask was slammed against her seat thrusting a gun in her face.

Turn the page for more sizzling romantic suspense from

Alexa Grace

Deadly Deception

Book Two of the Deadly Trilogy

Available Now

Deadly Deception

Book Two of the Deadly Trilogy

Is she able to forgive him, so together they can catch a killer?

In *Deadly Deception*, the second book of Alexa Grace's *Deadly Trilogy*, enter the disturbing world of illegal adoptions, baby trafficking and murder with new detective Lane Hansen and private investigator Frankie Douglas.

Lane Hansen has a problem. He needs a woman to portray his wife in an undercover operation and the only females on his team are either very pregnant or built like linebackers. Then he remembers gorgeous P.I. Frankie Douglas — a woman who could take his breath away by her beauty and take him down in 2.5 seconds. Unfortunately, she's the same woman he treated like a one night stand six months before.

Frankie Douglas has a problem. She wants to rid the world of one baby trafficking killer. The only way to do that is to partner with Lane Hanson, the man who hurt her by disappearing from her life after a night of mind-blowing sex.

They've been warned! Getting personally involved with a partner can put cases and lives at risk. Going undercover as husband and wife, Lane and Frankie struggle to keep their relationship strictly professional as their sizzling passion threatens to burn out of control.

Excerpt from *Deadly Deception*

"Lane, I know you're ready to do undercover work, but with this case I need two cops who can pose as a married couple. Unfortunately, we've got three women on the team. One is built like a linebacker and the other two are pregnant."

"Sir, for this case, why don't we go outside the department? I know a Private Investigator who can handle herself on a job like this."

Newly appointed Sheriff Tim Brennan's brows drew together in a suspicious expression. "What's the PI's name?"

"Frankie Douglas. I worked with her last year on the Charles Beatty serial killer case. She's a former sharpshooter for the Army."

"Is this the same Frankie Douglas you shot?"

Lane's face flushed with the guilt he still felt about the shooting. "Yes, sir. It was an accident. We were heading down the stairs of Beatty's cellar to apprehend him when one of the steps gave way and when I fell my gun went off and hit Frankie."

"Has Frankie Douglas done police work before?"

"I heard she's a former detective."

"I think I've heard about her. Isn't she a pretty tall blonde woman?"

"Oh, she's smokin' hot. Think Victoria Secret hot."

"Is that right? Do you have a personal thing going with Ms. Douglas?"

"No sir. Strictly professional." Of course, if he'd had a chance, he'd have made in personal in 2.5 seconds.

Brennan glared at Lane then picked up his phone and dialed a number. "Hello, Frankie, this is *Uncle* Tim. I may have a job for you. Would you please drop by my office?"

Available in the Spring 2013

Profile of Evil

Book One of the Profile Series

Carly Stone is a brilliant FBI agent who's seen more than her share of evil. Leaving the agency, she becomes a consultant for Indiana County Sheriff Brody Chase. He needs her help to catch a savage killer who is luring teenaged girls to their death in his community.

The two are determined to stop a dangerous predator before he takes another life — at any cost.

Excerpt from Profile of Evil

He pulled up in front of a two-story gray house in a
nice neighborhood with palm trees lining the streets.
Flicking on the interior car light, he checked the address he'd
been given. It was the correct address so he parked his
rental car in the driveway. There were lights on inside the
house which was encouraging, for he had a critical need to
talk to the resident.

Impatiently, he rang the doorbell several times then
pounded his fist against the front door. Damn it. He had
not come all the way from Indiana to Florida to miss talking
with this guy. He had to be home. He desperately needed
his help before another teenaged girl lost her life. Sheriff
Tim Brennan had written to him about how good this guy
was. And if Brennan recommended him, he had to be
excellent. He hammered at the door again, and then peeked
into the front window. There was no one inside, but from
his position he could see open sliding glass doors leading to
the backyard.

From the side yard, he opened the iron-gate to the back
of the house. The second he entered the backyard, he
noticed a woman diving into an Olympic-sized pool.

Transfixed, he watched her as she swam to the far end of the pool, and then kicked-off to swim to the other end, this time on her back. Her body, slick from the water, glowed in the moonlight. The tiny glittering lights surrounding the pool made her look ethereal as she sliced through the water.

He should do the gentlemanly thing and leave, but he couldn't move. His frozen legs seemed attached to the ground. He could barely breathe as she lifted herself out of the water. With long black hair as shiny as glass, she had an athletic build, with full, uplifted breasts, curved hips and endless legs. His jeans grew tighter as his arousal strained against the zipper.

Moving to a deck chair, she wrapped a white towel around her body — then picked up a serious-looking handgun that she pointed straight at his chest.

"I don't know who you are or why you're in my yard, but I've got a little secret I'd like to share with you," she began. "In the past two years, I've shot two men. Neither man is here to talk about it."

He stiffened as a wave of apprehension hit him full-force. He'd been shot before, remembered it well, and had no desire to repeat the experience. He cleared his throat and said, "I apologize if I frightened you. I pounded on the front door but no one answered."

"That doesn't tell me who you are and why you are here," she returned, assuming one of the best shooting stances he'd ever seen.

He hesitated for a second, and then responded, "I'm Sheriff Brody Chase from Morel, Indiana in Shawnee County. I'm here to see Carl Stone."

She quirked her eyebrow questioningly, and asked, "Who told you Carl Stone lived here?"

"A fellow Indiana county sheriff gave me your name and address in an email. Tim Brennan's his name," he replied.

She slowly lowered the gun. "Sounds like Sheriff Brennan made a typo. It's Carly Stone that you're looking for. Why do you want to talk to me?"

About the Author — Alexa Grace

Alexa's journey started in March 2011 when the Sr. Director of Training & Development position she'd held for thirteen years was eliminated. A door closed but another one opened. She finally had the time to pursue her dream of writing books — her dream since childhood. Her focus is now on writing riveting romantic suspense novels.

Alexa earned two degrees from Indiana State University and currently lives in Florida. She's a member of Romance Writers of America (national) as well as the Florida Chapter. Her first books *Deadly Offerings* and *Deadly Deception* have consistently placed on Amazon's Top 100 Bestselling Romantic Suspense Books. She was recently named one of the top 100 Indie authors by *Kindle Review*. A chapter is devoted to her in the book *Interviews with Indie Authors* by C. Ridgway and T. Ridgway.

Her writing support team includes five Miniature Schnauzers, three of which are rescues. As a writer, she is fueled by Starbucks lattes, chocolate and emails from readers.

For more information on her upcoming releases: Check out her website at http://www.alexa-grace.net/ Visit her on Facebook at https://www.facebook.com/AuthorAlexaGrace Email her at alexagrace@cfl.rr.com

Follow her at http://twitter.com/AlexaGrace2

Made in the USA
San Bernardino, CA
05 March 2014